HOT & BOTHERED
3

HOT & BOTHERED 3

SHORT SHORT FICTION ON LESBIAN DESIRE

edited by

Karen X. Tulchinsky

ARSENAL PULP PRESS
Vancouver

ARSENAL PULP PRESS
103-1014 Homer Street
Vancouver, BC
Canada v6b 2w9
arsenalpulp.com

The publisher gratefully acknowledges the support of the Canada Council for the Arts and the British Columbia Arts Council for its publishing program, and the Government of Canada through the Book Publishing Industry Development Program for its publishing activities.

"The Ridge Runners" was originally published in *A Fragile Union* by Joan Nestle, copyright 1988, Cleis Press, San Francisco, CA.

"Girls, Visions, and Everything" is an excerpt from *Girls, Visions, and Everything* by Sarah Schulman, copyright 1986, The Seal Press, Seattle, WA.

Text design by Solo
Printed and bound in Canada

CANADIAN CATALOGUING IN PUBLICATION DATA:
Main entry under title:
  Hot & bothered 3

  ISBN 1-55152-102-4

1. Lesbians' writings. 2. Lesbians-Fiction. I. Tulchinsky, Karen X.
PN6120.92.L47H67 2001   808.83'108353   C2001-911287-4

For Terrie
Still keeping me hot and bothered
and in love. . . .

CONTENTS

ACKNOWLEDGMENTS

Many thanks to Brian Lam, Blaine Kyllo, and Robert Ballantyne of Arsenal Pulp Press for editorial support, administrative assistance, encouragement and for taking care of all the millions of details it takes to publish a book and operate a press. It is always a pleasure to work with Arsenal Pulp Press, and an honor to publish with a publisher that produces such an impressive list of progressive and engaging titles. Thanks to Dianne Whelan for the gorgeous cover photography, author photo, and ongoing support and friendship. Thanks to Val Spiedel for the amazing book cover design. Much appreciation to Richard Banner for bailing me out of countless computer nightmares on an ongoing basis, and to James Johnstone for administrative assistance, support, and friendship. Many thanks to Lois Fine, CGA, for ongoing emotional support, friendship, music and accounting advice. Thanks to all the small, independent, gay and lesbian, feminist, and alternative presses and bookstores that against great odds stay in business providing the widest selection of gay and lesbian literature for readers. *Arigatô* to my lover and fiancée, Terrie Akemi Hamazaki, for loving me, keeping me on my toes and continually hot and bothered, and for wearing sexy, slinky, black lacy things. Thanks always to Charlie Tulchinsky-Hamazaki for unconditional cat-love.

INTRODUCTION

WHEN I WAS A SMALL CHILD I thought I was going to grow up and marry a woman. I believed this with all my heart and soul. When my mother read fairy tales to me at bedtime, I imagined myself riding atop a majestic horse, dashing off into the countryside to slay dragons for my one true princess. Imagine my surprise when I discovered at the age of eleven that as a girl, I was supposed to be the princess and that I was supposed to wait for a prince to rescue *me*. For a while I complied. I bent to what was expected of me. I pretended to have crushes on boys. I tried hard to fit in with the other girls as they tried on clothes, experimented with make-up, and giggled over boys. I tried for a while. A short while.

By the time I was eighteen, the loosely latched lock on my closet door sprang free and I burst out, and into the local dyke community of the large city of Toronto. And I never looked back. But I was lucky. I lived in a large urban center, a city with a visible gay community. There were gay bars, a gay and lesbian community center, a Gay Pride Day Parade every June. I wasn't alone. There were others like me. But even with all these resources, it wasn't always easy. My first relationship ended soon after it began and I felt alone, at odds with the rest of the world. If I switched on the television, went to the movies, or flipped through the newspaper, I likely wouldn't see myself. My lesbian self. It was to books I turned to see mirrors of my life: books written by other lesbians.

This is the third in a series of books on lesbian desire. *Hot & Bothered 1* was published in 1998; its first printing sold out before it was even launched. The second *Hot & Bothered* was equally popular. Both remained on many bestseller lists for many weeks.

In the beginning of the twenty-first century it is as important as ever for lesbians to be writing and publishing books about our desire for one another. To that end, I present *Hot & Bothered 3: Short Short Fiction on Lesbian Desire.* This is not a book of erotica. This is a book on lesbian desire. Desire covers a broad range of themes: it's about all aspects of intimacy between women, whether it's dating, having a crush, unrequited love, lust for an inappropriate person, betrayal, breaking up, revenge or one-night-stands; it could be group sex, phone sex, club sex, long distance love, sex in long-term relationships, sex through illness and disability, or cross cultural sex; it could also be about coming out, cruising or growing older. So long as it's about getting hot. And getting bothered.

Lesbian desire is complicated. We are bothered as often as we are hot. Lesbians in long-term relationships go through waves of desire over the years, desire that ebbs and flows like the tides. Sometimes in synch with each other. Sometimes not. Single lesbians' desire is sometimes requited. Sometimes not. Lesbians are sometimes monogamous. Sometimes not. Sometimes faithful. Sometimes not. Sometimes we desire our lovers. Sometimes we desire someone else.

And some of us are brave: those of us who see a girl we like who will march straight up to her and ask her out. Or buy her a drink. Or invite her home. But some of us are not so brave: when we spot a beautiful woman in the bar, instead of approaching, we will stare at her all night from across the room, swooning long distance, never working up the nerve to say anything. We lesbians can be predictable on some matters, but sometimes we surprise ourselves with our desire. In *Hot & Bothered 3* you will find many surprises: sex on a sweltering Manhattan rooftop, sex on the road, sex in the bath, sex on the work site; butch on butch desire, forbidden desire, lusting after straight women, getting together, breaking up, sex on a Greyhound bus, sex with Barbie, sex in a 1960s television sitcom.

This volume of short short fiction stories which are 1,000 words or less includes the work of 72 writers. Some are well established authors such as Sarah Schulman, Lesléa Newman, Joan Nestle, Jess Wells, Ruthann Robson, Lucy Jane Bledsoe, Cecilia

Tan, Elana Dykewomon, and Susan Fox Rogers. Emerging writ-ers include Rita Wong, Donna Allegra, LaShonda Barnett, and Terrie Akemi Hamazaki. Some contributors are being published for the first time.

We are a diverse community and desire is a subjective expe-rience. Wherever your personal tastes lie, I invite you to sit back and enjoy being hot and bothered. All over again.

Karen X. Tulchinsky
Vancouver, BC
June 2001

GIRLS, VISIONS, AND EVERYTHING

Sarah Schulman

"LILA, SOMETIMES I JUST NEED TO BE QUIET."

It was Friday night out on the stoop and Emily didn't feel like talking. So, they watched the street a while longer until Lila got involved in a detailed conversation with an Italian Buddhist. Then they started walking slowly over to Washington Square Park, where they sat on the littered grass until it was too disgusting. They moved to some benches until men harassed them away and ended up at the midnight show of *Blade Runner* at the Saint Mark's. They walked in late and Lila couldn't figure out what was going on. Since she didn't have a TV, she found it harder and harder to tolerate movies, or even just to follow them. Her eyes hurt from too many screen flashes and all the marijuana smoke in the theater and she didn't understand why Emily was being so stiff.

Finally they left that scene and wandered a bit, ending up on Lila's roof, lying on a blanket between the tarpaper and the open sky. Emily stayed distant and cool.

"I think touching somebody's body, well, I take it seriously, it's so personal. Sometimes I get afraid of being abandoned. I like being with you Lila, like I said, but I'm not sure which way every friendship should go."

Lila watched Emily consider whether she should be her lover or not. She watched her have a thought, decide to articulate it, and then do so.

"You know I'm not sexually adventurous. I'd rather not have sex and wait for something important and good for me to happen. You seem to have a lot of girlfriends, or at least try to, like you're not worried about being thwarted. How do you handle sexual fantasies about so many different people at once?"

"I always need to have some image in my head. Sometimes I

GIRLS, VISIONS, AND EVERYTHING

feel like a certain kind of sex, then I look around to see what's out there."

Listening to her own words made Lila consider that she might actually be crass, promiscuous, coarse, and in every way stupid. It was just at that moment that Emily abruptly put her face to Lila's breasts and started to kiss them. She put her face into Lila's lap and caressed her bare, hairy legs. This time Lila knew that Emily's cunt lived in her breasts and she looked at them, smelled them, felt their textures dry and wet, pressed her nipples, flattened them with her tongue and forgot that a few minutes before she had felt like a complete jerk.

"I love breasts," Emily said, and Lila felt so close to her that she saw a glow of flush and neon light vibrating around Emily's face, like she was enchanted or emanating power. Lila wanted to talk while they were touching, to drown Emily in mush, to tell her how beautiful it was to make love with her.

"Lila, are you falling asleep?"

"No, no, sorry, I just got lost in feeling you."

"Because I want to have sex, so wake up." She laughed out loud.

"Okay," Lila said, grinning. "Let's have sex."

But first, they stopped to share a cigarette, naked on the rooftop. Sitting together, they both reached over and felt each other's wetness while Emily smoked. Lila sat behind her, easing her into her arms, holding Emily's head on her breasts.

While they watched the night lights of the city, the red, white, and blue Empire State Building, Lila reached down into Emily's cunt.

"Have you ever been touched like this before, while you were smoking a cigarette?" she asked.

"No. Why?"

"Because of the suspense," Lila said and stroked Emily's clitoris around and around while the ash burned. As the smoke went up in a straight line into the sky, Lila held Emily's breast, feeling each duct of her large red nipple. Emily smiled, holding that glowing cigarette, moved and quietly came, curling up relaxed and natural.

Later, after different kinds of sex and feelings, Emily was so soft that Lila kept thinking as she watched her, I want to be close to this woman.

Morning on the roof began at five-thirty when the sun suddenly and brutally came pounding down over the still-tired refugees from hot crowded apartments, starting the day off grimy and stale. They woke up and Emily's affection was gone again. Lila could have taken a shower and sucked Emily's breasts all morning but Emily went off to do something, leaving Lila sitting there sweating on the roof, watching the city get ready for another sweltering day.

ONE FINE DAY

Lesléa Newman

for M. V.

IT COULD HAPPEN ANYTIME, ANYWHERE. Today, for instance. When you least expect it.

It's one of those snappy-cold New England afternoons when the air is crisp as the first bite of a sweet, red Macintosh apple and the sky is crystal clear, miles above you, a gorgeous shade of blue that has no name but is exactly halfway between cornflower and periwinkle. An afternoon like this is a gift, a reward for slogging through all those thick, humid summer days that used to end in August, but the past few years have dragged themselves into the better part of September.

You're on your lunch hour, standing in line at the bank, the check you need to deposit clutched tightly in one hand, a steaming take-out cup of coffee in the other. Usually the line is full of grumblers: "Why are they taking so long?" "Will Friday ever come?" But today has no room for collective misery. Instead everyone remarks on the beauty of the day, the glory of the afternoon. You do not shift your weight from one high heel to the other, glance at your watch every other second, let out sigh after frustrated sigh. You just stand there and when the man in front of you who reeks of garlic glances back over his shoulder, looks you up and down and smiles with open admiration, you actually smile back. What the hell. Today you have all the time in the world. So what if the young, blonde bank teller is bending the ear of a customer with a long, drawn out, and probably pointless story about her impossibly cute four-year-old. What do you care? You raise the coffee cup to your lips for a sip and turn your head to gaze idly out the plate-glass window at this surreal day, exaggerated in its perfection like a Dali painting, when suddenly you see her. Across the street. Wow. You almost choke on the steaming brew, for as if this day wasn't perfect enough, now it offers you proof that the Goddess really does exist. No one else could have possibly created such a masterpiece. She stands tall, proud and patient as a ship, as she waits to cross the street. Jet black hair that ends right at the collar of her leather jacket. Jeans that fit just right. Shiny shoes. A handsome face filled with kindness. And something more. Joy, mirth, playfulness. Even from inside the bank you can see she's got a twinkle in her eye.

Your patience flies out the window and you actually start tapping your foot. You've got to get out there before she gets away. You're just about to forfeit your place in line when the teller calls, "Next," so you dash to her station, and slap down your check. Hurry, hurry, hurry, you think, keeping one eye on the teller and one on the handsome butch who is now crossing the street. A woman on the corner stops her and though you flare up with jealousy, you are happy she's been detained. Now you know you'll make it. You grab your deposit slip, stuff it into your purse, and race out the door, screeching to a halt right beside her.

"Hi." You breathe out the word, your heart pounding, your knees actually starting to buckle at the nearness of her. She turns, and her eyes widen with surprise and then delight at the sight of you. The moment is frozen in time as you take each other in, and then, as if she senses your wobbly legs are about to give way, she catches you in her arms and bends you backwards to plant a kiss like you only see in the movies right on top of your trembling lips, right out there on the razzle-dazzle street, right smack-dab in the middle of this show stopper afternoon. You've never been kissed like this before out on the street in broad daylight, or anywhere else for that matter. You swoon, you melt, you ooze into her as the other woman vanishes, your coffee cup drops to the ground, the bank disappears, as does the sky above you and the ground beneath your feet. All that remains of the world is the butch who holds you tightly in her arms, grinning madly as you shake your head in disbelief, realizing you hardly know her at all, this tall dark handsome stranger who has been your one and only lover for a dozen years and counting.

ON BEING A COW

Susan Fox Rogers

WHEN I WAS THREE MY FATHER ASKED: What do you want to be when you grow up?

"A cow," I answered.

When I left Margaret, I didn't leave New York, as I told everyone I would. I stayed, sleeping for four months wherever I could find a bed.

Often that was at Eva's on Avenue B and Second.

East Village: the bathtub in the kitchen and the toilet in the hall of the five-floor walk-up. Eva hadn't paid the rent in nine months when I first slept there. Since her mastectomy a year earlier, she hadn't worked. I had no idea what she lived on. All I knew was that she made love to me for hours, like a teenage boy who won't stop, rocking on top of me, coming on her own hand that was inside of me. As we lay spent in bed I pet her chemo bald head; the scar where her left breast once was, I kissed. Her round, cream-black face spread into a wide smile, and then she'd leave me. As I drifted off to sleep, always near three in the morning, I heard her chanting: *Nam myoho renge kyo.*

A few hours later I'd wake to dress in pantyhose and a skirt for my corporate publishing job. Eva was awake too, warming up little buns. She bought those buns at a bakery down the street, fifteen cents each. Buttered, they were delicious with the Pico coffee she brewed strong.

And then one night after making love I got up, sat on the end of her rumpled bed. Eva looked over. "What are you doing?" she asked.

"Chanting," I said.

She walked over, took me by the hand and led me back to her altar. She pointed to where she was in the text of *Nichiren Shoshu.* With her I chanted, quietly at first, a little confused by the words, how to pronounce them, and no sense except in the sound itself: *Myo ho renge kyo. Hoben-pon. Dai ni.* We sat on small stools in front of her altar, which included an image of the Buddha, a half-wilted cluster of daisies, some small stones that were token gifts of faith, and candles. Her smooth face glowed in the flickering light. We chanted, louder and louder, the words reverberating in my chest. We chanted until dawn.

She calls at eleven in the morning to talk. I answer the phone at my job where I work as the managing editor for a university sex journal. We provide a lot of services at the journal but phone sex isn't one of them. I close my door. The room is small, a converted dorm room on a small college campus, with white painted brick walls and thin windows that don't seal tightly. But it's spring, so the windows are open, allowing in the sounds of student music, musicians I'll never know. My student assistant is sitting at a computer near my desk, logging in information about manuscripts read and rejected. She's a young lesbian, head shaved, skinny shoulders exposed in her loose-fitting tank top. She does all my drudge work: Xeroxing and mailings, but she also reads every manuscript, charging into my office filled with curiosity or fury. There, under humming neon lights, and academically sanctioned, we discuss anal penetration and oral sex, orgasms. Only occasionally do we slip into the personal but I can tell already that she is far too smart, too full of questions, to have a relationship that makes her happy. For other reasons, none of my relationships made me happy either, including this, whatever it is, on the other end of the phone. She's twice as old as me, a famous writer, and has piles of money that she teases me with. "How long could you live on one hundred grand?" Probably forever. My therapist doesn't know about this, no one does, not even my lover or my best friend. Even so, my therapist keeps using a word I find irritating: boundaries. I translate boundary to exposure and tune her out, stare into the space above her head like the crazy person I'm supposed to be.

I listen to my caller, the ritual now familiar. "Uh huh," I say. I'm no sex kitten in this phone sex world. And, after all, I'm at work so the vocabulary of sex is reduced to a nearly unerotic minimum. Yes. That's it. Uh huh, over and over again, while at her end she weaves words into the phone line from thirty miles away. Then I have this idea: her life is so public, but not this, the private obsessions. I reach over and tap the speaker phone.

"Oh baby I'm going to come," erupts like perfect canned phone sex.

My assistant swivels in her chair, her round blue eyes expanding in exaggerated surprise. I scrawl my caller's name on the yellow legal pad. She shakes her head as her face lights up. She probably doesn't believe me, and that's okay. I don't either.

Where I lived in my twenties, five miles back on a dirt road in the mid-Hudson Valley of New York State, rested a small farm. In that narrow valley it perched precariously above a slim strip of field, the sides of the barn sagging down toward the river. Sun warmed that valley for only a few hours every day; snow lingered on well into spring. Only then did the cows emerge, six or seven, black, always too thin. Spring weekends in 1995 I was single, living there in the middle of the woods with my two orange cats and blue pickup truck. So when, like the land, I rolled into heat, I drove the two hours down to New York City. My destination was usually the Clit Club. I danced body to body, shoulders bumping against each other on that crowded small dance floor. I waited for a while before letting myself head down the steep steps to the basement. The low ceilings, the dim lights in the three small rooms, made it dungeon-like. Over the one pool table women, cigarettes dangling from their mouths, leaned over, taking aim. In the basement darkness, it was a hand here, an elbow sticking out there, lips colliding in the dark more with force than passion.

Just before the club closed at four a.m., I'd slip into my pickup and drive north, up the West Side Highway, then onto the Thruway. By the time I pulled onto my road, bouncing over potholes, my bladder full from that last beer I probably shouldn't have drunk, the cab of the truck was warm. But I felt cool. Just wanting the softness of sheets, not skin, against my legs, just wanting to pee and to brush the smoke from my teeth, I raced down that road. From a distance I could see the lights, glowing eerily in the morning dark. Once, caught by that light, I stopped and rolled down my window. The hum of the milker, the warm buzz in the clear air soothed me. I leaned my head out the window and sucked in the sweet, perfect smell of cow shit and warm hay.

THE RIDGE RUNNERS

Joan Nestle

A LESBIAN COUPLE WHO, LIKE US, were summer inhabitants of this Catskill region, came by for an afternoon lunch by our pond, bringing with them a friend who had visited the summer before. The attraction between my lover and this young woman, a teacher–artist who painted huge canvases in her downtown loft, was palpable in the summer air. The young artist swirled around us in an earth–colored sarong and halter top, her skin sun browned, muscle and breast all swollen with victories. In a moment of playfulness, she removed her skirt and then pushed my jock lover into the cold waters of the pond, diving in after her to make sure her conquest was complete.

I heard their shouts and turned to see Lee, my lover, climbing out of the pond, standing with water dripping off her lean, muscular body, shorts and t–shirt plastered against her flesh, hair flattened against her head. She stood there half–stunned by the audacity of our guest. The young woman, continuing her challenge, danced a few steps away from her, half poised to flee. This is what I saw and what I knew. My lover would have this woman, not in that late–summer afternoon light, but in a darkened room somewhere back in the city. I was older than the newcomer by twenty years and had been ill. Illness, like floods, washes away the simply loose things first, and then it pushes at the bedrock. Too many nights I had turned away from Lee's desire. Anger, sickness, disappointments, and hurt rose like a wall between us, and while Lee could still make love to me, I did all I could to numb myself to her. For her, desire meant strength and reaffirmation of self; for me, it meant weakness and loss. Yet I wanted everyone to know what a wonderful lover she was, and as if she were a superb possession I could no longer use, I offered her to others.

I told her that I understood her need, that it was alright if she had an affair. I thought it was. I would be the slowed-down older woman who with great noblesse oblige handed over her still-vital lover to the passion she herself could not provide. Old Bette Davis movies were running through my mind; elegantly bereft, I would be. In control of things, I would be. But watching their foreplay in the summer heat, I began to feel uneasy with my own scenarios.

Later that afternoon, the three of us planned a journey up the mountainside to find a secret waterfall that Clarence Hartwell, the elderly farmer who was our neighbor, had told us was hidden in the folds of the mountain. As a young boy, he had taken delight in running barefooted over the ridges of the surrounding hills. "I would rather run then eat when I was hungry," he had told us one morning earlier in the summer, challenging us to retrace his youthful discoveries.

That day was hot and heavy. We made our way through the meadow, lit by an almost unbearable sun until we reached the beginning of the forest. The stream was just a short distance ahead of us, and we had our first choice to make—to follow the riverbed or to go along the bank. I chose the riverbed, they chose the bank.

In its first meandering, the stream was easy to travel on. I stepped from stone to stone, looking down at the river bottom, hoping to see some exotic river creature. Then the stream narrowed, and the footing became more treacherous. Several times I slipped into the cold water, reaching out to grab at a branch or tree trunk to keep myself from falling.

At one point, the younger woman came back to me, offering to help me over some especially rocky places. At first I was grateful, but then I wanted to push her away, push away her perfect body, her kindness based on sureness. "I know about you and Lee," I said at one resting place.

"I knew you would understand," she said. "You write so beautifully about passion, you of all people would understand." My breath stopped for a minute. I did not tell her that my body was breaking. I nodded and sent her on. For a long while I rested, breathing in the damp smells of the streambed and sipping water from my cupped hand.

For an hour, I traveled in the heart of the stream. No part of it escaped me. Slowly I was climbing the mountain. My two fellow explorers, walking on higher ground, had left me far behind. I could hear their shouts through the trees, "Here, it turns here." Soon I had to climb more slowly, clutching at whatever the bank offered me by way of support.

My lover's shouts alerted me to their discovery. I looked up and saw them both standing high on the edge of a huge stone outcropping, far above me. Now I was crawling up the mountainside, my head close to the moss-covered earth, my fingers digging into water-softened rootbeds. Ancient smells of mold enveloped me. Above, massive stone slabs like giant steps formed the basic structure of the falls. This hard old break in the mountain's side, its waters gushing out all around us, was the ridge runner's secret.

When I finally joined Lee and her new lover and sat with them, our feet dangling over the edge of the flat black rock, I knew that whatever fantasies I had entertained about being in control of their mutual desire had been ground out of me.

Now far from me, they are consummating the need that flared up on the way to the waterfall, the young dark woman, all bared desire, and my lover, ready to answer the call. On the way back from the falls, they fell far behind me on the trail, and as I made my way over the now-familiar riverbed, I lost sight and sound of them. Younger and stronger than me, they had fallen behind–to look for fossils, they would say. I did not look back; I did not want to see the kiss or the hurried touch. I had given away my lover one time too many.

The water in the stream was low, tired in the late summer, but I had seen its source, seen the ancient table of stone over which it had journeyed for thousands of years. I had dipped my hand into its stone cradle of caught water. How could I make sense of all of this–my own scheming against myself, the beauty of their physical love, the enduring wetness of the seeping earth? On the way home, I was not as careful in my footsteps. I walked resolutely away from the silenced excitement behind me.

Now my lover is entering the young woman, her muscles bunched up in her arm, her intense face hanging over the woman below her. She will push at her, in her. She will not stop until she has completely exhausted the woman under her. She is that kind of lover, relentless, selfless, and yet she grows big with each thrust.

I am back in the city. All the bittersweet dramas of the summer are behind me. Mr Hartwell and his stories of floods and late night run-ins with the ghosts of the mountains have been replaced by the gritty reality of sirens blaring and the loneliness of my room when I know my lover is elsewhere. Now the words come pouring out of me. I re-create their sex play, a drama I know so well, as if my words could carry me into their passion, into their gathered intensity, where all is concentrated muscle and thrusting hips. How I have fooled myself, and how careless I was of Lee's offerings.

I will write a story about how it all happened, how the summer and the water and an old farmer and his boyhood habit of running over the hills gave us pieces of meaning, how they led us from a half-buried cemetery where bones picked clean of passion were growing down deeper and deeper into the earth to a scar in the ridgetops that poured forth endless, and sometimes sad, possibilities.

I used to run over the hills too, the hills of lovers' bodies, the mountains of touch. I had made trails for myself in bedrooms and bars, a young girl wanting and always saying more, please more.

Now I sit, as the night grows later, in a room in the city trying to put up words to stand against the flood of knowledge and of memory, words to hold at bay the pain of a failing body, words that commemorate the persistent need to touch, to discover, to survive the loss of assured beauty. Words of water and stone, flesh and desire, reality and imagination, equally fragile, equally enduring–the fossils of our human way.

LA MONEY GIRL

Cecilia Tan

SHE TAPED PENNIES INTO HER PANTIES when she was six years old.

She was never sure where that idea had come from – if something she had seen on a TV show or heard some adult say had planted the suggestion, or if it had just seemed like a good idea at the time. She was afraid to get caught fingering herself in school. So she taped the pennies down where they would click and rub, so they would tap her gently when she skipped rope, so if she ran around the playground once or twice and then got a jumprope, by the end of recess the magic thing would happen.

When she turned twenty she discovered spirit gum and shaving. A Susan B. Anthony dollar on each nipple, she dotted her cunt with nickels and dimes, and discovered that she could hold a penny on her clit with no glue at all. She would go down to bars with esoteric names, in a rayon knit top and a miniskirt, and find a woman to dance with, and always, though sometimes on the dance floor, sometimes in a dark corner booth, that woman's hand would stray across her nipple. They invariably considered her eccentric – which she expected – but she was looking for one who would consider her eccentric, and who wouldn't mind.

She lies in bed with pesos and shillings and plasticky-feeling yen spread across her stomach, clamps a silver dollar between her lips (her lower lips, I mean) and presses her vibrator to it. She imagines that some day she'll go down to the bar, she pictures a dyke with a James Dean swagger, who will slide her hand under that knit top, who will peel a Susan B. free, who will flip the coin into the air and catch it smartly in one hand, saying "Heads your place, tails mine, baby."

And whatever the outcome, it doesn't matter, because what happens next in her fantasy is this: the other woman gets down

on her knees, peels away her panties with her teeth, goes hunting for the penny with her tongue, comes up with copper between her teeth, with her fingers between her legs ... nickels
and dimes are flying everywhere, the loose change on her belly
leaping and flipping as she shakes, as her stomach and her
thighs and her hips rock while she comes and she comes. . . .

Someday, she thinks, someday, someone will get down there
and hit the jackpot.

THE TENTH COMMANDMENT

Terrie Akemi Hamazaki

HER BELLY WAS SMILING UP AT HER. Cindy's slender fingers pulled the skin at both sides of the scar up, then down into a frown. Her head dropped back onto the pillow. It had been another bad day. She waited for Chaya to return from the bathroom.

"Am I hurting you?" Chaya quickly pulled back from where she had been leaning over Cindy. Her earnest brown eyes searched her lover's heart-shaped face.

"Just don't lean on me . . . it still hurts."

"I'm sorry, I didn't know, I'm sorry," Chaya stammered. She moaned and shook her head repeatedly.

"Honey, sweet baby, don't worry about it. I love you," Cindy soothed. She stroked Chaya's cheek. "Kiss me," she whispered.

Chaya's lips were ferocious.

What was it the nurse had said? Or rather, didn't say. Cindy frowned in concentration. The nurse had been listing off postoperative care instructions to Chaya for Cindy. The yellow legal-size sheet of paper had fluttered nervously in the nurse's hands.

". . . and secondly, give patient two iron tablets twice a day with water," she sniffed as she adjusted the octagonal metal-framed glasses on her nose. She squinted at Chaya.

Cindy wasn't listening. She lay with her eyes closed, focused on breathing. Three days had passed since her surgery and it was her first afternoon without morphine. She noticed the sharp pain in her abdomen now. Glass shards embedded in an empty gourd. And she certainly didn't feel giddy anymore.

The numbered instructions continued, then stopped. Cindy breathed deeply.

"I thought you said there were ten things. That was only nine," Chaya said.

Cindy opened her eyes and turned her head to look at the nurse.

"No, there's only nine, my mistake." She rose from her seat.

"Well, I'll take that, please." Chaya's right hand reached for the paper. The nurse reluctantly passed it over. She smiled at Cindy.

"You take care now," she said. "Your stitches look great and you'll be going home tomorrow." Cindy noticed a dark smudge of lipstick on the nurse's front tooth.

No penetration, no intercourse. The tenth item. Ever-vigilant Chaya had followed all the instructions on the list, up to and including the anal administration of anti-gas tablets, when needed. She'd also heeded the last item: no penetration, no intercourse. Her lovemaking embodied mellow restraint. Cindy yearned to break the tenth commandment.

"Are you sure you want to try again?" Chaya sat up in bed.

"I don't know," Cindy hesitated. "I think so."

"But is it safe? I mean, you had a ruptured ectopic pregnancy, babe. The doctor said if we'd been twenty minutes later to the hospital, you would've. . . ."

"So," Cindy interrupted. "Lots of women have that. Why shouldn't I try again? Don't you love me? I'm almost forty!" She screamed the last words out.

"Okay, okay. I'm sorry. Of course you can try again. I'm just worried, that's all." Chaya rubbed her eyes. She adored this woman. This spirited femme whose silky, lace-wrapped charms had bound their hearts together six years ago. Poetic sorcery.

"I just want to be a mom – why can't I be a mom? Why?" Cindy pounded the bed with her fists.

"We'll try again, baby. Anything you want. Anything." Chaya gently caressed the heartbroken face of her lover.

Cindy stared up at the calico kitten on the ceiling. She recognized the colorful poster from seven months ago. Her bare feet rested uncomfortably in the stirrups. Her sixth attempt at pregnancy. The staff at the fertility clinic whispered to each other when they first walked in.

"They think I'm crazy," Cindy mouthed to Chaya.

"So what, you have a right to be here," Chaya said loudly.

A soft knock at the door announced the nurse's return. Chaya set down her styrofoam cup of milky tea beside the sink as the nurse eased past her.

"Here it is," she proclaimed. "FR237B, right?"

Chaya checked the number on the vial. She nodded.

Cindy chewed on her bottom lip. It had to work this time. She gasped as the speculum's cool metal frame was eased into her vagina.

"Sorry, Cindy," the nurse grimaced. "I should've warmed it up before we started. Shall I go on?" She peered at Cindy from between her bent legs.

"Yes, I'm fine." Cindy squeezed Chaya's hand tightly.

The nurse filled a syringe from the vial before attaching it to a long, narrow plastic tube. Her practiced hand quickly maneuvered it into place.

"All right, Chaya," she announced. "You can push the plunger now."

Cindy watched as Chaya carefully pressed down the syringe. The sperm flowed directly into her womb through the nurse's improvised medical instrument.

"Good," she declared. "All done!" She quickly unscrewed the speculum and gathered her supplies. "I'll keep my fingers crossed for you. No need to leave right away. You can stay and relax if you want. Just pay the receptionist on your way out." The door closed behind her.

Cindy felt a slight cramping in her uterus. These should've been labor pains, she thought. A thin trickle of liquid tickled her vulva. Pink remnants of the sanitized insemination process. She passed a finger over the wet skin and held it to her nose. The lavender scent she detected was from her morning shower.

Chaya searched Cindy's face. "Does it hurt, honey?"

"Just a little."

"Do you want to rest a bit?"

Cindy shook her head. She tugged at the bottom of Chaya's shirt.

"Let's do number ten now," she giggled.

"Huh?" Chaya's head tilted to one side.

"Remember? No penetration, no intercourse. The last one on the list."

Chaya's eyes lit up.

"I love you, Chaya. Your name means life in Hebrew, right? And that's what you did, Chaya. You kept me alive." Cindy's voice was low and insistent. "I'm sorry I've been so upset lately," she continued. "I'm just really scared. What if it doesn't work again? What if I can't. . . ."

Chaya stared at her lover. She's so beautiful, she thought for the ten thousandth time.

"Fuck me," Cindy urged. "Forget about rule number ten. Let's make a baby."

Chaya grinned.

Her fingers were wicked.

STRAWBERRY GIRL

Judith Laura

SLOWED BY THE ARTHRITIS THAT HAD WORSENED over the years, Anna took the strawberries from the refrigerator. Each spring when strawberries were fresh at the supermarket, she picked out several of the largest and juiciest just for this moment.

She took a fancy glass bowl from the cabinet, placed the strawberries in it, and took them to the table. Seated comfortably, she picked one up with her thumb and third finger and, pulling off the leaves with her other hand, sucked it into her mouth.

Anna had been in her mid-fifties when she had met the young woman she had come to call Strawberry Girl nearly two decades ago. She never did ask her name. Perhaps it was that everything happened so quickly. Or perhaps, at the time, she simply didn't want to know it.

Anna hadn't had a lover for over two years, since Kay, her partner of twenty-two years, had died. That, together with menopausal changes, Anna told herself, had made her lose interest in sex. Her intellectual pursuits were sufficient for pleasure now. She felt fortunate to live in a city that provided a wealth of art museums, classical symphony concerts, theater, and foreign films.

One evening during the break of a museum lecture on Renaissance art, Anna was standing in the foyer alone when Strawberry Girl approached. She looked so much younger than Anna, reddish blonde hair tumbling to her shoulders, black miniskirt high on her thighs, white leather boots rising to her knees. She didn't introduce herself or ask Anna's name, simply started chattering about luminosity – or was it numinosity? Her breasts bobbled beneath her white sweater as she elucidated the Renaissance concept of the Virtues, babbling on about depictions of Prudence and Abundance by Veronese. Anna could see the outline of her nipples under that white sweater but couldn't tell if Strawberry Girl was really braless since some nylon bras were now so sheer.

When they went back into the lecture hall, the young woman sat beside Anna. After it was over, she asked Anna if she'd like to go for a drink or snack in the restaurant up the street.

Sure, Anna thought, why not?

Anna wasn't hungry, and didn't order any food. Just two vodka tonics, one after the other. Strawberry Girl had strawberry cheesecake. She dipped the strawberries into the champagne cocktail she had ordered, then loudly sucked them partway into her mouth, running her pink tongue around their bumpy red surface before slowly chewing them and emphatically swallowing.

Anna made believe she didn't notice this seductiveness. You never could tell with young people when they might just be joking.

They ended up at Strawberry Girl's apartment in the area of the city near the university. She said her roommate was out of town for a few days. Anna stood on the hardwood floor in the disheveled living room as the young woman put "Strawberry Fields Forever" on the stereo. Then Strawberry Girl kissed Anna, her tongue rolling around Anna's tongue and teeth like it had rolled around the strawberries.

When their long kiss ended, she stepped back from Anna and slipped her white sweater up over her head.

No bra.

Her breasts were round and high, with pink nipples. She brought Anna's mouth to one of them.

When Anna came up for air, Strawberry Girl stepped back from her, took her hand, and led her into the bedroom. "I want to show you some stuff that really turns me on," Strawberry Girl said, opening a bureau drawer. "I have some silky underwear." She held up a pair of red and ruffled crotchless panties. "Would you like to put these on?"

Anna shook her head.

"Would you like me to put them on?"

Anna could hardly swallow, let alone say anything or even

move her head to indicate her preference.

Strawberry Girl turned around and stepped into the underwear, exposing the back of her thighs, her incredibly white, smooth derrière, then slipped the black skirt back down over the red panties. She rummaged in the drawer some more, then turned toward Anna holding something that looked a small hand-held hair dryer but wasn't.

Strawberry Girl turned it on and the round thing on the end whirred.

"What do you think of my toy?" Strawberry Girl laughed her strawberry laugh as she leaned back against a desk next to the bureau.

Anna didn't know what to think. Once Kay had talked about getting one of these things. She tried to get Anna to look at the selection in a new store specializing in products for women, but Anna had demurred, had told Kay she didn't want anything coming between them. Besides, Anna had said, the electricity seemed rather risky. Suppose the device malfunctioned and delivered a shock?

How ironic, Anna thought, as she watched Strawberry Girl wave the vibrating wand in the air, that a shock was how the medics had tried to save Kay's life. Over and over they had urged the defibrillator on Kay's chest. But to no avail. Kay's heart had stopped.

Anna's own heart pounded as Strawberry Girl turned the gadget off and asked, "Why don't you sit on the bed while I sit on the chair?"

Anna sat on the bed. Strawberry Girl took the wooden chair that had been pushed under her desk, turned it around, and sat down. Slowly, she moved her legs apart so that her black skirt slid up to the top of her thighs. Anna heard Strawberry Girl's boots reverberate off the wood floor as she moved her legs even further apart.

Anna could think of nothing else as she looked at those red panties framing strawberry lusciousness. Anna swallowed hard. She wanted to touch herself and Strawberry Girl at the same time. But she sat on the bed not moving a muscle.

"Here's what I like," Strawberry Girl said as she turned the gadget on again. She moved it slowly and purposefully in the opening of her panties.

Later, Strawberry Girl removed Anna's clothes and showed Anna how to use the toy on herself. She watched as Anna moved it slowly over her body, over her mound, then lightly over the area of most intense pleasure and when Anna was lost in sensation, Strawberry Girl began stroking and sucking Anna all over. Anna's body danced as Strawberry Girl's fingers danced inside her.

When they finished, neither of them said anything about seeing each other again. And they never did.

Anna slipped the last of the strawberries into her mouth, glad she hadn't added sugar. They were sweet enough just as they were. The juice tickled as it ran down her chin. She leaned back in the chair and licked her lips. Then, massaging the ache out of her back as she stood, she took the bowl to the sink, washed and dried it carefully, and set it back in the cabinet.

PORTA-POTTY PASSION

Sarah B Wiseman

MOST DAYS, I WOULDN'T CONSIDER the porta-potty on my work site a good place for a quickie. Most days, all I feel about it is grateful that it's there to give me a few minutes of refuge from long days of lifting, measuring, cutting, and nailing into place, two-by-four after two-by-four. No, I wouldn't have thought it would be the ideal spot for a little one-to-one. But where did I find myself, week before last, in the middle of a sweltering August afternoon?

You betcha: rocking away in that damn porta-potty.

Nobody particularly noticed when she walked onto the site that day. And if they did see someone step into the porta-potty, they probably assumed it was a teenage boy from the high school across the road.

I was pounding a joist when I noticed her walking up the gravel road. First off I couldn't tell, but it didn't take long before my gaydar kicked in and I got a hint of dyke in her boy swagger. She looked up to me on the second floor I was framing as she walked towards the john and the first thing I thought was, Man, she has balls. And then, What a gorgeous smile. I followed her with my eyes, careful not to draw attention from the other guys on my crew, and watched the blue door bang shut behind her and the green Vacant sign shift to a red Occupied.

I continued to pound spikes into the joist I was working on, and when I looked up again, I saw the porta-potty sign reading Vacant.

I looked around the site and didn't see her. I turned to my crew to see if they had taken notice of the hot bulldyke in the porta-potty and this hot bulldyke's reaction to her. Seeing they were indeed oblivious, I made my way down the ground ladder and across the street to the porta-potty.

I opened the door to find a partially startled, partially expectant, beautiful fat butch dyke sitting on the lid of the can, her legs planted wide. I locked the door behind me.

"Hey," I said, putting my hard hat on the floor and running my fingers through my short sweaty hair. She wore a baseball hat backwards.

"Hey," she laughed deeply. "My name's Al." She sounded calmer and cooler than I felt.

I took a small step that put me between her legs.

"Joe," I said and put my hand against the back wall beside her head.

She smirked. I could tell she was twice as cocky and just as easy as I was. "Joe Blow?" she said, turning her hat around to the front.

I laughed and took her question as an invitation. I bent down so our faces were a few inches apart and put my other hand between her legs.

"Do you want this?" I asked. Meaning, a good fuck in the sky blue john on a hot afternoon in the middle of August.

"Fuckin' right," she said, standing up.

She kissed me, soft at first and then hard. I kissed her harder, and she fell back to a sitting position on the lid of the john. I crouched over her and pressed my hand into her thigh. Sweat slid down the crack of my ass. It made me feel like fucking. I pushed her hard against the back wall and she started biting and pulling at my lips. My hand squeezed her thigh, working its way up and against her cunt, applying rhythmic pressure, while she clutched at my shoulders and moved her hands around my waist, pulling up the Midnight Oil shirt on my back.

She kept the rhythm going as I unzipped her cargos and slid my hand in to find briefs and sticky thighs. Her hand snuck under my shirt to my hard nipple and rubbed it. I put my fingers through the cock hole of her briefs and did the same to her hot wet clit.

Then I pushed her into the wall again and slid my fingers inside her. She reached down around my ass to pull my body, thigh, arm, tight against her pussy while I fucked her. Her feet kicked at my hard hat on the floor and my hammer banged against her thigh as she came. My ass and nipples stung from her clutch.

I cupped her cunt, and when she started to relax, just for the hell of it, I slid my hand past her clit one more time, as far as I could get into her, only to have her come again, stifling long moans in my ear that told me this orgasm was twice as good as the last.

When Al eased her grip, I stood up and put my hand on the top of my hammer to stop it swinging on its hook.

Al leaned back on the john and zipped up her pants.

"Nice hammer, Joe," she said, a cocky smile on her face.

"Estwing, twenty-eight ounces," I recited the brand name and weight proudly.

We stood staring at each other for a minute. Then, turning her baseball hat backwards again, she squeezed past me and out the door.

I laughed as it swung closed. Before leaving the box myself I took a few deep breaths and a long piss, relishing the thrill of pushing her butch ass against a wall.

When I got back to the crew, I heard an earful.

"Jesus, Joanne, where the hell have you been? We're gonna have this fucking house built without you."

"I had to piss like a race horse," I told them. Which was almost the truth.

Getting back to work, I fondled my hammer and wondered if anyone had noticed the porta-potty swaying a little in the invisible breeze of the day.

YOU CAN'T JUDGE A BUTCH BY HER COVER

Elizabeth Ruth

CLEO STOOD IN THE AISLE of the Greyhound bus searching for a free seat. Sam noticed her round face immediately, the hint of mascara, dark lipstick, her thick black hair pinned neatly to one side with a single barrette. Cleo waved, and with a long painted fingernail, gestured to the empty window seat. Sam reluctantly removed her knapsack and resumed reading her novel.

"Thanks," Cleo said, squeezing past.

"Sure," Sam nodded.

"Look, I brought my own." Cleo waved an anthology with a cover photograph of two naked women.

Sam tried not to roll her eyes. Erotica was strictly the territory of bottomy femmes as far as she was concerned. And lesbian erotica was the worst – so full of clichés. She preferred gay male porn; at least the boys understood fucking. Sam didn't know how anyone with half a brain could fall for such predictability. And reading it in public!

"I read for relaxation," Cleo continued, pushing the silver button on her armrest, and tilting the chair back. "Among other things. Besides, you never know who you'll find yourself sitting beside, right?" She winked, cracked the spine of her book, and started flipping pages. Every few seconds, she stopped, skimmed, licked her lips, sighed, and then continued flipping.

Typical, Sam thought. *She's looking for the dirty parts.*

"Oh," Cleo said, sensing disapproval. "I see you've brought something more refined."

Sam shrugged. "Just your regular old mystery."

"Wouldn't be caught dead with one of these, I bet?" Cleo held up her book to reveal its title, *Wet and Horny.*

Sam shifted in her seat. "To each her own," she said flatly.

"Yes," Cleo said, uncrossing her smooth legs. "But you sure can tell a lot about a person from her reading material."

Sam cocked her head.

"For example," Cleo offered, leaning closer, "I can see you're the adventurous type."

"Not really," Sam said, clearing her throat.

"Oh, admit it. You're wondering what kind of woman reads smut on the bus?"

Sam blushed and Cleo, vindicated, returned to reading. A minute later she began to casually brush the bottom edges of the book along her nipples until they became erect. Then she undid one of the glass buttons on her blouse, revealing the lace trim of a brassiere. Sam, always a sucker for lingerie, squeezed her legs together. She heard herself breathing harder as the Greyhound sped along the highway. *Get a grip!* She chastised herself.

Just then, Cleo stood.

"Excuse me," she said, sliding past with her breasts at eye level and one leg on either side of Sam as the bus lurched, changing gears. Cleo pressed up close and Sam breathed in her musky odor. Cleo touched Sam's shoulder, pulled her left leg over and into the aisle, and whispered, "I'm waiting." She walked off toward the washroom leaving Sam speechless and with a swollen clit.

Don't move, Sam told herself. But she couldn't resist.

When Sam opened the door she found Cleo topless and facing her. Cleo's tongue was fast and probed her mouth, her hands slid down Sam's jeans, her shallow, wispy breath filled the cubicle.

"Cocksure, I see," Cleo said, pleased to discover that Sam was packing.

Sam furtively pushed Cleo's bra up to her clavicle without unhooking it, and sucked her right breast. She reached under Cleo's skirt and twirled her fingertips around and around, as if tracing some illicit script. Sam pushed a wet g-string aside and teased her way along the grooves of Cleo's cunt, tugging the engorged lips. Then she unzipped her jeans, let them fall to her knees, ready to plunge her rubber dick into Cleo's available cunt.

Elizabeth Ruth

But before she had the chance, Cleo bent Sam's left arm tightly up behind her body, and unsnapped her plaid shirt with one hand.

"So you do like a good mystery," she said, exposing Sam's bare chest. "Now let's see if you can handle a little science fiction or fantasy." Cleo slid the barrette from her hair, and clamped it over Sam's fully erect nipple.

"Hey!"

She pushed Sam up against the wall, suddenly snapping off the barrette. Sam squirmed as the blood rushed back in a torrent. Her cunt was dripping, despite the pain. Or maybe because of it.

"You can't read me," Cleo chided, "any more than you can judge a butch by her cover."

"Yes," Sam groaned. She ground her clit against Cleo's leg, but Cleo pulled away, bit Sam's earlobes, cheek, shoulder. She tightened her grip until the tendons in Sam's neck strained. Then with one hand Cleo reached down between Sam's legs.

"Please," Sam panted, no longer caring about appearances.

Cleo flicked Sam's swollen, throbbing clit with her sharp nail. Sam flinched but immediately tried to ride Cleo's hand.

Cleo smirked, withdrawing stimulation.

"Guess you like a good cliché as much as the next girl, huh?"

"Don't stop," Sam begged. She raised one leg onto the toilet seat, spreading herself wider. Both women felt the vibrations of the bus's engine below.

Cleo released Sam's arms, but they held each other for balance as the bus pulled into the terminal. Cleo's palm thrust against Sam's pubic bone, then she carefully eased three fingers, four, her folded thumb, and finally her entire hand into Sam's wet cunt, and pumped violently. Sam felt a blanket of heat cover her, pinning her to the finish. Cleo swung her right leg over Sam's trembling thigh. She thrust with one hand, and dug her nails into Sam's back with the other, breaking skin. She bit hard on Sam's upper lip until Sam shook, gasped, and fell forward.

Seconds later, in the absence of words, Cleo stepped back, buttoned her blouse and quickly splashed cold water on her face. As Sam dressed, Cleo blotted her face with paper towel, removed a tube of lipstick from her skirt pocket, applied a fresh coat and, just like she was stepping out from the pages of a trashy book, opened the door and disappeared.

SPICE GIRL

LaShonda K. Barnett

I OPEN THE DOOR TO YOUR APARTMENT, close it behind me and
lock it. A strong, spicy aroma greets me. I don't recognize it right
away but as I walk closer to the bathroom (I hear water splashing), the scent becomes familiar.

What a beautiful picture. You are soaking in the tub; your
head resting on a small pink plastic pillow, your breasts bobbing
in a sea of suds, your legs bent causing a wreath of bubbles to
hover above your sex. Four patchouli candles flicker to the syn-
copated rhythms and soulful words of Bob Marley coming from
the portable stereo. In your right hand the last inch or two of a
joint burns. You take a drag. Out with the smoke comes the
question: "How was your day?"

I want to share with you but by the looks of things you are
higher than any bird has ever flown and probably won't com-
prehend what I'm saying. This realization irritates me until I realize I want to forget the happenings of a miserable day anyway.
I decide that you have the right idea.

"Hey Spice Girl, got any more of that?"

"Sure do."

I know where you keep it so I turn on my heels to go look
for some.

"Before you go –"

I stop, turn around.

"Take your clothes off."

"We can't fit in the tub together. There's too much water and
we're too tall."

"Drop those clothes," you order teasingly.

I open my blouse, do a dance with my shoulders until it
slides down my arms onto the floor. Unsnap my bra. By this
time, you've put the joint out and widened your legs.

I unbutton my trousers. They crash around my ankles silently and I step out of them. Your eyes travel the length of my legs and rest on my upper thighs. I know this because my thighs grow hot from the intensity of your gaze. You move your fingers in a gentle swirl, dispersing the collocated bubbles that hide a triangular mass of curly wet hair. I mumble something incoherent. Having lost count of the times we've been together I am still shy, then surprised and excited every time I see all of you. I determine that you are full of good ideas this evening. I put my hand inside my panties and am stunned by my own wetness.

"Touch your nipples for me."

With my free hand I obey your command and fondle my left breast, then my right one. I watch your nipples grow even more erect. I slide my fingers between my swollen lips and bite my tongue – an attempt to prevent the moan that escapes anyway. You tell me that you want me to come for you and I begin to finger myself wildly. I feel the muscles in my thighs contract and release. I tell you how hot you make me, amazed that I can even finish the sentence before coming. You begin to writhe in the tub and I know you are there with me.

SERENA

Leah Baroque

"SERENA?" I DIDN'T THINK SHE WAS REFERRING TO ME. The way my name rolled off her tongue, slipping out of her mouth like seductive cigarette smoke in a black and white film. She made the name sound so exotic, so sophisticated, so mature. It didn't belong to me at all. I was embarrassed to claim it as my own; it felt too big for me, like an older sister's shoes I was trying on without permission.

"I'm Serena," I acknowledged. She didn't seem disappointed that I was the owner of the name.

"Hi, I'm Cathy."

It wasn't really an accent, just the tone of her voice. I loved the way she spoke my name, as if it were almost a prayer. She made me feel like me, and I'd only just met her.

"Have you done this sort of thing before?" she asked.

"This sort of thing" was meeting a woman through an Internet personals ad for "friendship, fun, or more." My own agenda was a new experience; I agreed to meet her thinking that even a nice drink over light conversation wouldn't be a disappointment. But now that I had met her I would be disappointed if I couldn't get her to say my name many more times, in high pitched tones, in uncontrollable gasps, begging me to let her come as I fucked her. I had never had this kind of confidence before. Just being near this woman filled me with a feeling that I could take on anything – even her. My mind was racing with the deviant possibilities of what I'd like to do with her.

"No, I haven't," I said. "But now I'm wondering what took me so long."

She smiled. "Well, it's a bit of a risk, you never know what you're going to get." She looked me up and down as she took a sip through the straw of her Black Russian. A signature drink of hers, I later learned.

"Life is a risk I'm willing to take." I bought myself a vodka and lemonade and her another Black Russian.

"So what are you hoping to develop by meeting me?" She was weighing me up. If I said I wanted friendship would she try and persuade me to go to bed with her, or would she gracefully bow out? If I said I wanted a relationship would she finish her next drink and leave me here unsatisfied? If I said I wanted sex, plain and simple, hard and hot, sweaty, dirty sex, would she take me to the toilets right now? I enjoyed watching the options playing through her mind.

"I came here with no agenda," I said. "But now I'll be disappointed if I go home alone."

"Well, who said you had to go home at all, Serena?" I'd felt we were equally matched until she spoke my name again. There was something about the way she formed the word that made me giddy in the stomach, weak at the knees, and wet between the thighs. "You like the way I say your name, don't you, Serena?" She did it again; she could already read my sexual response like a book with large print and pictures. It was a wonderful quality to have in a lover. I couldn't answer her. "You think you can make me call your name in ecstasy, don't you? But I think you'll be the one begging me to call it out, begging me to say Serena, Serena, Serena."

She'd got me, she knew it. It was a challenge and I was happy to fold, because I won either way. "Okay, take me home."

In no time we were pulling into her driveway. She held the power. Just by speaking my name I was hers. But there must be something that I could use over her. She seemed like a woman who enjoyed a challenge. Something about me must make her feel desperate and sexually vulnerable. I just had to work out exactly what it was.

She asked me to unlock the door. I saw her fixate on my hand turning the handle. It was my hands that got to her. I wasn't sure why, perhaps because they were small and cute; maybe she wanted to see just what they could do to her. Once we were inside the door I took hold of her hand, watching the sexual energy just beneath her skin shifting, and she led me to her bed. I climbed on first and beckoned for her to follow with my fingers. Her eyes melted as she sat next to me. I ran my hand up her thigh, she said my name, the rules were simple and clear. I pushed her back onto the bed and climbed on top of her, kissing her. She couldn't say my name with my tongue in her mouth, and thus I had the power. My hands caressed her hair, her breasts, creeping under her skirt and rubbing her upper thighs. Wrapping her arms around me, she rolled me over onto my back and pushed her thigh between mine. She pulled off her top and pulled my hands to her bare breasts. I squeezed and stroked and pinched at her nipples as she moaned my name. I pushed my clit against her thigh and maneuvered one of my hands underneath her skirt, inside her underwear, and ran it along the wetness of her cunt.

"Touch me, Serena!" she shouted. I pushed two fingers inside of her, my other hand playing with her nipples, and she called my name again and again, causing my cunt to clench and convulse just as hers was. I pushed hard against her thigh, which she rammed between my legs. Pinching her clit, she came, calling my name over and over as I came from the hardness of her thigh between my legs and the magic of her voice.

BUZZ

T. J. Bryan

SURE, I HAD MORE ON MY MIND than the state of her kinks. And this one, tall and thick with nuff attitude to boot, must'a known it, too. Her eyes on me promised things I wasn't sure she could deliver. But damned if I was gonna pass up a chance to find out.

I said a nice clean fade would do her good. Her flat-top was obviously getting a little outta control 'round the ears and in back. I knew just what to do about that. So I came in close enough to whisper and invited her on over to my place. Offered to fix her up real nice.

She gave me the once over. Must'a liked what she saw. Said she'd bring the drinks. We parted ways and I began to strategize, confident that I'd control our fun.

Next afternoon I open my apartment door and invite her in. She's rockin' a leather jacket, wine colored shirt with matching tie, carefully cuffed dungarees, and some square-toed boots. Before I get the chance to comment she steals a kiss and a handful'a my butt. I don't protest. But I'm not brave enough to admit that her bad behave' ways and bravado have already won me over.

I stammer something 'bout stubble and her shirt getting covered with it. She grins and, without taking her eyes off me, sets the wine she's brought on the kitchen counter, then removes every stitch of clothes she's got on. And I can't seem to find a reason to stop her.

Her brown skin is ruby-tinged with the last of the summer sun's color. Breasts are fuller than I usually like. Areolas are huge and dark. My mouth waters. A happy belly, well-rounded, sits atop her smooth shaven mons. It takes a supreme effort of will to stop myself from closing the space between us and positioning my face right there.

She slides herself into one of my kitchen chairs and lights a cigarette as she waits for me to prepare the clippers. No easy task since my hands are shaking. I combust internally when she reaches out and fingers the flimsy cloth of my dress asking if I'm not worried 'bout bits of hair too?

No need to ask me twice. I quickly slip out of my frock, black lace bra, and matching panties. I stand head bowed, skin flushed, suddenly every inch the shy femme. A girl out of her element. Feeling so very new and startled when she grabs my pubies and pulls.

She takes the clippers away and gently pushes me down into the chair I had prepared for her. The clippers are cold and hard as she runs them over my nakedness. She hasn't even flicked the switch but my body is already stiff with anticipation. One smooth leg forces its way between my thighs. Fingers smelling and tasting of cigarette enter my mouth and I suck greedily.

One dexterous motion sends electricity flowing to plastic and metal. I try to close my legs. She looks impatient. Gives me cut eye and kisses her teeth. A warning.

The intense vibration makes me wet. Makes me wanna move seeking pleasure in danger. That sharp cutting surface could slice into my soft flesh. Could make me bleed. But right now I don't care. I don't wanna stop. And why should I? Her focussed, deep brown eyes are all business. She is so confidently trimming my bush. So carefully seeing to my pooni's beauty that all I need to do is lay back and enjoy the ride.

Her free hand comes away from my mouth and she uses it to spread my cunt before the clipper's jagged teeth. I feel her hand graze my clit and inner lips gently, covering them, protecting them from harm. But even so, I take in shallow scared breaths whenever the blade moves in close.

Eventually the clippers are quiet. She takes her hand from between my legs and I sit up. The kitchen floor is littered with tiny clumps of hair, but my skin is smooth to the touch. I try to get up but her free arm circles my waist holding me tight. Her smile chills and entices simultaneously.

I pull her to me. We kiss hungrily, briefly. She reaches for the clippers and the buzz begins again. Only this time the clipper's position has shifted. The metal on my clit is warm from use. The flat of the motorized blade presses against flesh and bone. I hesitate and consider pulling away. Her eyes are hard, demanding but I know that if I want to, I can call it off, stop everything. Can't I?

She watches, nudging the blade in time with my need. I find a way to rock without getting hurt and my clit hardens. I am a flood, wetting my own skin and the chair beneath me. Thoughts of electrocution and risk swell my clit.

I wanna reach for her but don't dare make a sudden move. I want more of her lips on mine. Her hot breath. Her words whispered in my ear. But I have to be content with her free hand clenched 'round my neck.

I scream and cuss and struggle to keep still as the vibrations take me, become my whole world, my very reason for being. Rhythmic pulses echoing through my body increase unbearably and peak in waves rushing over me. I collapse limp.

She turns the clippers off, rests them on the table and retrieves another cigarette from her jacket pocket. She offers me a drag but I wave her hand away, too conscious of the cliché. I manage a smile and hope that my hands are steady enough to do her hair.

SUNSETS

Denise Seibert

SHE DOES NOT KNOCK WHEN SHE COMES HOME. I hear the key in the lock and the door opens, and she glances in my direction, to see if I am present, I suppose, but she does not greet me. I hear her toss her keys onto the kitchen counter. I hear her ask the nurse how my day was. The nurse replies fine. No problems. She lets the nurse out the front door. I hear her enter the bedroom and open drawers.

I am sitting in front of the patio window, looking at the sun reflect off the little stream below, one storey down. The sun glimmers off the leaves, making the whole view look watery. From the time I have been sitting here, watching, the sun came into my view from overhead, slowly slid down towards the horizon, and soon will dip into vibrant color and then, finally, disappear. This is my favorite time of the day, after the nurse has left, and she has come home, and the sun is sinking, and she may sit and watch with me. I have no way of telling her how much I would like that.

She returns from the bedroom in more comfortable clothes. She bends over and kisses me on my cheek, then gazes out the window. "Nice day," she says. She is weary from her work and I hear it in her voice. She goes to check the refrigerator for our supper.

"Did you eat lunch?" she calls out to me, as though I might answer. I blink once, for yes, but of course she cannot see me from the kitchen. "I guess we will have TV dinners again, is that okay?" It is okay with me. I do not care much for eating. I hope she will come sit with me to watch the sunset.

I hear the freezer door open and close. I hear paper tearing, the oven door closing. I hear the click of the timer being set on the counter. I hear drawers of silverware opening and closing.

Outside a sparrow is hopping on a tree branch. He has disturbed the leaves at the end of the branch and they are also hopping, up and down, waving to me. The sun has sunk a little lower; it is now below the branch the sparrow is sitting on. When she first came home, it was above that branch.

She stands beside me now.

"Did she put a diaper on you again?" she asks.

I blink yes.

"Hell," she says disgustedly, and slips her hand into my sweatpants to feel if I am wet.

"Let's change," she says shortly.

She wheels me into the bedroom. I do not blame the nurse, who does not want to sit and ask me every hour if I want to use the toilet. I do not blame the nurse for not wanting to leave her soap operas to lift me. I am not heavy, but I am an adult, and I am just dead weight. I am grateful that she allows me, has figured out somehow, that I prefer to sit and watch the sun.

Her arms are so strong. She lifts me in one smooth motion to lay me on the bed. I feel her hair float against my face. I breathe in her smell. I would like for her just to hold me in her arms, rock with me in the chair in front of the fireplace, to let me stay within range of her scent, her hair, her breath. Her hands are firm and soft. She pulls my sweatpants down, takes off the diaper, dries me with a towel. I watch her work. Is this work for her, I wonder? It does not seem to be.

When she has dressed me she places me in my chair and wheels me back to my window. The colors are beginning, outside. The timer goes off and she brings our dinner.

It is a lucky evening, I think. There are just enough clouds to render the coloring adventurous. I remember, briefly, back to the time when I did not know to appreciate the sun. I remember, also, holding my lover, taking that for granted. I do not reminisce much anymore; I like to stay peaceful.

She feeds us slowly; a bite for her, a bite for me. She is quiet this evening. Sometimes she will tell me of her day, of the world that is so far away from me, and that is alright. But I like the tranquility of this quiet, now.

"Is it too hot?" she asks, and I blink no.

I cannot tell her what I have discovered in the sun and the trees and the sparrows. I would like to. But perhaps it is not something I can teach her anyway, if I could say it aloud. It is something that took me months to learn, myself.

She asks me the same question she asks every night. "Do you want something?"

Tonight I surprise her and answer yes.

"More food?"

No.

"Are you uncomfortable?"

No.

"Should I spell it?"

Yes.

"Does it start with an 'A'?"

No.

"A 'B'?"

No.

She goes through the alphabet and I look at the colors, waiting for her to get to the right letter. Finally, she does.

"An 'M'?"

Yes.

"Is the next letter a vowel?"

Yes.

"An 'A'?"

Yes.

Again I wait, this time for a "K," and finally, an "E."

"Make?" she says.

Yes.

"Make what?"

I wait.

"Does it start with an 'A'?"

No.

It only takes two letters before she gets the idea.

"Make love?" she says, gently, incredulously.

Yes.

She is quiet for a moment.

"With me?" she asks.

I laugh with my eyes.

We finish our suppers and she puts the trays in the trash can. If she would have gone on, I would have told her I want to hold you. I want to kiss you and feel you and give you pleasure. I am sorry I cannot. I am so sorry.

The sun has gone to hell, as Dire Straits once told me. The sky is blood red. Even as I watch, this is fading. I will watch until there is no light left, and then I will watch the stars, until she puts me to bed, where I will watch the ceiling.

She returns from a clean kitchen.

Without a word, she wheels me into the bedroom.

She lifts me, but this time it is different. There is a tenderness in her touch now, which is different from the tenderness with which she lifted me to change my clothes. She lays me gently on the bed. As I watch, she undresses. She removes her blouse and drops it on the floor. Her breasts are small and firm. She tugs at her jeans; lets them fall to the floor also. Her movements are slow, hesitant. She takes off her socks and underwear.

She wiggles my pants off. She slides my shirt, my bra, my underwear out from under me.

She lays her full length beside me. She does not know that she can lay on top of me, it will not hurt me. I want her to. Instead, she lightly strokes from my neck to my pubic hair with her fingers. Goosebumps appear on my body. I can feel them. She kisses me on the cheek and pauses.

"Okay?" she asks.

Yes.

She kisses my mouth, my neck, my collarbone. She moves to my breasts and lingers on the nipples, which grow hard.

"I didn't know," she says.

Slowly she drifts to my legs, parts them, kisses. All of my mind, all of me, focuses on her, on the way she makes me feel. I remember this, I remember, I think. My thoughts disappear and all I do is feel. I am a blank slate and she is drawing on me, her movements my only existence. My breath catches, releases, again and again.

"Did I hurt you?" she asks, now, moving up to my face.

No. I must touch you, I think. I must.

She whips her head around, suddenly, feeling something on

her back. My hand has floated up, somehow; it moved up, and rests against her warm skin. She smiles brilliantly. My eyes smile back.

We lay for a while, together. I draw energy, by osmosis, from her closeness. Finally, she rises, dresses, dresses me. She wheels me to the window and together we sit and watch the stars.

THE GIFT

Rita Montana

"RAY, THIS IS MARYANNE."

I try to smile a welcome. Janet has been telling me about Maryanne for a year. So here she is. She reminds me of Janet – same size, same silky, honey–colored hair.

"Ray and I are so glad you have come, aren't we Ray?"

Ten years ago I would never have agreed to meet Maryanne. But that was before my life changed forever. Ten years ago . . . on an icy cold Valentine's day, Janet and I sat in my red pickup, fogging up the windows.

"Let's get married," Janet said.

"Funny you should say that," I said, taking a ring from my pocket and holding it out. "I bought it last week, but I've been so scared and excited, I couldn't show it to you."

She took the ring and held it to her heart and said, "Let's get married right now."

"Here in this truck!"

"Yes, here. Let's just do it."

I took the ring and held it poised against her fingertip and said, "Do you, Janet McLean, take me, Ray Brown, for your wedded spouse?"

"I do – oh yes – I do, I take you as my spouse, forever, Ray Brown."

I slid the ring on. She kissed me deeply. There wasn't another soul in the parking lot, but even if there was, I didn't care who saw us. I just wanted to take her home.

Much of my history is lost, but this is what I remember. We held one another until our feet began to freeze. It was getting late and Janet had to go home. It was her mother's birthday and I wasn't invited, even though Janet and I had been together for ten years.

Now, Maryanne, Janet's lover, leans down, takes my hand in

hers and says, "Janet has told me so many wonderful things about you, Ray."

I bet she has, I want to spit. The memory of that February day rolls over me. In slow motion I see Janet climb down from my pickup and get into her Ford. We wave, make a few little toots on our horns – our wedding day bells – and I watch her drive out of the lot. Once she is out of sight, I exit the lot the opposite way and drive into a semi with my name on it. Red. That's what I saw in that split second.

For six months I was in a coma. I awoke to find I was paralyzed, unable to speak, barely able to see. The only organs unaffected were my ears. Many months later, thanks to lots of work with my occupational and physical therapists, I learned how to operate this laptop. They taught me how to use a head stick. It's always with me – my link to communication and relationships.

"This is a terrific experiment we want to try," Janet pleads.

"I know it could be a disaster. Or the best thing in all the world. You are incredible to be willing to try this out. I don't think it will be easy for any of us," says Maryanne.

I cry. Maryanne is staying over tonight. I said I was ready but now I'm not so sure. Maryanne and Janet both hug and kiss me and I start to feel excited and happy. Maryanne is tender. She has been so good for Janet. Janet wheels me into the dining room and we eat the delicious meal she and Maryanne have made in celebration of our new life. They take turns feeding me. Afterwards we sit in front of the fire and listen to some great jazz. I'm falling asleep, so Janet takes me into my bedroom, undresses me, tucks me in. She kisses me, then tiptoes out. I hear the two of them go up the stairs, stifling giggles, schoolgirls at a pajama party. In the morning, I awake to the sound of the bed bumping upstairs.

It's no surprise, but it's the first time their life together hits me with full impact. At the University of Texas, Janet, lecturing about the rights and needs of wheelchair–bound people, ran into Maryanne. They had gone to high school together twenty-five years ago. Over the years they kept meeting each other at conferences and colleges around the country and became best friends. Of course I heard nothing of this for the first year.

I feel something besides jealousy about the squeaky bed overhead. Desire makes me wet. That part of me was untouched by the accident. My body is still responsive. The bed noise stops. I hear Janet coming down stairs.

"Hello, my darling," she sings out as she comes to my bed. She says no more but begins to stroke me and murmur sweetness into my ear. Part of me wants to ignore her, but her touch is so loving and arousing and I want her more than breath. She knows how to get past my barriers and can open my body up to pleasure like that first time she made love to me after the accident. The memory comes back to me and meshes with the present. She had started to wash me and noticed I was getting turned on, even though I couldn't tell her. She cried as she held me and brought me to orgasm. Even now, I am feeling light, floating up to the ceiling. Lights whirl in my head – it's a miracle.

After the accident, nobody talked about sex. Not the doctors, not the therapists, not even Janet. It was just assumed by all of us that I would never even think of sex. Hah! Janet holds me for a long time, until I'm okay, better than okay. One of the saddest things about our sex life is that even though Janet can give me a really good loving, I can never return the favor. This is where Maryanne comes in. I will lose Janet if I can't be generous. She can be very giving. So can I.

MORNING NOTES

Zara Suleman

IT WAS THE SCENT ON THE RECYCLED PAPER I found at the bottom of a stack of letters that made me think of her. I had started sorting through all of her belongings; it had taken me a long time but I knew I would have to clear away some of her things or at least pack them up.

The letter smelled musty and musky but distinctly of her. A contradiction, like her, of sweetness and spice filled my head. On the outside she maintained her distance; a cold, almost perturbed look. Most avoided her. She was rough but inside was a gentle, uncertain, giving spirit. The letter was given to me twelve years ago, soon after we had met. She was thoughtful with her words and passionate expressions, every sentence sensuous, every image a slow seduction pulling me into her.

The letter was a morning note. She would leave them for me, on my car windshield, taped to my coffee mug or clipped to the bathroom mirror. Times were so busy then, going to university, working full-time, always running around. Some of our best moments were caught in our morning notes.

While sorting I had tried not to read anything. I wanted to strictly put things in "keep," "throw out," or "give away" piles, but it was the smell of this letter, the smell of her, so vivid, so intoxicating, so compelling that I carefully unfolded it and began to read:

"Did I tell you how much I love you, sweety? I didn't want to get up so early I'd rather cuddle with you, warm against your body snuggling into your soft skin, our hands clasped into each other. Some mornings, like today, all I can think is how much I love you. Do you really know how much I love you? This morning I watched while you slept and I couldn't imagine, for a moment, what it would be like if you weren't there. You're my home, my shelter, for now and years to come. I know we are still new and that we are still learning each other, but I want to learn you. I see the woman I want to grow old with, I see the woman I want to have kids with, I see the woman I want to fight with, make up with, and come back to at the end of each day. See you tonight. Love you."

I sobbed, the pain so fresh, tears overflowing and endless, the tightness in my chest made up of all the memories I carry of her, all the things I want to say to her and no one else. The words and thoughts caught in a space only she would have access to, are stored and waiting to be released over time.

It had been nine months and yet it seemed like yesterday. I was in the hospital every day after work and after her surgery I took a month off to stay home with her. She had decided to have both breasts removed. She was devastated, but she thought it would stop it from spreading. But it didn't stop. Chemo, radiation, more surgery, herbal supplements, prayer, meditation. She tried it all.

It was like a flash from her last major surgery to the doctor walking in and telling us about her latest test results. It had spread through her lymph system.

She had never cried in front of the hospital staff through all of it. Until that moment, she had kept fighting. We cried so hard that night; we did not say anything to each other. I remember my fingers enmeshed in hers. I remember my head on her belly away from all of the tubes and needles, her hand stroking my hair and then she whispered, " I love you, do you know how much I love you?"

I folded the letter carefully, and held it close to my face, closing my eyes and smelling her scent. It felt like she was in the room with me and I knew she was, I needed her to be.

I knew when I met her that she was the one. Not the "for three months" one, or the "three years and it's over" one, or the "we'll just be friends" one, but the "one." I never got bored, I never wanted another, and even when we fought hard and the honesty was brutal I still could only imagine sharing my bed, body, mind, and heart with her.

I missed her so much, her touch so firm yet soft at the same time. Her arms wrapped around me at the sink while I did the dishes. Her kisses full, deep, and generous at the end of a hard day. I missed the small of her back and curve of her hips, always hidden under too many layers of clothes. I missed the nights, days, afternoons filled with the wetness of our bodies, the sounds of pleasure we made and the look in her eyes as she watched me. I missed the way our bodies moved under, over and around each other's. I missed her laugh and I missed her making me laugh.

I had managed to get one box done. I hesitated before closing it and took out the morning note I had just read. I wasn't ready to put it away in some cold, dark storage space. I wanted it near, I wanted her near.

"I love you," I said. "Do you know how much I love you?"

HOLDING HANDS

Jean Taylor

MY PARTNER MAUREEN AND I were sitting side by side on the old couch holding hands that Thursday mid-afternoon over two years ago now when she simply stopped breathing and died.

One of the thoughts uppermost in my mind at that particularly significant point in time was that she had allowed me to be there with her when she took her last breath. It was another one of her generous acts that held me in good stead in the agonizing months afterwards without her great presence to comfort me. And another thing that became part of the legend of her life.

We were holding hands, something we'd been doing ever since we'd become lovers. And even more so over those final weeks of her life, when it finally and inevitably got to the stage that we stopped making love (in the genital sense) because it took more energy than she was capable of or could be bothered mustering.

To say that we made do with holding hands (although we still managed to do quite a bit of kissing as well) would not only put down or belittle what I consider to be one of the most essential points of contact between two people, but it would not do justice to the incredible warmth, love, and sensual comfort conveyed by the contact of our two hands.

All of the pleasure we'd given each other over the eight years we'd been together was contained in our fingers. The thousands of caresses – around our breasts, our nipples, our clitorises, our vaginas – all the love we'd felt and wanted to convey by our loving gestures was at our fingertips while we held hands.

Remembering this reminded me of a workshop I went to years ago at one of the lesbian festivals organized by various dykes in different states on a rotating basis.

"Going to the sexuality workshop?" someone asked me, as I

passed the pot-bellied stove on the veranda where the smokers congregated. If it was this cold in January, the middle of summer, it had to be Tasmania. A bit windy, but the view out over the hills towards the sea was awe-inspiring.

"Probably," I prevaricated. I was hesitant because I wasn't sure what to expect. It was mainly the s&m dykes who held sexuality workshops and while I had nothing against those who mixed pleasure and pain, the fact was I didn't and had no intention of starting.

As I passed the kitchen, I was encouraged by the numbers of us who were heading in the same direction and entered the designated workshop room along with everyone else. A popular workshop.

And well organized. To start, we had to call out every kind of sexual practice we could think of while the facilitator wrote it on the whiteboard. Not a problem. It wasn't long before the board was covered with everything from cunnilingus and breast sucking to penetration and finger fucking and everything else in between. Nothing was left out.

As most womyn were quicker off the mark and mostly saying what I would have said anyway, I waited until there was a bit of silence while everyone wracked their brains for one more practice we'd forgotten: "Holding hands," I called out.

To my surprise, everyone laughed. Not that I minded, and I continued to participate in what proved to be a lively and interactive workshop with lots of laughter.

It was only afterwards when I had time to reflect about why everyone had laughed that I thought to myself, they've forgotten. In this society we live in where we want instant gratification for all our senses in a non-stop orgy of sexual delight they, we, have forgotten what it's like to simply hold hands with someone. We've also forgotten how absolutely electrifying it can be: to hold hands with someone for the very first time when you're still too young to fuck or you can't fuck for whatever reason. You hold each other palm to palm, the fingers squeezing, massaging, one hand held by the other so you feel cherished.

The challenging statement to the world as you walk down the street holding hands says unequivocally that you're lovers; anyone want to make an issue of it? Sitting in the picture theater, or anywhere really, her hand takes yours and for that moment there's nothing so important as the burning in your body from that all-encompassing and riveting contact.

I kept on holding hands with Maureen for several hours after she died, still sitting next to each other on the couch, neither of us going anywhere, only wanting to be there together.

I made the necessary phone calls, other people made cups of tea, brought food. I stayed next to Maureen on the couch, holding her hand that had become like a lifeline to another world.

By late evening the small flat was full of friends crying and laughing, telling stories, making jokes, and remembering. The last woman to arrive held out her hand and I took it in my free one. It was freezing. "You're even colder than Maureen," I exclaimed.

Maureen's beloved hand, because I'd been holding and stroking it, was like smooth white marble, and was still warm in mine.

FALLING

Nina D.

A WRENCHING TEAR, PULLING FREE, I topple and I am falling. The sudden lurch of my body as it begins its descent. My lungs gasp and clutch at the air crashing through them. The wind grabs my body and sucks it into her. My winter coat batters insanely about my body, buttons straining to burst open. Wind billows up the sleeves, rushes through my pant legs, seeking to claim every possible crevice, every hollow. I notice that already my shoes are gone. My red chenille scarf twists around my neck and caresses my face in its escape. I am plummeting at a treacherous speed. This is free fall.

And as abruptly, I am caught, suspended in an updraft, hovering in one spot long enough to see landmasses far, far below me. The intimate warmth of the current slips away from me and again I tumble. A sister slipstream embraces me and I am caught again, then float. My body breathes, dares to connect with this moment, acknowledge my presence in time. And I notice the almost complete lack of sound. The ubiquitous wind is palpable, but it is wind devoid of any other cadence. The wind here is the rushing sound of God.

And now I am floating sweetly. I watch as cloud tendrils race across my palm, reading the path left there by my life. A gull wheels close, its curious eye catching mine. He hangs with me for a moment or two, gliding effortlessly to be with me. And then he spins up and away. I am alone again.

The wind lashes at my face, reminding me of my peril, my fall. I see evidence of humanity below, still just indistinguishable specks of color bobbing on the inky sea. The wind laughs in my ear.

I feel the shift, the sudden surge of acceleration again as the earth pulls me homeward, her claim. My heart clamors in my chest, its rhythm exploding in my head, blocking out all sound

of the angels' fluttering wings. I know there is only a dusting of
sand left to fall through the narrow waist of this hourglass.

And there they are, the gnarled arbutus trees, scattering
across my glazed vision, nanosecond images of jutting coastline,
luminous wave crests, blue sky colliding in my brain. A child's
party balloon, purple, happily intact, hums along the horizon.

I smash through the iron surface of the water, limbs bursting,
the pain searing my soul.

Lauren calls to me, "Hush, sweet one, come awake to me,
hush." I swallow, feel my legs slick with sweat, the tangle of hair
clenched in my fist. My face is molten with tears.

"Open your eyes, little one, it's okay, see where you are,"
Lauren's reassuring voice coaxes me. "It's alright, hush."

I reluctantly peel open my eyes, and adjust to the silver light
slipping across the room. The hulking wardrobe in the northwest corner, the plexi-chrome print glinting quietly on the wall.
My body shudders. I am here. I am safe.

Lauren slips her long arm under and around me, pulling me
tight, my hip fitting below hers. Her hand, warm, ah, Lauren always so warm, gently easing the wrinkles from my forehead.

"You are drenched, sweet girl. Was it the ocean again?" she
asks and I nod, gulping back the tears.

She pulls the quilt along me, absorbing the dampness that is
chilling my feverish body.

"Let it out, darling, let it go," she urges me. And the sobs un-
fold, searching for the angels that flock to take them away.

Slowly, my chest quiets and the waves recede. The silver light
in our bedroom has shifted across and down the wall.

I float, but in warmth, in safety.

Lauren holds this embrace for what seems like forever and
then she slips seductively down my body, her lithe limbs tumbling along my surfaces, her breath intuitively finding the path.
And as she lays her tongue ever so gently inside me, the warm
wet of my underwater fall begins.

This incredible woman carries me, sucking and calling me to
the safest place I know.

And she cradles me again, body length against mine, her tender intent wrapped about me.

I whisper to sleep, asking for its forgiveness, its undemanding solace. I feel the tug as the water softens, pulling me under, my hair trailing down from the surface. I catch the scent of salt-water on my mouth, the delicious taste of my fall.

THE ISLE WOMEN WATCHING

Denise Nico Leto

IN THE CORNER OF A CORNER I WILL FIND YOU. On a long stretch of beach, near the nautical, the wet, the wind I will find you. When I first saw your gaze you were silver, you were green, you were yellow and maroon. I remember your hair; it was unplanned. I remember your smile; it was an ellipse. There were stars behind the night as your eyes followed. You were falling; you were not falling. It was autumn, it was winter, it was spring, and it was summer. I know because the sun set early and late; the day was cold and the day was hot. It was light near your body as I passed by and it was just getting dark out. You were not a window or a mirror; you were clear but you were far. I heard the old sky gather. Your arms were not wings, but they glided near and then over. I saw rain on your skin although it was dry out. I imagined this. I did not. I know this because I love you now.

In order to meet we polished the street lamps clear, crisscrossed city streets, and sampled the odd repast. We studied Latin, smoked hashish, flattened mounds of dirt with our sandals, and we traveled through books and electronic mail. It took years. It took two boats in the water. I rowed and rowed. Of course it was foggy. I could not find you at first. Of course you capsized. I couldn't see to save you and you swam a long way under. Later, I saw your face through the scrim. It was unposed yet flawless. I held out my arm. You climbed into the boat. To start out balmy is the best way.

Do I take you to me here in the boat or do I wait for land? Should I ask you your name or should I name you allure? Do we promise to last or do we surrender uncertain? Do we latch our boats together or do we lilt them apart? Or do I just say: Come wake with me; incite the weather.

We rocked my boat, but not as wood in a lake lapping, rather more slowly and slippery, as aromatic oil in water would sway. We lay heavy and floating, unmixed while swirling. You leaned back in my arms and there were edges and curves and an arithmetic sorrow, an uncalculated joy. There were grand breaches of mainland etiquette and the only law upheld was ancient, saline, and Sapphic. This is not a metaphor. Her body took a shape – feline. This is not a cliché. When she curled up, there were triangles, purrs. Everything was in threes. Oh holy trinity of her body unto mine; her pussy could only be called divine and worldly. As in: it had not yet been given, but knew all. It had not been lorded over, occluded or cleansed. It smelled of a deep Eurydice–river descending, and when I turned back to the upper air to look and taste again and again I did not betray, almost from wanting, but I did not. She was wet and it was vital. She was a body within a body. This is not a theory. We could perish for this love. It is called hate. But I was able to orchestrate her hum and we sang when she came.

And her breasts could rule the world. They could negotiate their way through a treacherous grove and prove the flavor of freedom. The beautiful beast in us swallowed and we were breathless and wild: no scribe, no lack, no god. When we kissed we were swollen together. When we did not kiss we were swollen together. When she moved near without touching I felt her untethered reach always imminent. When I moved near her without touching, she watched and she waited till I grazed her nipple with my tongue.

Years later and our boats remain unmoored. You may see us in the bay, rocky seashores, outlandish inlets, marshes, swamps, and peninsulas. We are naked. We are imperfect. We have jobs. We exist as much alone as together. Her body is not a castle. My body is not a moat. We are not a poem. We climb over scraps of memory, paper fragments. We watch women to see what you watch. We are infinitely interested in recreating the world in your image. We saw each other first in your eyes. We are often ecstatic. We are often imperiled. Last week a man threatened to throw a pile of rocks at my head. The week before a drunken boy tried to push my lover down an escalator. "Dykes!" they yell.

We may only live a short time. We may live to be a hundred. We are never far from water. We are everywhere near you. When we love each other, we love you. This is how we came to be together.

DINOFLAGELLATES

Elana Dykewomon

IN THE MOONLESS, HUMID NIGHT a rusty school bus pitches over a sand track, swatted by palm fronds as if it were a large yellow bug. Elaine holds Sorah's hand, low, against the torn brown plastic of the bench. Sorah is being a good sport about adventures in the Vieques heat, although at night the heat is greased by breeze, and this close to the coast becomes pliable, buttery. Sorah finds she can breathe in humidity, recovered now from the ten-seater plane ride from San Juan that tipped her within scraping distance of the giant bamboo groves in El Yunque, the rain forest.

As the bus inches along the hidden road, Elaine and Sorah use the lurches to press their thighs together in secret pleasure. They are middle-aged Jewish dykes and for the six years of their alliance, traveling has increased their appetite for each other. Aside from the obvious – no phones, no routine – they thrive on visual stimulation and slightly edgy situations, moments when they must find their way and succeed. Joy embroiders their small successes. Desire is a map with half the roads obscured by the creases that come from folding it so many times and carrying it in your pocket. In unknown terrain, what star can you use to navigate the way to your lover under the mosquito netting? Traveling is a search for signs that lead us not back to some easy habit, but forward, or sideways, into raw presence. We push on, among strangers, towards revelation, discovering anew how meeting another woman startles us into contact: lover contact, and through that, contact with the pulse of the world.

Tonight they are among eighteen tourists, a female tour guide, and a male bus driver who waits by the bus, smoking. The other tourists are heterosexual couples or families, three pre-adolescent children among them. In order to get the full wonder, tours to the phosphorescent bay are recommended at the new moon, when the night is black as squid ink stippled only by the Milky Way. On this side of Vieques, away from the military base so often the site of anti-U.S. demonstrations, few lights pollute the dark. The woman who runs the tour is ecological and nature-minded – she uses an electric engine on her boat to cut down on oil entering the water.

Elaine spent part of her childhood in Puerto Rico and over the last thirty years she has taken several lovers to see the more famous phosphorescent bay on the main island. Even though a relatively small percentage of tourists leave the beach and casino strip around San Juan, the double-decker boats that stream out to the bay in La Parguera have been carrying too many people for too many years – Elaine's last trip with some hundred tourists was disappointing – and she'd read how the dinoflagellate population there, the one-celled creatures that sparkle in the Caribbean dark, is endangered now.

So this time she altered the tour, having found a lesbian-owned guest house on Vieques. In the guest house, which straddled a volcanic hill covered with dense green vegetation, they were the only lesbians besides the owners. The hammocks had views of both the Atlantic and Caribbean seas. It was gorgeous enough, but Elaine, inured to the more blatant charms of the topography, restless, had spied a notice about the phosphorescent tour tacked on the bulletin board, and persuaded Sorah to give it a try.

Sorah likes being gently persuaded, lovingly cajoled into trying things she hasn't imagined. She likes to taste new things if they come vouched for, and Elaine likes to vouch. Elaine is too big for the life jackets that the tour guide offers, and she has a cold, but she has been pushing herself because, after all, how many chances do you get to show your lover the sights of the tropics? Really, they've come because her father died nearly a year ago; within a week they must circle back and stand by his grave with Elaine's mother and brothers in a rural Puerto Rican cemetery that has a small Jewish section. But not yet.

Tonight they are gliding out on a small boat that rides low in the water. The guide cuts the engine and a large shape zips by, outlined in yellow light. "That's a turtle," the guides says, clearly pleased. "Watch for other fish." As they adjust to the obsidian shine of the water ringed by mangrove trees, fish part the surface with electric jaws, snapping at bugs that must leave footprints for bait. Dinoflagellate, who wouldn't swoon to say it, roll it around in her mouth, suck at its undulation?

The guide says they can swim in the bay. Elaine would never admit to being terrified of getting into the opaque water, even if the creatures that lie still in the deep will flash, betraying themselves when they move to snap. Anyway, she has a cold. Anyway, the life jacket doesn't fit. Sorah has her bathing suit on under her clothes, and is swept up in Elaine's encouragement. Usually it's Elaine who takes the dare and dives into the cold wave or snorkels along the shallow shore, only a little concerned about scraping herself on the purple spines of sea urchins. But she can see the spines. Sorah does not know until she reads this story how glad Elaine is to have the cold and life jacket problem to fall back on, so Sorah bravely, happily even, descends the ladder off the boat into the dark bay with about ten of the other tourists, shouting, flapping, making a sudden carnival splash of color in the night, setting the dinoflagellates into panics of bioluminescence.

Sorah hauls herself back on deck, laughing, sweeping Elaine up to her dripping body. The other tourists are paying no attention to them – everyone is transfixed by the glittering that washes over the deck from the wet swimmers. Elaine pulls the top of Sorah's bathing suit down and stares between her breasts. Here the constellations spark against Sorah's flesh, showing the way – between her bathing suit and body lie a thousand stars.

POWELL STREET

rita wong

BIKING DOWN THE AUGUST STREETS OF VANCOUVER i find my pride at powell street. reverberating into the crowd as exuberant taiko. walk into a sea of issei, nisei, sansei pride, generations of pride playing in rock bands, doing park clean-up, serving corn on the cob, making videos, doing a post-atomic dance. loud, juicy watermelon smashed open pride. lazy summer sweet, sweaty orange pride that turns your quick stride into a languid prowl. an icy lemon kakikori pride, melting on my thirsty tongue. once found pride somewhere on the curve of her nape, on the pout of her lips, in the welcome between her thighs. now i rummage through the ashes looking for stubborn, black, swishy strands of girl pride recently shaved off. a bare nun pride. a coldblue tightlip heartbruised pride that holds your shoulders rigid, your back sad. pride on Salish land. kaslo, slocan, new denver, greenwood, black & white archived internment survival pride. ragged ass bi any means necessary random trigonometries of pride. oppenheimer park downtown eastside strung out on the street scowling pride. oxymoronic cop in a uniform pride. not just the usual suspects, the flashy buffed fag dancing on a float or glittery drag queen strutting pride but a burnaby correctional centre prisoner pride, a mom and dad marching in pflag pride, an every day in high school pride, elementary pride, endless legal battles to win pride, child-friendly pride, a jenny shimizu is everywhere hello kitty hello pussy pride. kiss me like you mean it pride. finally coming out to your momma pride that is actually relief. scavenging alleys for art materials pride. creating our own rituals because we need to pride. give me graffiti pride over the glossy commercial brand any day. a constantly inventing what we desire pride.

with acknowledgments to adrienne rich whose words help close this piece

COME TO ME IN COSTUME

Jess Wells

COME TO ME WITH A TIE COURSING between the sweet spot of your breasts. Wear a vest to bed.

Let the slits of a leather bodice slow my fingers, make them search.

Wear something from another time, another culture, something to get us outside our minds, our mail–stops, our past and joint possessions. Any costume at all that will make you a clit, a tit, a length of hip edged in somebody else's life.

You see, I lust after wonder, long for awe, for the deep, weapon-less stranger bearing no grudges, storing no resentments as ammunition in the closet.

Don a sports jacket to dream of fucking me on the subway.

Hide our life behind fringe, beneath chaps – make me hunt for you in the folds of a cape. Remake your body under the cling of gauze.

Be my plumber, firefighter, my priest, my boss. Be anything but naked, well–scrubbed, utilitarian, married, and plain.

REST STOP

Mickey

DRIVING THROUGH TEXAS. Almost halfway. The sun is high, the sky burnt blue. The wind is hot. I'm looking for a diner or even just a rickety old gas station with an out-of-order pump. Anyplace where I can get something cold to drink. I haven't seen a soul for 100 miles. Buildings appear in the distance. I pass the first one and see crumbling plaster, broken chairs, an overturned table. Graffiti covers the walls. I see something up ahead, in front of the next building. It's a motorcycle. Black, a lowrider, coated with a thin layer of desert dust. A well-traveled backpack is strapped on. There's a sticker on the tank that says, "This bitch don't ride bitch." I pull in. It's the only sign of life and I am set on finding something to quench my thirst. I shut off the engine and get out. Dust rises where my boots hit the ground. I hear a splash coming from behind the building. I follow the sound. Around the side I get my first sight of you. Your head thrown back as you pour water from a canteen over your face. It trickles down your back, which is bare except for the straps of your black bra. A tattoo shows itself above the waist of your jeans. Your ass is firm inside your black jeans and leather chaps. I clear my throat. You turn, spilling water on the ground. Your breasts push out over the top of your bra. Our eyes meet. You say nothing and turn to the old well where a bucket balances on the edge. Using a rope you lower the bucket, tipping it so it fills. I watch your muscles work as you hoist the bucket. You walk over and wordlessly set it at my feet. I scoop water with my hands, bring it to my face, let it run down my neck, over my chest. I take more. My thin tank top gets wet. My breasts show through. You can see where my nipples are pierced. You pick up the half-empty bucket, put your hand under my chin and tilt my head back. You pour the water over my hair, being careful to spill some so that my top is now soaked through. You walk back to the well. I come up behind you. Run my wet hands down your back. You make a noise – the slightest intake of breath. I step closer. My nipples, wet and hard through my top, press against your back. Your skin wakes up with goose bumps. I reach up and around to your breasts. Your nipples harden under my fingers. I pinch. Your back arches. I bite your shoulder. You tilt your head. My lips wander up to your neck. You grab my arm and walk towards the building. We enter through the back door, stepping around a saddlebag you have left on the floor. We still haven't spoken. Only breath has passed our lips. You push me against the wall and pull up my top. My nipples are so hard they hurt. You make them hurt more as your teeth close around one, your fingers pulling the ring of the other. Involuntarily I moan. Your other hand loosens my belt. My cutoffs drop to the floor. Today was too hot for underwear. You smile. Your fingers trace my lips. My hips move. I want you to fuck me. I reach out for your breast. You slap my hand away. Your finger slips inside me. My legs move further apart. You drop to your knees. Your tongue brushes the edges of my cunt. My lips are swollen. I move, encouraging you to go in, with your tongue, your fingers, your hand. With anything. My head is against the wall. My eyes are shut, my mouth slightly open. My teeth hold my lower lip, biting back sounds. I do not want to break the silence. You stop. Your finger slides out. Your tongue moves away. I look down as you stand up. Your hand moves up to close my eyes. My breath is audible. I am panting. I hear snaps. A zipper. I hear leather sliding against leather. I hear your footsteps. I feel your breath on my shoulder, your hand on my waist. I move my hand to your leg. I feel your chaps. My hand moves up. Your ass is bare. I feel leather straps. I feel something hard against my thigh. I open my eyes and see a strapped-on dildo. You move your hand between my legs, my lips part. I am breathing through my mouth. When you enter me, my breath escapes. We move to-gether, your hands on my hips, my hands flat against the wall. You're watching. Looking to see how easily you're sliding in and out. You push all the way in. I gasp. You pull all the way out. And then you just stand there smiling. I grab your shoulders and push you to your knees, then onto your back. I straddle your waist. I lower myself, my cunt wrapping around you. I move. Slow, then faster. Riding you. Hard. Our eyes meet and lock. Minutes pass like hours. I fall into you, coming in waves.

Slowly I stand, releasing you. I pull you to your feet. My hand moves between your legs. You push me away and walk outside. I pull on my cutoffs and follow you. I see you, your head thrown back, water trickling down your back. Your ass is bare, straps gone. I clear my throat. You turn slowly. I blow a kiss in your direction. You snap your head as though it struck you. I walk around the building. I get into the van. I start the engine and pull out. I'm looking for a diner. Even just a rickety old gas station with an out-of-order pump. Anyplace where I can get something cold to drink.

RECKON

T.L. Cowan

THE MOMENT OF RECKONING HAD ARRIVED and she had failed. It was obvious and conspicuous. Glaring fluorescent in her face. It illuminated the fact that she had spent an hour the night before squeezing blackheads on her forehead. It made her cotton maxi pad bunch between her legs. It whisked the clotted stench of dried-blood-clinging-to-pubic-hair from her crotch to her nose. It filled the bus with the exposed smells of shed and spun uterus. Failure crept wet into her armpits.

The hole in her left sock gnawed at her heel and she knew that her pant-leg was hitched inside the ankle of her boot, betraying the ribbing of her cheap, white tube socks – white tube socks in brown leather boots. The bra she was wearing had slackened, and rather than graciously lift, it drew her breasts downward. As a result, her erect nipples (because of the bite in the air) were pointing directly toward her belt buckle. Her purple shirt was not as tight as it used to be. It folded under her long breasts, creating the effect that the shirt was not one item of clothing, but two separate pieces: a top and a bottom attached under her breasts in exactly the same faded color. Her brown cords were faded too. She knew that she had left the house that morning wearing purple and brown, but only now saw how ridiculous she looked. Her own reflection accused her from the bus window and she was hit with the devastating realization that she was at least five years too old for the "grunge" look. Slovenliness, she now understood, loses its carefree appeal once you have crow's-feet around your eyes.

It was almost dark outside.

More devastating then the mess of her clothes, was her chaste and bulky fleece coat. It was fine for camping, even for playing Frisbee, or dog walking, but she was out in public in a coat covered

in cat hair, girlfriend hair, fluff, and lint. This coat had no purpose other then the practical. It was about as sexy as a dryer
filter. She might as well have been wearing a sign that read: "I
haven't been out of the house on a weekend night for eight
months." She figured that if she did have her own sign, there
would be letters missing.

In her right hand she carried a beige, cotton grocery bag full
of library books. Her backpack also bulged with the mangled
angles of books. The immense weight of the pack made her
shoulders hunch and her head jut forward like an osteoporotic,
nosy neighbor. The hip strap of the backpack was cinched tightly
at her waist flaring the thick fleece coat over her ass like a lumpy
wool tutu. She had an old, plastic travel mug attached to the
pack. She knew what she looked like. It was abundantly clear.

Condensation clouded the air, stifling breath and sound.

The moment of reckoning arrived at exactly 4:31. Right before
5°C. Right after 'FREE PARKING.' As the bus passed the Biltmore
Hotel's sign, she saw who had gotten onto the bus at the last
stop and was now heading her way. In that moment she saw the
open vintage leather jacket and the polished black boots. She
knew about the freshly shaved neck and sensed the scratch of
three-hour stubble against her cheek. She saw that cocky raised
eyebrow and felt like she would vomit from nerves. She glanced
quickly to the deliberately flat chest. She knew about the tensor
bandage that kept it that way. She felt her own breasts bounce
and sway obscenely, albeit rhythmically, in time with the jerky
motion of the bus. The tug on her unconfined chest was humil-
iating. Her cheeks colored and she wished that she had taken
the time to do something about herself that morning. As she
bowed her head to avoid making eye contact, she reached over
to yank the stop cord, all the while willing the enormous white
man who stood between her and this moment to grow roots
through his feet and stay where he was.

This moment of reckoning was absolute.

It contained thirty years of lovers and passions; it was every
insignificant crush and every raunchy affair; it was every success
and every failure. Every moment existed in that moment. Every
fuck, Rachel knew, existed in the eyes whose gaze she could not

look up to meet. Not like this. This moment contained the girl she licked like a pro in a tool shed when she was twelve. It had in it the boy she ditched at a drive-in movie when she was seventeen. It was the asshole who picked her up when she hitched home that night. Right there on the bus, she could feel the hands of the professor she seduced over and over again because he wore v-necked sweaters and Birkenstock sandals and knew how gay men fist fucked. This moment was the roommate she couldn't have when she was twenty-five: lovely, naked, wet, and sleek, out of the shower, running to her bedroom, steaming and untouchable. It was the horny girl in that Atlantic bar who bit her neck and sucked her clit in the bathroom while her customers waited for more bread. She imagined this moment when she whacked off to get rid of cramps.

This moment reached out and drew a face on the clouded bus window.

Rachel frowned. This moment should have extended into the future. It should, she thought, represent the first moment rather then the last. But as she left the bus hauling her bags and tripping on the last step, she didn't look back to see if those eyes followed her. She let this moment pass her by with a sneeze of gutter and a yawn of exhaust and promised herself that when it came back to her, she would be up for the reckoning.

NINE DEGREES LATITUDE

Jules Torti

AT NINE DEGREES LATITUDE WE ARE HORIZONTAL. I know every longitude of her body, especially the unchartered territory of "down under." The Great Divide. Every elevation, each inlet of pleasure, creek of fervor, canyon of arousal, bay of pleasure – where the four winds collide and calm, dividing the tropics and racing towards the meridian.

We are sticky, slippery, sweaty, and syrupy in all the right places. On a bed of warm sand with the salty Pacific at our toes, we whisper fantasies and desires to each other that make us both salivate. We kiss between breaths, our mouths sweet with pineapple, our lips velvety with coconut milk. We caress under the palms, groping at times with pounding hearts, taking time out to feed each other ripe papaya and bites of banana.

I picked a deserted isle on the horizon – exile wouldn't be such a terrible thing. I'm not talking about an island and a battle for a tidy million; we just wanted a bit of land surrounded by ocean to call our own. *Sexile.* Imagine running barefoot in pristine waters, making love under stars that seemed to shine brighter every night. When you're in love you see more constellations. The air smells sweeter, everything you eat is an aphrodisiac, and the sunsets hang in a gallery that no artist can enter.

On our own island, far from everything familiar and comfortable, we howl like monkeys with every climax. We watch every sunrise and sunset with a poet's eye and a songwriter's heart. Climbing the ocean battered cliffs to the highest spot, where our hearts beat so loudly in our ears we think we might faint, we plunge into the depths, leaving fear naked on the cliff.

We imagine erotic play in the exotic wilds. This endless playa, the tide of bliss that follows the path of the moon. She waxes poetic, like she's stealing words from a Jewel song, and then she blurts out a fantasy with Elvira Kurt eating Hungarian goulash off my body. Yes, Elvira would be wearing that bad-ass Catholic school girl kilt with no underwear, like she did that year at Michigan, crouching down in such a position that every lip-licking lesbian in a lawnchair wished she had her greedy hands on a pair of binoculars. When Elvira Kurt is in a kilt, there is no binocular sharing.

We contemplate mountain-biking, naked of course, somewhere mucky on the west coast. Melissa Ferrick would be naked too, or clad in leather chaps – whatever turns you on – riding on the handlebars, *my* handlebars.

"How 'bout a *ménage à cinq* with the Butchies?" my gal pipes up, eyes wide with a devilish expression. I thought the only French she knew was fries, well, *poutine* for that matter – but a *ménage à cinq*? Five bodies, ten nipples, probably five nipple rings and five clits, all begging for equal opportunity. Her tongue is wagging like a happy dog's tail.

I want something with Carole Pope, and lots of leather (but not in the sand – too hot and expensive). Maybe pleather would do. She'd whisper sweet nothings or sweet somethings in our ears (or other parts), or hum Rough Trade lyrics – a Bananarama tune (who cares, it's Carole Pope), and send me to all the planets. Men are from Mars, women are from Venus, but Carole Pope's from the Leather Galaxy of Bodies that make you pant, moan, and scream all at the same time. Yeah, I'm a High School Confidential cheerleader. Give me a C-A-R-Oooooooooooooooooh.

We both figure a night with Annie Lennox and Dr McGillicuddy would go over well. A little vanilla Schnapp's and Godet on our lips, gyrating hips and a 104-degree hot tub steaming in snowy Northern Ontario. Or Northern Ireland, or England – it doesn't matter because when you look in the eyes of Annie Lennox, you're transported to another world anyway.

The girlfriend wants Martina. Martina and martinis on the clay court. Who wouldn't want that body, her muscles all flexing with startling definition. She can bounce balls on the court, and bounce quarters off her abs. It would be . . . love, love.

I interrupt, dizzy with the thought of my breaking daydream – "licking cappuccino froth off that Starbucks barista with the nose ring. Nibbling cranberry and pistachio biscotti out of her navel. . . ."

My girl opts for the Tim Horton's babe who's a dead ringer for Mary Stuart Masterston, who always throws in a free maple dip with her large black coffee. Always. Mmm, maple dip lesbian.

Fantastic fantasies. I could write an encyclopedia set of *Hot & Bothered's*. Sexcapades, a climax at the IMAX – I could arouse myself into a frenzied stupor. A masturbation manual for armchair nymphomaniacs. Something to cuddle up with in your La-z-Boy – or, rather La-z-Girl. Everything is erotic, and in the sand and sun of nine degrees latitude, our fantasy is each other. We don't need Martina and her muscles or mussels in a white wine sauce, or Carole in leather or Elvira in a kilt. We have each other, and when I look in her eyes, we are always on that island.

We make love all day – hard, relentless, soft, and tender. Like nymphos, like angels, like barstool strangers and long lost lovers. From the breath of dawn to the sigh of dusk, until the moon climbs to its highest arc.

Insatiable, desperate, begging on bended knee for yet another climax of our souls. Our bones and bodies ache as though we had climbed Everest and K2, cycled the Tour de France and traversed five raging rivers somewhere in between.

I have mapped out all her erogenous zones with a blind compass. I've discovered every intricate plateau of the human heart – how to tickle her fancy, and other parts too. Life is sugar and spice and everything nice, every endearing kiss brings me closer to the brink of addiction.

That's when fantasy becomes a breathing reality, and a dream becomes a story that you can hardly believe. That's what happens at nine degrees latitude, somewhere between the Tropics of Cancer and Capricorn with the Pacific at your toes.

THERAPY

Karen Woodman

DREADING HER, I CROSSED THE PARKING LOT from the bus stop. Lately there was always something wrong. The till would be twelve cents short, the garbage was in the wrong bin, or a book would be filed in the wrong category. I knew she was in the store, ready to pounce.

I had been hopeful the day I saw the "Help Wanted" sign taped to the front door. Melody looked me over and said, "Nice tennis shoes. You're hired." I noticed her gold pinky ring and the beaded, daisy chain rainbow bracelet around her left wrist. *Right on*, I thought. *Finally I get to work for a lesbian.*

The first day I thought she was sweet. On a shelf behind the cash register she displayed cute little kitten books – some were shaped like kittens, others were filled with kitten stories. Melody leaned against the counter peering at customers below partially closed eyelids. Her pursed lips never moved. She spread her elbows on the counter top and one hand covered the other, like a kitten, I imagined.

My biggest mistake was not coming out right away. We never talked about personal things. She talked *at* me and it was difficult to make conversation. Melody believed in a no–nonsense work ethic. She had managed a grocery store for twenty years and there was always plenty of work before any chit chat. She taught me how to hand scrub linoleum with Javex. She demonstrated how Fantastik worked on the inside of a garbage can. When someone offered a box of old books, reeking with basement mould, her spotless hands would contract into tiny fists and she would lean forward and say, "This whole box is infested with spores," enunciating each word, slowly. The person would disappear, forever.

I loved the job but my relationship with Melody began to deteriorate. We started to dislike one another. When I suggested we move the Modern Warfare and Weapons of Destruction books away from the window to a less conspicuous area of the store, she muttered "Little snot" under her breath as she continued to scrub the counter.

Another day, I was doodling on a scrap of paper. She pulled it away, whispering, "You little witch," and crumpled it into a ball. I tried to make conversation one last time and asked, "What sort of books do you like to read?" She pointed to the wall of General Fiction and blurted, "None of this crap." She paused for a moment and added, "Non-Fiction." *Self-Help?* I wondered silently.

A studious-looking woman wearing gold, wire-rimmed glasses entered the store and approached the counter. She asked if I had anything by Toni Morrison.

"No," I replied, "we just sold our last copy of *Beloved.*"

"I'll go and see what else you have," she added, browsing along an aisle of Science Fiction. "I can't find anything for myself," she said, returning.

"Maybe it was poetry you were looking for," I suggested.

"Maybe you're right," she smiled over her shoulder, walking out the door.

After work, I noticed the same woman pull up in front of the store. She was waiting. I was trying to get a better look at her car when Melody slipped into the passenger seat and they drove off together.

What an unusual couple, I thought.

The following afternoon, the studious-looking woman entered the store again and approached the counter. She offered her hand. "I don't believe we've been introduced."

"I'm Julie," I said.

"She's my roommate," Melody said, approaching the counter. The telephone rang behind me. Melody placed one hand on my left shoulder and reached behind to answer. I felt her breasts against me. Her hand released my shoulder and I felt it between my thighs.

She's fondling me right in front of her girlfriend, I thought incredulously. She began to stroke my clitoris. I felt tingly, queasy, shocked. Aroused. I felt as though I could orgasm right there. I leaned towards Melody's girlfriend and asked, "Can I kiss you?"

When I arrived at the store the next morning the "Help Wanted" sign was taped to the door. In black marker I added, "Self," so the sign would read "Self-Help Wanted." That was all I could think to write at the time.

HAPPY

Carol Demech

HAPPY FANTUCCI'S BEDROOM LOOKED like a hospital dispensary. Next to her bed was a rolling cart with four shelves filled with bottles of medicine, syringes, IV bags, and medical equipment. Two tall bookshelves held more bottles of medication and supplies. Happy sat on her bed with an IV drip attached to her arm. She was especially tired today. Each day, she had less and less energy. Each day, she knew that she was closer to death. She had survived years of living her life on the edge and knew she was about to tip over. Her greatest fear was that if there were a heaven, she'd never get there.

Waiting for the IV drip to finish, she closed her eyes and prayed. "I know there ain't no God but in case there is one, I need to talk to you. I know I've done some bad things that I wish I hadn't done but I ain't doing most of them no more. I really need to get them protease inhibitors. If you let me get into the study, I swear I'll do something good. I'll straighten out, I swear. I'll only charge a thousand on them two stolen credit cards then I'll cut them up. I won't use the stolen cell phone. No, I need that. I promise I won't get another stolen phone when this one gets cut off. Please, if you can do it, I want to get into that study. I know I got some things to settle with you, some things to get off of my chest."

Big tears rolled down Happy Fantucci's cheeks. She was scared. "Please, don't let me go to hell. I know I done bad things but I was fucked up. That fuckin' prick Hector. He shouldn't have never tried to fuck me over. Hector, suck my dick, I ain't gonna let you make me lose no more sleep. I gotta think this through."

Jean called from the kitchen, "Hap, where are the papers for Dr Berman?"

"Try the drawer next to the phone."

Jean was on the kitchen telephone talking with Happy's health insurance company. When Happy had a problem with a creditor or her health care provider, she called on Jean for help. Happy knew that Jean could always get them to cooperate because she used them big words. Happy got frustrated when she talked to bill collectors. She was only two or three months overdue and they wanted their money immediately. Happy thought they had a lot of fuckin' nerve and she would tell them to kiss her big fat ass in Times Square. "Hey Jean, bring me a glass of water when you're done with them assholes and roll me a joint. . . . I'm just kiddin', I know you don't smoke, but can you come in here? I want to talk to you about somethin' important."

Happy was glad Jean was her friend. Jean made her laugh and didn't give her "aggita." Jean was real smart but she never made Happy feel stupid the way most people did. When Happy had a serious problem she always went to Jean for help. Jean could always find a way to get Happy out of a jam. Jean walked into the bedroom with a glass of water.

"Hey, Jean," Hap smiled, "I wudda let you have sex wid me if I wasn't so tired."

"Thanks, Hap, I'm honored," smirked Jean.

Hap grinned. "Ya know, to tell ya the real truth, I was thinking of letting you be my lover if I hadn't have met Chris."

"Lucky Chris, guess I blew my chance."

Happy and Jean smiled at each other. Jean turned to go back into the kitchen.

"Jean, wait a minute, sit here on the bed next to me, I gotta tell ya somethin', real serious."

Tears welled up in Happy's eyes. She stuttered with anguish in her voice. "I, ah, did, I did a bad thing. It was real bad." Jean couldn't imagine Happy telling her anything that could be worse than what she already knew about her. Happy continued to speak in a soft, gentle voice that was unfamiliar to Jean.

"When I was seventeen, I was the toughest-assed butch Brooklyn ever seen. Tell me, Jean, how many dykes can say they was a pimp? I had four girls workin' for me. It was when I was livin' with Katherine and her kids. Me and Katherine was shooting dope and we always needed money, between the dope and the kids always wantin' somethin'. Katherine said she would turn a trick for money and I knew this guy Skinny Hector, what a scum bag he was. A slimy, skinny-assed, low-life Puerto Rican. Real short, about five-foot-three, and he'd wear them Cuban heels to look taller. He was only nineteen, and had seven kids, and used to beat the shit out of his kids' mothers. He had no respect for nobody. He'd mug old people and give them a beatin'.

"Anyway, he says he could find me some johns. The rest was easy. Skinny Hector got the guys and I got the girls. Katherine and me was dealing and our house was like a shootin' gallery, a lot of dykes used to come over to buy dope and get high. Only, they didn't have no money sometimes so I'd tell 'em they could get dope if they fucked some guy or gave him a blow job. They jumped at the chance to get free dope. After I had four girls working, I told Katherine You ain't doing this no more. I didn't want her with those disgusting pigs and besides, her pussy was losing its sweetness. Then that prick Skinny Hector makes Katherine suck his dick and for no money or nothing.

"I wasn't lettin' Skinny Hector get away wit' dat. I went lookin' for that motherfucker. About two in the morning I seen him by them warehouses near the Dean Street canal, walking by himself. I got outta my car and I told him to pay up or I'd kick his fuckin', skinny, low-life Puerto Rican ass across the Brooklyn Bridge. He started yellin' at me in spic talk. Called me a 'maracone', a faggot. Katherine told me he had the smallest dick she ever seen. So I says to him, Yo, Hector, I hear you can't get nobody to suck that small dick of yours, and I grabbed myself and told him to suck my big dyke dick. He got real mad and he grabbed me and tried throwin' me on the ground. Skinny Hector and me was strugglin' and he says he's gonna kill me.

"I was wild, I wanted Hector to pay for what he did. We was fightin' and then and I, ah, ah, and then I had my knife in my hand and I caught his neck with it. It happened so fast. He started moanin' and I pulled the knife out and then Skinny Hector was dead. His eyes were wide open starin' at me, blood gushin' all over. There was blood everywhere, on my clothes, my hands, everywhere. I was so scared. I threw the knife in the canal. My mind was racing. I didn't know what to do. I jumped into the car, a big '61 Caddie Eldorado. It was a good thing Katherine made me get them plastic covers to protect the leather. There was blood all over me, even on my face.

"When I got to my building, I was scared somebody would see me. I went in real quiet and got to the elevator and it would-n't open. I started kicking the doors. Then this old Jew bastard and his dago wife opens their apartment door. I yell at them, 'What the fuck you looking at?' They knew to mind their own business and closed the door.

"When I finally got to my apartment, I wasn't thinkin' straight. I got into the shower, shoes, clothes, and all. I had to get rid of Skinny Hector's blood. I kept scrubbin' and scrubbin'. I wanted to scrub out my brain, my mind. I wanted to get rid of the blood, of Skinny Hector dead, his eyes starin' at me. I scrubbed and I scrubbed, but I kept seein' Skinny Hector starin' at me.

"I ripped off my clothes and shoes and I got brillo and scrubbed my body until I couldn't scrub no more. I put the clothes and shoes in a bag and threw them down the garbage chute. I was shakin' so bad. I had to stop seein' those dead eyes lookin' at me. I wanted to get off but I couldn't even get the spike into my arm, I shook so bad. I didn't want to wake up Katherine to get me off, so I snorted the smack, and passed out. I never told nobody about Skinny Hector and nobody ever asked."

Jean was stunned. Happy had told her something that was worse than she could have imagined. Jean knew that Happy had done many awful things. She had been a pimp, a thief, a drug dealer, had beaten people and cut off a man's ear, but murder? Jean, too shocked to speak, took a deep breath and said a quick prayer to herself. "God, forgive her." She put her arms around Happy and rocked her as she sobbed.

COALS IN THE SKY, SAFETY FIRST

Sook C. Kong

WHAT DOES A LESBIAN BODY DO LATE IN THE NIGHT, Lilian wonders, as she completes her pre-slumber flossing in her pre-war suite, tucked anonymously on the ridge of Mount Pleasant. When the night is not hazy, you can see the nocturnal ritz of downtown Vancouver, against the imposing North Shore mountains. Vancouver seems even more sectioned-off and divided when downtown is seen from afar, from across the tattered East End schoolyard that Lilian passes on her way home from work every day.

Ten years in the city, and Lilian cannot recall every day she has lived in this West Coast village grown large. But she does remember the quiet of several late fall evenings.

Sometimes, in the overwrought fragments of a harried life, Lilian wishes for time to slow down so she can savor the basic rhythms of life. But sometimes all that Lilian, the dyke-of-color, can do is roll with the riptide, doing her best not to fall on her face, in spite of the relentless suds under her feet.

These days, she wishes that the walls of her apartment were soundproof, insulating her from the din of the business of other people's lives. More than once, she has been startled out of her sleep by what felt like a long bad dream punctuated by an endless whimper riding to a crest. She feels the pathos, the struggle, and the imploring, before she realizes it's Myrna, her heterosexual next-door neighbor and her current boyfriend, in the no-nonsense throes of good, old-fashioned sex, fast building to its climax.

Lilian is honest when she thinks to herself, *Good for Myrna*, but she also wants to be spared the human sound effects and crashing furniture of their frenetic trysts. Once, when Myrna had a particularly driven stud for company, the headboard of her bed kept slamming hard against the bedroom wall; so hard that

Lilian sat up, wondering when the walls would come tumbling down. She hurriedly lit some incense for protection.

There is more than one woman on Lilian's mind these days. Away from people, tucked behind the forcefield of self-protectiveness, Lilian's mind wanders through the kaleidoscope of lesbians, bisexual, bi-curious and questioning women she's met during this intense year of the Metal Dragon, the year 2000. But she keeps returning to thoughts of one particular woman. Lilian has recently received a gift of dried flowers, with pictures and text, from her, who lives out of town. She always knew the woman had the oomph factor, even before their paths actually crossed, that allure a dyke both dreads and desires. Lilian knows that in the last two long-distance phone chats they had, it was Lilian herself who seemed keen on getting off the phone. Lilian, the veteran dyke, came up with a bunch of limp excuses, like having deadlines to meet, pretenses that would never convince anyone. What Lilian knew but could not bring herself to say was, "I miss you too much. I cannot afford to miss you even more. I have to get off the phone, so we don't bond too much and before my blasted photographic memory, once again, recalls every single thing you've said, including your subtle promises that we will one day live in the same town. I don't want to remember some things too sharply. I cannot afford to."

Lilian knows too well what it is to miss a woman every day of your life. Gabriel Garcia Marquez wrote about a hero who waits more than fifty years for the love of his life. But that's in a novel, something to think about, but not easy to replicate in one's own life.

But much as Lilian does not want to remember too much of the fabulous time she spent with her woman-artist-florist-friend-ideal-babe, she does recall a lot: the textures of her voice, the warmth in her coal-black eyes, the caress behind her every gesture. This woman continues to challenge her, with her gifts of flowers and fecund words.

Lilian looks out at the night sky. She knows that when she sees a certain constellation in the east, she sees the woman whom she knows she can love without restraint. It's the sort of love she fears.

Echoing in her is that long-ago lesson from elementary school traffic negotiation games: "Safety First."

By turning away, we keep ourselves safe – especially, from those we love.

Coals in the sky do land at our feet.

THIS IS A PROMISE

Cathy McKim

I WON'T CALL YOU BABY WHEN WE FIRST MEET.
Let's say we're at a party. I'd walk across the room to where you're standing, probably after noticing you sometime earlier chatting with your friends, maybe someone we both know. I'd have a shy, crooked grin on my face as our mutual friend introduces us. I'd say "Hi" and we'd shake hands. It's then that you might notice the silver claddagh ring on the middle finger of my right hand, turned with the crown facing inward, my heart open and unoccupied. You might already know this, or you might ask me about it. I'd probably blush a little as I tell you about the mythology of the ring, then I'd look sad when I mention that when I first put it on my finger I was in love and the crown was turned outward, ring on my left hand.

We'd talk and drink and tell each other our stories. If the music is right, we'd dance – maybe only to fast songs at first, but then a slow song would come on and we'd have lost any blush of shyness by then, drawn by the first flutterings of attraction. Your hands on my shoulders, my hands on your waist, bodies close together, we'd sway in rhythm to the music. And maybe we'd be about the same size and the warmth of your cheek against mine would make me long to kiss you, but I'd be too shy for that and instead I'd breathe in the fragrance of your hair, the scent of you, and I'd commit every sensation to memory in case I never see you again.

And I definitely won't call you Baby when I ask for your phone number.

I won't call you Baby when we go out on our first date.

I'd probably have that same goofy grin on my face when we meet at a movie theatre or restaurant – or maybe we'd meet in a café that plays old jazz standards, and sit in the sun on the patio sipping cappuccino. We'd talk and smile and notice the color of each other's eyes. Maybe I'd make you laugh and I'd think, Wow, you've travelled to such exciting places and chosen an amazing career and, God, the sunlight makes your hair shine like a halo around your lovely head.

When we kiss goodnight, I'd lean in to you gently, maybe brush a stray strand of hair from your face as I gaze into your eyes, hoping that you want our lips to meet as much as I do, and I'd pull you close to me, my arms wrapping around you as our mouths meet softly, sweetly, neither of us knowing if the warm glow in our bellies is coming from the inside or the outside.

And I won't call you Baby, certainly not then.

I won't call you Baby when we make love for the first time.

But I'd revel in the heat of your body, my skin on your skin, breathing you in and out as lips and hands touch the places that ignite us further. I'd explore every inch of you with my hands, fingers, mouth, tongue, your sighs, your moans directing my movements. And maybe I'd find a spot I could dwell upon, to tease you, to arouse you further and then undulate with you as your pleasure crescendoes.

I would lose myself under your touch, every cell coming to life with each of your caresses, planting a kiss on whatever part of your beautiful body comes near my open, hungry mouth. And as my body rises, burning for that inevitable explosion, I'd call on God, on Jesus – recovering Catholic that I am. And when my tingling wet flesh sings its final notes beneath the dance of your fingers, I would call your name, breathless and hoarse as my fists grip damp sheets.

But, never will I call you Baby.

I won't call you Baby the day one of us asks the other to share a home, a life, together.

My answer would be "Hell, yes!" if you asked me. If I'm the one who asks, I'd hold your hand and tell you how much I love you and how I want to grow old with you and our two cats and have wheelchair races down the hall. And I would take that ring off of my right hand and put it on my left, crown facing outward, and I would have one picked out for you to tell the world how our two hearts are occupied.

And we'd debate over what color to paint the living room and you'd compromise by letting me stencil the bedroom. We'd divide up the household chores; I'd be especially glad that you actually liked vacuuming and you'd be relieved that I didn't mind cleaning the bathroom. And we'd christen every room with wine and love-making, with music playing and the cats looking on, scandalized.

And if you should die before me, I won't call you Baby, not even then.

But I would hope to be there with you when you go, so you wouldn't be alone and I could say goodbye. And then I would hold you close and whisper "I love you" in your ear, knowing how I'd miss you so much, but I probably wouldn't say it. And after the last sweet breath has left your body and your spirit soars away, I would close your eyes and kiss you our last goodnight.

I would play your favorite songs and have bunches of your favorite flowers and sing "Amazing Grace" for you. And I would bring flowers and crystals to your grave – or maybe you'd have asked me to scatter your ashes at a spot that was very special to you.

All those years together and I won't call you Baby – not even once.

But I might call you Sweetie. If you don't object, that is.

ONLY ONCE

Suki Lee

for WJW

ABOUT HER: HER BODY IS ONE LONG CURVE. She lives above me – my neighbor. Her bedroom is over mine. In the mornings before I get up, I hear her getting out of bed, staggering, putting clothes on maybe, sleep in her eyes. I watch for when she passes by my window. I watch for her hand when it takes the railing. Her hands are beautiful, her fingers too. And she has nails on their tips. They excite and terrify me. I think only once about her using them to taunt my nipples.

But she never has. Sex for her is customary, and she has it often, but not with me. She has it with men. She tells me about it when she comes back from work and sees me in front of my open window. She makes up different names for them: the pimp, the Italian, the French guy, the photographer, the German. That is how she refers to them. I think it is strange. I invite her in, offering her a cold beer. I think only once how we could be there, on the floor, naked, her body on mine, her hands with those nails running along my back.

Clean olive skin. I am looking at her. I have her in my apartment. I think only once of how I would like to touch her, to feel her flow.

Do you like women? I think only once of asking her. Her hips curve like a road, arching.

Eat my hot, wet fruit, I think only once of saying to her when she sips her beer, and asks me how my day went.

Fuck me hard, I think only once of answering her instead of talking about my editing job. I want to see her smooth knees and her thighs. Her legs slim and strong like her arms. I want her to leave her rings on her fingers as she parts me, and I envelop her.

Gasping as we hold onto each other. I think only once how her body is perfect, while she talks about her plans for the weekend.

Hold onto me forever. I think only once of how she is like a hot poker driving through my body. I watch her mouth as she brings the beer bottle up to it.

I am in love with you, I think only once of telling her as she looks out my window at the sunset. Her body is both heat and cold. When I turn my head up to breathe, there she is, like the sea. She is a drift of water before me. My body is like a ghost floating through her liquid forest.

Juiced right through my underwear. I think only once of telling her how wet she makes me, as I watch her walk through my kitchen.

Keep me, I think only once of saying to her. I want to bow down over the peaks of her breasts. I want to see their shadows when she bends over, the outline of her nipples, challenging me when I speak to her.

Love me, I think only once of saying to you as you touch the cold beer bottle to the skin on the inside of your elbow. You are like a leaf, full and wet.

Move your hips quickly. I think only once of our cunts, that first moment when we put them together.

Naked. I think only once of you kneeling on your bed. The color of your nipples is the color of something I have never seen before. Your jaw is clenched, and then open, taking in air. You are touching yourself. Your breasts are quivering. Your hair is down. Your whole body looks wet – the small Y where your ribs meet, the thin flesh of your arms. I am aching.

Orgasm. The vision of your body is like an unruly dream. I think only once of how much you love me. You are wearing nothing but a necklace, tight around your throat. I can see the curve of your shoulders, the shape of your body. It is teeming.

Pleasure. I think only once of my body spread like a starfish in the sun, your face between my legs.

Quietly. I think only once of how we cradle each other afterwards.

Reveal who I am. I think only once how you really know me, like no one else in the world.

Staring into your eyes. The beautiful hazel of them. They are yellow. They are gold. I think only once of how I can see the entire planet in them. I think only once of you running your hands through my hair. I think only once of you touching my face, your fingers across my lips.

Truthfully, I think only once of you.

Unhinge me. I think only once about how you are so gentle, so majestic.

Voluptuous you are, I think only once.

Will we be together? I think only once of asking you.

Yes, you answer me. I think only once of how you answer me, yes.

THE SIREN

Connie Chapman

THE BLACK RAVEN SWOOPED OVERHEAD and let out a raucous caw as I docked and climbed out of my kayak at Hot Springs Cove. The forest was so thick, the wooden platform and a small clearing on land was all I could see. As I reached into the kayak to unload my yellow sack, a husky voice asked me softly, "Do you want help?"

I turned, throwing the sack onto the pier. She stood with delicate hands resting on her hips and looked at me with green twinkling eyes. She was about my height, five-foot-five, slim and fine-boned. Height was all we had in common. I was large and peasant-boned with short, curly silver hair. Her khaki shorts hung like moss on her narrow hips and the long-sleeved silk green shirt with a deep purple scarf tied at her waist more than hinted at what was underneath.

"No," I said, jumping out and grabbing the kayak, thinking to myself, she's gorgeous, but I promised myself no entanglements. "Thanks, but I've come here to be alone."

"Is it alone you want or to heal? Lots of us come here for that, you know."

Who wants to cry and soul-search? I can do it after she leaves. "Alright, let's go to the hot springs. My name is Helen, by the way."

"Franca," she said. "I'll help you set up camp later. This is the best time of day to walk up there. Let's go now."

We walked the cedar-planked boardwalk. Franca was a great storyteller, making me laugh with tales of the ecological activists and Aboriginal residents who had ensured the preservation of the springs. I relaxed and stopped thinking about Angela who had walked out on me three weeks ago for my best friend, telling me I was frigid and too uptight for her. In several places, the trail narrowed, and Franca brushed up against my arm. I felt her touch all through my body.

Finally, we reached the trail. Large rocks, some grey and impenetrable, others black and mossy, lined the cleft in the hillside. Steamy water seeped from the center of the earth, cascading over one large black cliff face, running into several pools before meeting the ocean.

Franca quietly came up behind me, put her arms around my waist, undoing the button on the front of my shorts. "Relax," she whispered in my ear, "I've been waiting to touch you since you pulled into the dock."

"Yes," I squeaked as she unzipped my shorts and slid her hand down between my legs, thrusting two fingers in me. The memory of Angela's barbs was still in my body. I involuntarily jerked away. She stopped and gently held me until the memory passed and I was back in her fingers.

Leading me into the first pool, she pleasured me in ways I'd only dreamed about. My body responded deeply and passionately. It was as if she could read my mind and body. Whatever I craved, she either did to me or had something in her bag to satisfy me. She wouldn't allow me to touch her, explaining that healing means being able to accept. Frigid, my foot, I thought, as I came for the third time. Franca moved me from one pool to another, pleasuring me more deeply each time until the sliver of a moon disappeared into the black hills. I was falling asleep when Franca poked me.

"Time to walk back," she said, pulling me to my feet.

For the first part of the trip back, we walked naked, our bodies steaming. On a small bridge, we stopped and dressed. When we arrived back at camp, Franca led me to a seat on a stump and set up my tent, her grin wide enough to light the night. Curling under my unzipped sleeping bag, I whispered to her, "Tomorrow it's your turn."

When I awoke, I was alone. I climbed out, stretched, and went looking for Franca. I saw her tent was down, and my kayak was gone. It was then I remembered I hadn't seen a boat in her camp the afternoon before.

Maybe she's gone for a paddle, I wished fervently as I walked toward the pier. Sitting, I hugged myself, and watched the water until I accepted that she wasn't coming back.

I consoled myself. I had enough food to last four days or more, and someone was bound to arrive. Thinking of food, my stomach growled. As I got up and walked back to my tent, I felt surprisingly calm and peaceful for a woman who had been seduced and abandoned.

I opened my pack to get food. Sitting on top of the items in the pack was Franca's black leather backpack. I pulled it out and held it to my face. Then I started laughing. I didn't know the punch line, but I did know I was part of a cosmic joke.

After lunch, I walked back to the pier with the leather backpack on my shoulders, sat, dangled my feet over the side, and wondered when the trickster would show herself. Although dark clouds were increasingly covering the sky, the obsidian-colored water in the inlet was still calm. It was then that I saw a solitary kayak making its way between two small islands on the horizon. Opening the black pack, I rummaged until I found what I was looking for and knew would be there. Putting the glasses to my eyes, I adjusted the lens and brought the boat into focus. Paddling with a look of serene concentration on her face was a woman with short, greying hair. Suddenly, I laughed to myself, got to my feet and quickly walked back to camp.

Now I knew. Now I was ready. I changed into clean dark blue shorts and a powder blue shirt. Wrapping the purple scarf around my neck, I walked back to the pier and waited.

A VERY SPECIAL
ISRAELI SOUVENIR

Rachel Kramer Bussel

IT WAS DECEMBER 31, 1996, and I was in Israel on a two-week
college student trip. We were all virgin visitors to the holy land,
young Jews learning about our heritage and history. We'd done
some socializing, but were mostly busy being tourists, visualiz-
ing our ancestors walking these same lands thousands of years
ago. But that night was a break from our more serious pursuits.
We were in Tel Aviv, there to venture out for some fun at a local
nightclub and celebrate the new year, an outing I'd come utterly
unprepared for.

While my tripmates dolled themselves up with fancy designer makeup and even fancier dresses and shoes, I donned the
only thing I could find that was even remotely suitable: a faded,
sheer dress that hung loosely around my body. When I say
"sheer," I don't mean "sexy," like lingerie. I mean a pale, faded soft
cotton fabric that resembled something you'd use as a washrag.
Since the dress was so sheer, I wore jeans underneath, completing my disaffected anti-fashion look. And off we went.

We arrived at the club, which was quite full of European and
American tourists, with a few Israelis thrown in. Music by
Madonna and the Spice Girls assaulted our ears. One of my
friends bought me a drink, which had so much rum in it I had
to hand it back. I'm not a teetotaler by any means, but I need a
little sweetness in my drinks (and my women). We proceeded to
stake out our own little area in the back and boogie. I pretended
I had on the most glamorous outfit ever and shook my ass with
the rest of the crowd. My eyes were closed and my hair flying
all around as I really got into the music.

I was so into the blaring beats that I had little time to notice
a slim, blonde girl who wiggled her way through the crowd to
our area. I saw her rebuff two of the more macho members of

my trip, and thread her way next to where I was dancing. She was only inches away and staring at me as she gyrated her hips. She seemed to be flirting with me, but I couldn't be sure. I continued my own gyrations and waited to see what would happen. I didn't have to wait long; the next thing I knew, she was running her fingers down my arm, smiling up into my face. I smiled back and slithered into her arms; if a hot girl wanted to dance with me, who was I to say no?

We danced close like that for a few songs before she pulled my face to hers and kissed me deeply, her tongue swirling into my mouth, leaving my whole body weak.

"Do you like girls?" she yelled over the music.

"Yeah," I said casually.

"Really?"

"Yes, don't you believe me?" I grabbed her ass and pulled her next to me so I could suck on her ear.

She stepped back and waved her hand in front of me, showing off a sparkling diamond ring. "I just got married five days ago," she said proudly.

Her statement puzzled me, but if she was happy about being married and still wanted me, I wasn't going to worry about it.

I could feel all my fellow travelers eyeing us with envy, so we moved to another part of the club. I met her husband, who scurried off to buy us drinks. Her body was so compact, her breasts pushed together under her tight white top. I leaned forward and nuzzled my face in her cleavage, while she tossed her head back and reveled in my explorations. We kissed passionately, holding onto each other as our tongues mingled and our bodies buzzed with sexual energy. It was like a dream, something that happens in movies, or to someone else, but not to frumpy old me, who had to be dragged out to the club. I wondered briefly why she'd chosen me, but then brushed that out of my mind as I felt her hand squeezing my ass through my jeans.

"You're really turning me on, do you know that?" I groaned into her ear.

She smiled at that, a big grin that told me she knew exactly what she was doing.

Guys were coming up to us, pestering us to join in our little love fest. She shunted them off and returned to kissing me. She was so free and open with her lust, it was a refreshing change from going to clubs and eyeing a girl all night only to go home alone, with neither of us even working up the courage to speak to each other. She kissed me ravenously, squeezing and stroking my body as her tongue worked its way all around my mouth. She brought her lips to my neck, sliding her tongue along my sweaty skin and causing a mini-earthquake in my cunt.

As she planted kisses all over me, I thought to myself, *Who knew Israeli women were so wild?* I'd been hearing about Israel my entire life, but as a state of righteous political drama, with Zionists staking their claim for the rights of Jews everywhere. Now I had an Israeli girl, blonde and pale like me, staking her claim on my body. She twisted my preconceived notions around as easily as her fingers twisted my nipple beneath my dress.

Her husband finally returned, and though he seemed like a nice person, a threesome wasn't really what I had in mind. It was quite late by now, several hours into the new year, and as the Spice Girls sang "If you wannabe my lover, you gotta get with my friends," I bid them adieu. From that point on, my class-mates looked at me with envy and respect, and I got to take home my memory of that night as a very special Israeli souvenir.

WHAT CAN TWO BUTCHES DO TOGETHER?

Donna Allegra

THE KISS STARTED LONG BEFORE Lynne opened her mouth to mine. It began in that other lifetime, when I came to the job a day-and-a-half ago, and she smiled at me through the crinkles around her eyes; when those eyes took an infinitesimal second to scan my body from tits to crotch as I faced her two rungs up a ladder; when she cruised me from behind and I caught her stare in the mirror. Or maybe the kiss began during the work day when my back brushed hers while squeezing through the door, when she allowed me to snuggle around her in the crowded hall or to squinch by on the carpenter's scaffold, my skin pressed against her flesh as we held a light fixture high in the air. But it could have begun when I climbed up the back of her ladder and faced Lynne on the fourth rung from the floor as she spliced the wires in the ceiling: my being there just to talk, to tease, to make her laugh when she was helpless with tools in both hands, screwing the silver threads of a bolt to an octagonal nut that would secure the light in place. But surely the kiss began when Lynne became open and playful with me, when she let us be boys together.

Her mouth in that kiss tasted of baked apples, cinnamon, and rolled oats – the granola from dinner. We stepped apart and Lynne pulled open her jacket. The sound of velcro – more a rip than a zipper opening, and sexier – tore at me.

She pulled up the dark jade ribbed tank top to expose her belly button. A sudden itch nipped her back and I watched the way her shoulder blades twitched, hinting at wings. Her breasts, bigger than my speed bumps, drew and deflected my gaze like bright lights, but my eyes were more seduced by the arc of muscle curving through her forearms into her shoulders. Muscle in the shape of a Christmas tree radiated across her abdomen over the slight bulge in her belly.

All day long I'd been stoked with desire. Maybe the state of being unrequited is what's truly exquisite. Fulfillment and aftermath aren't as intense as the uncertainty of wanting someone and not knowing if they want you back. Still, I shucked my clothes quickly.

We wrestled, as if to see who would go on top. To break the tie, Lynne sat on me, incubating my butt, then pressed her vulva against my rump like a cat rubbing its scent on a person to mark ownership. That touch set off a such a charge that the petals between my thighs unfolded a vestigial limb with the revelation that I didn't always have to be the boy.

Our thighs clasped and I felt greedy for pleasure. I went at Lynne like an animal in rut. She twisted against me like a wiggling pup when I needed her in one place so I could get off. "Stay still," I said as I humped her hip and didn't check her facial expression to see if she was getting where she wanted to go. I strained to reach that urgent crest of release, riding the wave to shore until it kneeled against the sand.

I swelled like a sponge in warm water as tingles of eruption rose through the bulbs at the tips of my hair follicles. Then I wanted the fullness crushed like a juiced orange, flushing aching pleasure through my pussy parts.

Lynne spread her legs wide to fold her thighs around my back, wrapping me like a tortilla. This rekindled the embers and I coaxed them to roar with flame. Across the room, the silver midnight moon hovered at the window as Lynne wrote her touch on my skin. Pulses of pleasure became ribbons unravelling and my body conducted thought from Lynne's fingers. My mind heard talk about a sacred place, the religion that lives in your heart, a place called home.

I gurgled to a fullness that ached, a balloon longing for puncture to ease its too taut skin. I arched to open my all to Lynne, gave her my neck to draw mortal blood from or nuzzle me for life.

She pushed my legs apart, as if I could, like an acrobat, bend my limbs easily over backwards. I felt stretched beyond straddling, but inside, compressed like a coil eager to curl back to its fetal position. Pull me like a wishbone until I break, I thought as my toe tips yearned towards my heels.

Lynne carefully folded my vagina lips apart and a whistling sigh escaped me. Her mouth was firm and delicate, her tongue mining my vulva to excavate pleasure. I focused all my being to concentrate on the power ringing through me, on her touch that spooled new life from my core.

As I pressed against her mouth like a drill craving wood, I monitored the cross talk between my sexual hunger and desire for a mate. Maybe the bridge of longing for companionship and the biology of sex was fuzzing up my judgment skills, but I felt I was receiving the kind of love that made my spirit weep, sing, want to go out and save the world.

The gathering wave of sensation flooded toward release. A kettle of breath spouted and my sex chords trembled towards the high notes and it was as if I could see, like a star, in all directions at once.

Perhaps it was a few minutes or a week that passed with my eyes sealed tight as a newborn's. When I did awaken, I saw the world upside down: brain and optic nerve not yet in sync. In the wonder of it all, Lynne folded her body across mine like a new mother with the wisdom of the world and licked the eye of my elbow.

RAZOR

Rosalind Christine Lloyd

I WAS IN THE MARKET FOR A RAZOR. Not one of those ugly plastic disposables; I wanted something that screamed extravagance. This desire had everything to do with my ex-lover, Indigo, who had the kinds of beliefs that were rooted deeply in erotic ceremony. I'll never forget a candlelit evening spent in her tiny bathroom; both of us inebriated by the steam of scalding hot water transformed into a rainstorm splashing against the porcelain like hypnotic background music. Indigo kneeled before me, her drenched locks like an African wedding veil. She caressed my buttocks with one hand while her other hand maneuvered an 18-karat gold-plated antique razor across my oil soaked mons veneris. The glint of gold flickering was unforgettable. The sensation of the sharp blade gliding against my skin filled me with indescribable longing. The closer she shaved, the tighter her grip became on my buttocks, her sinking nails turned into burning talons ripping into my flesh. Not one bit of body hair below my waist was spared. Spreading my lips wide apart, while whispering "My sweet, Nubian butterfly," over and over, directly into my erect and volatile clit, the blade skimmed my soft tissue. Bending me over, gently applying the blade to the edges of the tiny pucker of my ass, I fell in love with her all over again. In a haze, I felt drugged while her moist lips traveled beneath me, her tongue inside of me. She rimmed me as if I were the best tasting thing she ever had and I could not predict that her plans included inserting herself up to her wrist inside of me. I've been obsessed with razors ever since.

That was over two years ago. Indigo is now involved with some young, super-dyke surgeon. She moved on to scalpels while I remained, painfully, still in love with her.

In my quest for the perfect razor, I headed for Bloomingdale's where I dodged beautiful women wielding perfume bottles that propelled feminine scented ammunition through the air. Defeated by the fact that women's razors were basically relegated to disposable hell, I navigated toward men's accessories in the back of the store.

Mahogany display cases offered an assortment of men's leather goods and an endless array of accessories. Every kind of grooming aid and gadget imaginable was in abundance.

"Can I show you anything?" The voice was soft yet breathy. Looking up, I noticed a divine face, dark and rich like the display-case mahogany. Shiny, jet black hair pulled back so tight it narrowed the soft doe eyes that were staring back at me. The tight black turtleneck stretched across a bounty of bosom. The matching tight black mini-skirt could easily be mistaken as an invitation. Long sculpted legs concealed in sheer black stockings and Italian semi-stiletto heels finished her look. In fact, she looked the type to be stationed in front of the store spritzing perfume instead of being stashed away in the back.

In her expertly manicured hands with dangerously long, crimson nails was a small, thin stainless steel case. The designs engraved on its surface were intricate, whimsical. Interested, I removed it from her hand to examine it.

"Do you know what it is?" she asked.

"No."

"Condom case."

"Really? Interesting concept."

"A little overstated, but worth a hundred dollars."

"You think so?"

"Sure. Why not? Do you need one?"

A bold assumption she was making.

"No. Why don't you try selling me something I do need." I decided I liked the sound of her voice. It was sultry, like a rainy, restless summer evening.

"What are you looking for?" She leaned in closer to me.

"I'm looking for a razor. Think you can help me?"

"Definitely. You came to the right place." She put the condom case away before pulling out four shaving kits, three in leather cases, one in suede. Two were stainless steel, one had a handle of Mother of Pearl, the other 18-karat gold. Handling each very professionally, she provided an impressive detailed presentation about each kit. Of course she was good. I wanted them all and couldn't decide on one.

Noticing my confusion, she asked, "Do you like any of these?"

"I like them all, but none of them stand out."

"Really? We have quite a collection suited to a variety of tastes. If price is an issue, there are others."

"Price isn't an issue."

"Will this be a gift for someone special?"

"Actually, I'm looking for myself." The smile that spread across those thick, juicy lips of hers made my afternoon.

"Why didn't you tell me? In that case I have the perfect razor for you."

She pulled out a velvet display with two very sophisticated, cordless electronic razors.

Selecting one, she stroked the power button while a low-level hum filled the air between us.

"I highly recommend this one. It provides a deliciously close shave, it's perfect for a quicky, the unit is rechargeable, and it performs exceptionally well during long showers. You will love this razor. I guarantee it. Try it yourself."

This woman was excited about this product. It resembled a miniature power tool although the design made an attempt at being somewhat sleek and elegant. Three sets of round blades whirled around in synchronicity. The vibrations were compelling. Reaching for a peach from a fancy bowl of fruit, she handed it to me with a knowing look on her face. As I applied the razor to the tender piece of fruit, the fuzz was gently erased by the razor blades, not at all abusing the flesh of the peach.

I was sold. As I handed her my credit card, she said, "I give complimentary private demonstrations."

"Do you now?" I purred lowly. In my opinion, it sounded like an awfully hard offer to refuse.

BEGINNING

River Light

CATHY PAUSED AROUND THE CORNER from Dev's place and wiped her sweaty palms on her non-absorbent leather mini-skirt.

"Damn!" She grabbed her scarf and used it to wipe clean the wet streak. She took a couple of slow deep breaths. Her heels pinched and she wondered again if she should have worn flats, but there was nothing like pumps and black-seamed stockings to catch the eye, and she suspected that Dev was the kind of butch who appreciated this look. The thought of Dev made her stomach flutter again and she took three more deep breaths. Adrenaline, fear, apprehension about not living up to Dev's expectations – a most delicious cocktail. There was nothing quite like a first date.

Ever since Cathy had become involved in the leather scene she had been watching Dev. She was older than Cathy, and considerably more experienced, which was part of what both interested and terrified her.

Dev moved like she had a right to take up as much space as she needed, as much as she wanted. She swaggered, not with arrogance, but with confidence. She wore no jewellry of any kind – no watch, no studded wristbands. She did not flag, it would have seemed redundant. It was this strength, this confidence, this relaxed self-assurance, which drew Cathy to her. She wanted to elicit desire in Dev, wanted to see the cool façade crack enough to show hunger play across her face.

Finally, a couple of months ago, they had bumped into each other at the birthday party of a mutual friend. Much to her pleasure Cathy had been able to keep her cool, stay calm, act interested but just a little distant – which she felt to be no small victory. At the next play party she had been able to screw her

116

courage to the sticking point and walk up to where Dev stood talking to friends. She managed a casual-sounding hello and felt a tingle run down her spine when Dev moved aside to make room for her in the circle. She introduced her to her friends, women Cathy knew by name and reputation only. Cathy stayed and chatted for a few minutes but left before there was any chance she could be perceived as having anything but a casual interest in the group.

Later that night Dev had approached, then waited for Cathy to see her, to focus and acknowledge her presence. Cathy's body was still in a state of suspended bliss from the scene she had just done with a current playmate who was off chatting with friends. Dev took the vacant seat beside Cathy.

"I liked watching you tonight." They sat observing the room. After a while Dev added, "Would you like to play sometime?"

Cathy was pleased to notice that she felt calm. She nodded, then let her eyes rove around the room. "But not here."

"No, not here," Dev answered.

In their subsequent discussions Cathy had been surprised at the subtext that had made itself immediately known. While the negotiations centred around one night of play, that was not all that was being discussed. They were both surprised at how quickly they seemed to connect. The buzz of sexual energy between them was never mentioned aloud but it saturated the air. A date was set. Cathy's mind was constantly distracted by the contour of muscle in Dev's shoulders and the way her eyes seemed to change color depending on the light. Even so, Cathy was able to keep her gaze direct, her voice steady, her nervousness well hidden.

Cathy's hand was on the doorknob. She closed her eyes, listening to her own breathing, to her heartbeat – finally feeling the calm she had been waiting for.

The door was unlocked and she stepped in. The sound of a flute drifted toward her. While she had never been here before she knew from Dev's description that the living room was straight ahead. She hung up her coat and scarf and walked toward it, passing the kitchen on the left – bright, clean, and neat.

The living room opened up in front of her and she stopped.

The room was warm and inviting. The lilting flute music floated from speakers mounted high in the four corners of the room. In its center, back to Cathy, stood Dev – black t-shirt, faded and ripped 501s, bare feet on a thick Indian rug. She stood still, hands clasped behind her back, legs firmly planted.

Cathy walked slowly up behind her until their bodies were almost touching, and watched as the hairs on Dev's arms prickled. Dev smelled of fresh sweat. She was nervous, a good sign. Cathy drank in the scent of her, and for a moment entertained a series of images: Dev naked on a bed, blindfolded, wrists handcuffed to the frame above her head. Cathy with her right hand around Dev's throat, left holding her own body up as she fucked her. Dev's body slick with sweat, writhing under her, on the verge of coming. Dev asking, "May I please come?" then gritting her teeth and struggling when Cathy replies with a whispered, "No you can't, not yet, not until you beg me." Cathy felt a hot flush warm her at the thought of Dev's desire doing battle with her pride.

Careful to keep them silent, she slipped handcuffs from her waistband and flicked them onto Dev's wrists. Dev jerked in surprise.

Cathy smiled. She had practiced that move for hours and was always pleased when it worked so well. She grabbed Dev's hair and yanked her head and body backwards and down, forcing her to drop to her knees. Keeping her head pulled back, Cathy hunkered down next to her.

"If you please me tonight, and I should choose to come back to you again, I will find you kneeling," Cathy said, keeping her voice hard, "or I shall leave and that will be the end of it, do you understand?"

Dev's jaw clenched, but she did not reply. Cathy left it at that. If Dev wanted her to come back, she knew what she had to do. Considering the heat that radiated from Dev's skin, and the wetness of her own cunt, she was relatively certain this evening would be the first of many.

A NIGHT AT THE CAFÉ

Mar Stevens

SMOKEY AND I ARRIVE AT THE CAFÉ on Wednesday night. It's ten-thirty, the bar is alive, and the music is bumping. It's a comfortable crowd, with plenty of interaction and scenery. I am excited to see Smokey, and she is looking fly, as usual, especially in the black leather vest she is wearing. Smokey is a fine sistah, with smooth caramel skin, and light brown eyes. She is a shapely woman with hips, ass, and thighs. She has a beautiful face, mouth, and her short hair as well as her attire is always neat.

I'm staring at Smokey, checking her out lustfully. I want her, and have fantasized all day about having wild sex with her. We order drinks, we toast, then I lean down and kiss Smokey on the cheek. She looks up and smiles shyly, trying to hold back her passion for me. We finish our drinks and head for the dance floor. The music is good. The Tanqueray kicks in.

The dance floor is full. Everyone is having a good time. Smokey and I are dancing close, and smiling. I feel good tonight. I check myself out in the mirror. I'm a tall, chocolate sistah, with distinctive features. I have a strong athletic body, which attracts not only women, but straight and gay men.

I move behind Smokey, pressing my body up against her backside, and slip my hands inside her vest, cupping her breasts. Her nipples stand at attention. Smokey screams playfully. The rhythm of the music changes to a slow song. I pull Smokey into my arms, placing my hands around her waist. Smokey presses her body tight against me, and holds me around the neck. I look down at her and kiss her teasingly. Smokey is getting hot, and she kisses back aggressively. She is oblivious to our surroundings. She inserts her tongue, which I grab with my mouth and suck. I kiss back aggressively then pull away gently. I look at

Smokey, grab her hand, and lead her off the dance floor. We go down the stairs into the ladies' room. It's empty, so we enter the bigger stall, and close the door behind us.

I look at Smokey, who is excited and curious about what's next. I position her body on the side of the stall. The ladies' room is like a dungeon. Everything is painted black, with a dim light overhead. The stall is clean with an open window enclosed with bars. The music is pumping from upstairs, making the walls vibrate. The mood is set. Anything goes at this point.

I can feel Smokey's heart racing with excitement. We kiss wildly. Smokey's tongue is darting in and out of my mouth, which I open wider. We grind our pussies together. Smokey removes her shirt and bra, and I watch her breasts fall out. She stands back against the wall. I move to her and lightly lick her left nipple. She moans silently while I continue to suck and tease both of her hard nipples. My right hand moves between her legs and parts them gently. I grab her crotch, causing Smokey to grunt. I unzip her pants and slide them down along with her panties. Her pussy hairs are cut short. I can see her juices running.

I look at Smokey with bedroom eyes, lick my right index finger, and place it on her clit. The hot spot. Smokey's back flattens against the wall and she grinds her hips to my finger movements. She is so hot and wet. She wants to give up her power. I whisper to Smokey that I want her to come quickly. I kneel in front of her. I position my hands on her ass and place my mouth between her legs, aiming my tongue straight for her clit, which is nice and hard. I feel Smokey's clit twitch, and her body rises slightly, then falls back on the spot. I know how to eat pussy. My own pussy tingles and throbs.

Smokey goes wild. She spreads her legs wider and grinds her hips forcefully into my mouth. My tongue is aggressive but tender. I am hitting all the hot spots. I grab Smokey's ass harder, rock her vagina back and forth on my tongue, sending her into complete ecstasy. Every movement of my tongue on her clit causes her orgasm to peak higher and higher. Smokey's climax is coming fast, and hard. She grabs my head and rides my face forcefully. She does not hold back. She grinds her crotch down hard on my mouth and tongue. I extend my tongue. Let Smokey ride the wave. She guides herself into ecstasy. The beat of the music vibrates against the walls. Her orgasm is strong. Her body jerks upward, but she holds on, to get it all.

I stand up and watch Smokey's body shudder. She holds me around the neck for strength, leans back against the wall, weak. She looks like somebody just worked her body good. She is sweating. Two women enter the ladies' room talking loudly. I quietly help Smokey with her clothes, then exit the stall. I wash my hands but not my face. I'm so horny and wet. My pussy is dripping. I need to be fucked. My nipples are hard. They need to be sucked. My pussy is pulsating with pain. My skin is burning for soft kisses. I want to feel ecstasy race through my body.

Smokey comes out of the stall giving me a satisfied look. The two women stop talking, and give us funny stares, then smiles. Smokey and I leave the bathroom holding hands. We look into each other's eyes and grin at thoughts of what's to come.

LOOK HARD

Angela Mombourquette

SHE HAS DARK HAIR, SHOULDER-LENGTH – she's straight, but looks kind of butchy. Strong.

Beautiful mouth. Dark lips. Like the dark nipples I can barely see under the white cotton of her shirt.

She likes me, she knows me well. We talk a lot. We hug, giggle, share gossip. Flirt. She has never slept with a woman before. I know this. I know she likes to fuck men. I know she comes when she is being fucked. She can't imagine how it could be any better with a woman. But there is a little hint of curiosity . . . she wonders what it would be like to kiss me, even though she has never said this out loud.

We go downtown, drink a few beers, hang out with friends, laugh, talk. I have a joint in my pocket. I keep it secret, save it, to smoke with her. Late in the night, I tip my head. "Let's go. . . ."

We climb the hill and sit on a bench where we can see the whole city. I light it up, inhale, pass it from my lips to hers, feel the touch of her fingers as she reaches to take it from my hand. We sit in silence, smoking, looking out at the lights. I feel my head spin, my muscles relax, my pussy get warm. She is sitting so close, I can feel her body, pulling me, like gravity, like magnetism.

We talk quietly for a while. Finally I am overwhelmed, I can feel her, smell her, I can't keep myself from touching her. I turn, hook my leg through the back of the bench so I'm facing her. I look at her, hard. She looks back at me, uncertain. I take a deep breath. She is so beautiful, the city lights are dancing on her skin. I lean, move close to her. My lips are swollen, they brush against hers and I inhale, gasp. Her mouth opens and I am all there, everything, my body complete in my lips, all I need is to kiss her, harder, lips thick and soft.

We kiss forever. When we stop, it is sudden and harsh, like a car accident. We blink like kittens. Desire is all there is. My cunt is burning; hers must be too, she kissed me so hard; it is intense, this feeling, this need to touch her.

"Come home with me," I say.

She hesitates – her husband, her identity; she's not gay.

"Come and kiss me," I push.

We get up, she is staring at me, not speaking. We get a cab in silence. I feel her arm against mine in the back of the cab. She is staring out the window. We climb the stairs to my apartment, still not speaking. I lock the door behind us; she looks uncomfortable now. This is far too premeditated to be a simple matter of being swept away. We are standing in the hallway and I glance at her sideways, then lean in to her, pressing her up against the wall. I look at her again, hard; I want her to know who I am, who she is kissing, why. Again, she looks back, not afraid of me.

I kiss her, lean into her, my body telegraphing my desire; I feel her hips push back at me. Lips touching, exploring forever. My knees are weak, her neck so soft and sweet, I am faint. Walking backwards, I pull her, sleepwalking, dreamily, to the bedroom. My lips are inches from hers. I make her wait. I light a candle, step up and pull her drowsily onto my bed.

She is on top of me, unsure of what to do, now that she is in control. She feels the power, though, and her hips push harder against my leg. She is hot, breathing heavily. She will not be stopped. Kissing me hard, ragged breath burning my ear, I roll her aside and unbutton her jeans. A small moan, her hips lift up as I slide my hand down into her panties and touch her cunt. She is so wet, her cunt is swollen and hot, her hips press up into my hand. My finger swirls around her clit as she moans, small sighs, arches her back and disappears into desire as my finger flits, teasing her, up and down, then around. When my finger rubs sweet wetness directly over her clit it is like an electric shock; she shouts, jerks, her head rolls back; she is so far away right now.

I pull my hand away and her breathing slows down. I press a finger to her lips and kiss her, my finger with her sweet smell

between our lips. She kisses back. I reach down and tug her
jeans off her hips, pull off her boots, her socks, her panties.
Beautiful curves, we are women; she looks at me and smiles
sleepily as my kisses move down her neck. I unbutton her shirt
and pull it open; my breath catches at the sight of her breasts, a
lace bra, her dark aureoles showing through just a little, her nipples hard. Reach behind, undo her bra, pull everything off.

She is completely naked on my bed. I am fully clothed, but
overwhelmed. For a moment, I pause. Then my lips are drawn
to her breasts, I am unable to think anymore. Soft, soft skin, I
pull at her nipples gently, suck, her hips lift slightly as I suck. My
tongue making circles as my hand moves again to her pussy;
sharp intake of breath as I touch her clit, circles of my tongue
matching the circles of my finger.

Again, she is far away until I move my lips, kiss her belly, her
thigh, and she is suddenly silent, still, as my mouth closes on her
cunt, hot, and my tongue licks a gentle path to her clit. A groan,
she pushes her pussy hard into my face. Her hips lift, now she
is bucking, she yells, she moans, my tongue flits and darts, circles and laps, my whole mouth is sucking her in now as she
raises her ass and rolls her head back, yells and comes, hard and
soft and wet, body jerking and eyes rolling and jesus christ holy
fuck and her breathing finally slows down and she looks at me
as I move up to kiss her lips and look hard at her and smile a
tiny smile.

LOVE LIKE A LOOSE TOOTH

Erin Graham

MEMORY CAN'T STOP THINKING ABOUT PEGGY. This has never happened to her before. Peggy is short and stocky with lanky arms and long straight hair. She calls herself a "no-neck-knuckle-draggin'-dyke." She laughs all the time, it seems to Memory, and she is kind to her friends.

Peggy won't stop thinking about Memory. Damn. She's straight. But she's smart, tough, and brave. Not that heterosexual women aren't smart, tough, or brave ... but usually they seem just a little bit frightened. Memory never seems frightened; even though she's a single mother and she has a Master's degree in some six-syllable subject and she's slinging platters of pasta around at Caper's Pizza and Ribs. She's lovely – short dark hair, slightly wavy, dark eyes, high cheekbones. She holds her shoulders square when she walks, and she is graceful, tall, and solid, though she is slender. Peggy wants to just stand beside Memory. She wants to just look at her. She doesn't want to touch her, she doesn't want to make love to her, or even imagine it, because then she would become too real. They'd start finding one another commonplace. Start to fight. She would forget the enchantment of watching Memory's hands move. Forget about the shiver that now moves through her when Memory asks her a question, or laughs at a joke, or leans towards her with a conspiratorial whisper on her lips. Peggy used to think she wanted more. She used to think she wanted a love affair, but now she doesn't. Now she wants a friend. She needs friends. She doesn't need a lover.

Memory savors the time she spends with Peggy; sharing a smoke at work, between the lunch and dinner rush; or laughing about that weird customer who sloshes beer into her ravioli to cool it off. She watches Peggy play with her eight-year-old daughter, Nadine. Peggy is easy with Nadine, like a child herself, but more solid, safe. She has taught Nadine how to juggle. They are friends, too. Memory doesn't want to feel like this. She has not felt like this for a long time, and Peggy is a dangerous woman. Sparks fall between them now. Memory doesn't know what to do with them. They burn her fingers. She touches them to Peggy's shoulder; in a friendly way, trying to cool herself. She burns. She waits. Memory wonders, when she looks at Peggy, what it would be like, to run her hands along Peggy's rib cage, to see Peggy's round belly pressed against her own. She tries to think of Ken, her last lover, sweet and gentle. Boring, really. But he played the bagpipes and how could she not fall in love with a man who played the pipes? Truth be told, he was in love with her more than the other way around.

Peggy doesn't speak of Memory with anyone. She waits. Because she knows Memory doesn't know. She knows Memory thinks they're just friends, though she seems to crave Peggy's company the way Peggy craves hers. But Memory's straight, so the subject of sex never comes up. Never. It won't, either. Peggy doesn't even fantasize about her. Because Peggy is already lonely. And if she were to make up scenarios of them together, it would be unbearable, the loneliness. She knows, now, that it will be only a matter of time before the urgency wears away, whether or not they act upon it. And if they don't, the urgency will last, like the splendid ache of a loose tooth. Remember that feeling? When you were a child and your teeth would ache with the wanting to be free? You couldn't leave that molar alone until it was wrenched from your mouth. You did everything and nothing to get it gone and then there would be the final small pull and it would be in your hand and then the other tooth coming in, pushing up, delicious under your tongue as you rubbed it and played with it, feeling the nerves on the gum as it gave way, leaving room for that new tooth to push through. Now there; a mouth full of grown-up teeth and nothing to look forward to.

She will not move this tooth of desire. She will listen to it in her mouth and she will let it be until it falls away (as she knows it will), and then she will have something grow in place of the desire. That's all. Because sex is like that. The wanting of it like the loose tooth, and then having it, like pulling the tooth and the new one growing in and then what is there to look forward to?

But then Memory decided to have a party to celebrate her final payment to the government's Orderly Payment of Debt Program, two weeks previous. She was finally debt-free and could now spend two hundred bucks a month on Nadine, or curtains, or her RRSPS. This first month, she spent it on beer and candles and invited her friends, including Peggy, to a celebration. During the party, Nadine danced with everyone and fell asleep in the coats on Memory's bed, and everyone cheered as Memory burned all her old student loan and Visa bills.

As she was leaving, Peggy congratulated Memory again and said, "What a relief, eh? You gonna get a credit card now?"

"Oh good lord no, Peggy. That was the scariest piece of plastic in my wallet." Memory laughed and took Peggy's hand. Their eyes met. There was a delicious moment when either of them might have said, "May I kiss you?" The loose tooth of love. But neither did. Peggy kissed Memory on the cheek, her lips leaving a trail of sparks in the air, and said goodbye.

As long as no one says anything. . . .

THE PHASE

Susan Lee

WHEN LISA CAME OUT LAST YEAR she kicked down the closet door with her combat boots and then proceeded to drag me around to the two gay bars in the city. I had known Lisa most of my life; she was a sister to me. So, being the supportive "straight" friend I followed her to all the meetings and homo hops. But after awhile, I started to question my own sexual identity. I was being exposed to a lot of options and wasn't quite sure where I belonged. I told Lisa I thought I might be attracted to women, but I wasn't sure. Perhaps I was just going through a phase. Lisa nodded her head and said she understood. It had taken her a while to come to her own decision and solidify her "phase." She then invited me to a housewarming party at Jackie's, her current love interest. She suggested it might help me get some perspective on things.

When Lisa and I arrived at the party we were greeted by a roomful of women. As I made my way around the room I discovered that most of the women were coupled off and I began to believe that lesbians only came in pairs. I walked over to a group of women in the kitchen who were deep in discussion. Hanging around the edges, I leaned against the counter, my beer pulled close to me, resting on the edge of my belt buckle as I took a drag from my cigarette. As I exhaled, I noticed one of the women looking in my direction. I caught her eye and smiled. When she smiled back I felt a wave of warmth and knew my cheeks had betrayed my act of confidence.

After a bit of an absence, Lisa and Jackie reappeared. Knowing Lisa, she probably wanted to give Jackie her house-warming present in the bedroom, and judging from their rumpled appearance I'm sure Jackie enjoyed it. They suggested we move the party to the bar for "Women's Night." We all piled into various cars and I found myself sitting next to the woman with the smile. Desperately wanting to make conversation, I asked her how she knew Jackie. She told me that this was the first time she had met her and she was just visiting a friend of Jackie's for the weekend. As we continued to talk our bodies leaned into each other as we rounded the curbs and I secretly wished there were more winding roads.

When we arrived at the bar, I ordered a beer and then sauntered over to a prime spot by the dance floor. By now Lisa was totally distracted by Jackie, while I was consumed with thoughts of this new woman. I was incredibly attracted to her. She had deep red lipstick and carefully styled short blonde hair with a little dip that hung just right. She wore a tight little t-shirt with black jeans. I watched her dance, and saw that she was comfortable with herself from the way she moved on the floor. She caught me watching her and flashed me a smile.

She motioned me over and I gathered my courage to dance with her. I watched her roll her hips to the music, catching every beat. There was a mischievous glint in her eye that reflected mine. I moved towards her, drunk in my confidence, while the beat of the music took me over. She smiled coyly, encouraging me along. My body against hers, we caught each other's rhythms, our legs intertwined, pussies on thighs, sliding up and down. I could feel every part of her moving with me. I pulled away slightly so I could run my lips gently against hers. I had never felt anything so soft. Sinking into her kiss, lost in the sensation, I didn't want to stop. I ran my hands down the length of her back and held her close.

She reached behind and took my hand and led me to a dark corner of the bar. Once there, I melted into her. She was pressed against me and I was pressed against the wall, exploring each other. I no longer heard the loud music or tasted the smoke-filled air. All of my senses were focused on her and what she was doing to me. Her tongue and lips along my neck sent a shiver down to that spot between my legs. I wondered if she could feel the pulsing she was creating there. Her hot tongue lightly licked my ear and I closed my eyes to drink in the moment.

I felt her tongue lingering long after it was gone and tried to concentrate on where it was going next. With a feather–light touch she brushed her lips slowly over mine. Her tongue teased my mouth while my hands explored her and I could feel that she wanted me too. I daringly undid her zipper and discreetly slipped in my hand. She rocked against my fingers, holding me close. I felt her breath quicken on my neck as she moaned over the music, while my fingers worked until she came shuddering against them. And in that moment, I instantly knew that this "phase" was going to be a long one.

ALL OF IT

Judy Grant

IT HAD BEEN A LONG, RAINY, boring summer. I worked at a day camp for kids; it was all work and no play. I like to play, I didn't have the energy or the money, or maybe it was the uncooperative, endless monsoon weather. Anyhow, summer came and went without adventure.

It dissolved into autumn and surrounded us with orange leaves and tender warmth. I have never been a big fan of autumn but this year was different: the crisp leaves, the brilliant sun, and women everywhere.

I met her in a coffee shop without being sure it was her. No, it wasn't a blind date. It was a blind ride to the World March for women on Parliament Hill in Ottawa. I was part of a group called Loose Lips and for once we were doing something more political than putting our loose lips around a beer. I always show up early for these things. Even if I am late, I'm the first one there. I went up to a woman who was purchasing coffee. "Elizabeth?" I asked.

She looked startled, said "No" and slinked away. Not used to being approached by a five-foot eight black lesbian, I reckoned.

I pulled out the newspaper and tried not to look lost. At least I knew who the other girls were: Sheena, the bookworm and Tamara, the voluptuous party-girl extraordinaire. *She'll show up eventually* I told myself as I sipped my java. Finally she rolled into the joint, or floated, I'm not sure exactly, but it wasn't a regular entrance. It was like she beamed off a starship. I approached her cautiously. "Elizabeth?"

Leaving Montreal, I lucked out and sat next to her in the front seat of her car. We talked the whole way and we saw the geese flying in v formation. When she laughed, she did so from her belly and slammed her hands on the steering wheel. I knew we would be friends.

The rally was an empowering experience of strong feminist sisters with a multitude of banners along the boulevards. After the rally, we walked along the Le Breton flats back to the car, joking that it might have been towed and we would have to keep each other warm with outdoor survival skills, laying naked next to each other. Along the way we saw a hot-air balloon lifting off, full of people. I knew we would be lovers.

Weeknight dinner at my place. Alexander approved and couldn't stop himself from jumping and licking her neck. I envied his direct approach, the confidence, and realized this was dog privilege. I'd have my chance later, I hoped.

She had cut her hair and looked mighty fine with a slick blonde coif. Her skin was white with ruddy cheeks; lips heart-shaped, soft, and giving. I was very happy to have her in my nest. After supper, we chatted as she had a smoke out on my balcony. I don't even think I finished my first sentence before my lips were caressing hers. I felt her passion, and she melted my walls, opened me up. We went into the living room and lay on the floor, and she wrapped herself around me like a black leather jacket, my hands on her breasts.

It seemed like things were swirling around us, and I felt drunk with desire. We traveled at warp speed. Stars flew past my window. Our bodies flowed into each other, blurring definition like a soft focus.

At one point I hesitated. It was happening too fast. I wanted control. But she wanted to me out of my head. She stepped out of her public persona and relaxed into a passionate lover divine. She was wanton and her hands ran freely over my body. I unfastened her jeans and slipped my hand in. She didn't disappoint. Her mons pubis cut made her delicate and smooth. She was breathing soft and hard in my ear, turning me on more and more.

"Can I spend the night?" she whispered.

This woman is bold, I thought, *and I like that.*

Naturally, I said yes. I mean how could I pretend that I wasn't involved at this point?

We made our way to the bedroom, and we kept the lights on as we dove into each other, breathing hard and fast. The clothes dropped and our bodies pressed together, riding the curve. She opened up. She gave her fingers, her heart, her electricity. Her touch was sure. I felt her heat and knew. How much? How deep?

"I want all of it," she said.

BUTCH GAMES

Karleen Pendleton Jiménez

"YOU BASTARD!" I SHOUT AT THE BUTCH kissing my girlfriend in the hallway of our home. She looks up at me startled. She is handsome, with wavy dark red hair, freckles, green eyes, and a broad jaw. She is quite muscular but endearingly softened by a round tummy.

I brought her into my home, asked her to come. As a butch who makes love to femmes, I know a lot of lines. I've got a pretty good idea how to make whoever I'm with feel wonderful, pride myself in these skills, though I don't know what to do with other butches. This fact never occurred to me until last year, when I was wrestling this same butch in a swimming pool, some kind of clichéd boy play. Looking up at her in the middle of the fight, it struck me that she was handsome, so I told her.

We made love the next night in a hotel room. It was nerve-wracking for both of us, as she is also femme–inclined. We kept throwing out our lines and recognizing them as ones we've both used. I kept sensing myself in her gestures. But when she put her dick inside of me, I fell for her, imagining myself her pretty girl, deserving this thick bone she kept shoving in deeper. And when I opened her, I found my image shivering in her body. So careful and hard with her, I felt I knew what she needed because I knew what I needed, what I am often ashamed to give. We both became these brave and beautiful butches in that room. We were men and women and queers in each other's hands at any given time. We made out a bit more in the parking lot outside and then left to our different homes, 3,000 miles apart.

That was okay. First, because I am in love with my girlfriend at home. Second, because I knew I would see her in another year at the same conference. And I didn't think I could actually handle something like this more than once a year.

"Look, I want to make out with you again, but only if you'll make out with my girlfriend too," I say this when we meet up again. I say this and think I've totally lost my mind. Even though we have a vaguely open relationship, my girlfriend and I don't often act on it. Things get messy and mostly just use up too much energy. I am willing to risk the jealousy of seeing another butch touch my girl, as long as I can get another piece of that night in the hotel room.

In the hallway, I think that I have lost. The risk was too great. Only moments before I had been crying. I told her I couldn't handle the situation. We were both so accustomed to taking care of our femmes that my girlfriend in the picture would make it too difficult to see each other. She agreed. She comforted me by saying we would find time alone later. She then left me in the bedroom, walked right out to my girlfriend and began kissing her.

"You bastard!"

Her eyes narrow and she lets go of my girlfriend. "Don't ever call me that," she says. She covers her eyes. I can't tell if she's gonna hit me or cry or what. To my surprise, she opens her eyes and asks me clearly if I would fuck her, and if my girlfriend could watch.

"No! I just told you I don't want it to be about her any more!" How much clearer can I get? She pulls me to her, says, "please," softly. She says to close my eyes and imagine that we are alone doing this. I am so mad and hurt that I begin to tear at her.

I push this taller, stronger butch down onto a couch too narrow and uncomfortable for this as my girlfriend watches. I throw anything in our way across the room. I tell her how mad I am, call her obscenities. I rip off her jeans and shove my hand between her legs. Her breathing is fast. Her eyes are squeezed together. I pound her. Fuck. Fuck. You fuckin' piss me off. Why did you do that when what we had had been so sweet? My muscles are hot. My hand is burning inside her. Everything feels red and wet. I am hurting her back.

I looked beneath me and found a mirror of myself in her tensed frame. I know this butch game too. Usually I have to practically get my girlfriend to rape me before I will give it up.

So I don't lose some kind of sexist bullshit pride. So I can claim that it wasn't my fault. That she forced some female animal part of me to the surface that I don't even know existed. The tender times are much less common and more often unsuccessful.

I don't know if these things were true for this butch too. But I know she felt me in the middle of my rage. Her heart was racing between her legs. I held her down with my weight as her whole body shook. But I still don't know what to do with other butches.

BROUGHT TO A ROLLING BOIL

Lisa G

I WAS STIRRING JAMBALAYA with a big wooden spoon, slopping the shrimp, the peppers, the rice all around in a spicy mush. It bubbled and smelled divine. The stove sat where I could stir and stare out the Dutch door, the top half open to the summer night air. I breathed in the sweet peas, the lavender, and the spices as they mingled together. The burner was up too high and the bubbling was getting crazy, making the juice fly. A few drops fell first on my dirty white t-shirt, tied in a summertime knot, and then a few more drops dotted my cut-off shorts that hung from my hips. Finally the pot spit up onto the place between the two fabrics. This only reminded me why a smart cook wears an apron as it stung and burned my belly. I was just about to bend over to get a look at the flame to turn it down when there she was.

She came out of nowhere, well, out of the bathroom I guess, or the sitting room. I mean, I knew she was around, she just surprised me with her mouth suddenly on the place where the spicy sweet sauce had landed. She pulled me into the hallway, her lips on my bare skin. Her mouth was open and she ws tonguing the place where it first tickled and then burned. I felt funny and guilty and giddy and hungry. Hungry for the jambalaya on the stove, I told myself – not anything else. Not the tongue or the licking or the slipping about ... my eyes rolled into the back of their sockets as one hand gripped the spoon, the other the counter. Her mouth moved perfectly. The tongue sunk into the folds of flesh as she collected every last drop of juice. Her tongue was moistening the fabric of my shirt and getting frightfully near the sagging old edges of my jeans. And I didn't stop her.

This tongue and this mouth were not my girlfriend's.

"You get your filthy mouth, lying lips, and that cheater's

tongue off me right this instant!" I called her names that deep inside were more reserved for me. Guilt and projection took over. I grabbed her arm and marched her like I imagined her mother would do, down the darkened hallway into the sitting room when she needed a scolding.

"You have just done something that ... something that.... What you did...." I was completely flustered and flushed, which I'm sure she could see, emotions mixing with the pungent air. The jambalaya! Still at a rolling boil. The perfect excuse to buy some time and besides, just because there was one fire in the kitchen that needed putting out, there was no reason to have two. I ran back to the kitchen hiking up my stupid shorts, still holding the wooden spoon.

"I can't believe this.... I was just.... You should never...." I was mumbling. My thoughts were fast and furious, overtaking any sentence I could ever hope to finish.

"I ... can't ... hear ... you...." Her sarcastic sing-song voice came slinking through the hallway, wrapping itself around my neck and trying to be oh so soft, caressing my earlobes.

"No cute boy act is going to help you right now!" I talked big but as I immersed the spoon into the stew and stirred right to the deepest part, where it had a tendency to burn, I remembered similar situations that had presented themselves in much the same way. I stirred the spoon around and around, slowly, tightening up the circles, reliving the previous indiscretions in an odd sensuous medley. I eventually made zigzag patterns as if erasing these images, making sure no surface was left untouched by the spoon. If I didn't want a burned bottom I had better put the bitch to simmer.

She always did whatever and whomever she wanted. It was part of her charm. But her escapades never made me an accomplice. Now here I was all kind of turned on somehow with that excitement of taboo and the adrenaline of lust. Like a drug. It usually ended in disaster ... but what a ride.

"I just wanted a ... taste...." She was still singing to me in there. I couldn't look in at her but I didn't need to. Her little eyes would be all crinkly and smiley. I've seen her get away with murder with those eyes.

"Stop it! Just stop it! This is ridiculous!" My voice, still low, was saying all the right things while my loins felt uncomfortably horny. I noticed some stray shrimp that hadn't made it to the pot, and I desperately needed to find a lid to cover this mess. I picked up the chopping board where the shrimp lay and tilted it so they could slide easily into their inferno.

"C'mon ... it was all in fun." Her voice was now as sexy sweet as honeyed gravel. I'd heard that tone before, but now, directed at me, I imagined myself as one of those shrimp.

"Fun? Fun? As in 'good, clean' I suppose?!" I raised my voice. "After-all-the-times-the-four-of-us-sat-here-laughing-and-drinking-and-carrying-on!" I was working myself into a veritable frenzy, my words getting incrementally louder, a practice learned from my father as he had learned from his father before. "A bunch of friends, your girl sitting on the arm rest of your chair playing with your tie and me sitting on my baby's lap all romantic and laughing and drunk and silly and me so many evenings spent alone with you, bullshitting and carrying on, trusted by our partners and me, that one time, sleeping here too stoned to go home and sleeping on your couch and no raised eyebrows when I finally made it home. No way. No need to be. And now this with you two all busted up, it isn't my fucking fault. I'm still in love and she's still loving me and you do this today after our fine day in the sun. I immediately think it's my fault because of what I'm wearing or how I'm acting, hanging out, smelling like summer and tasting like shrimp and unintentionally turning you on ... what are you on, crack cocaine?"

I had rummaged around in the cupboards and then I was on my hands and knees, crashing and banging pots and pans just like my mother and her mother before her. I realized that my ancestry really was getting the better of me.

"Aha," I breathed quietly, suddenly calm. I located a pizza pan that would do in a pinch as a lid. I stood up, stirred the pot one last time, thinking of her tongue and my skin and how good it felt. I thought about the pizza pan and wondered if I was settling for something that would just do in a pinch until I found the real lid, or did the pizza pan actually become the lid because I used it thus? Was the actual lid really better anyway? I dipped the spoon in and pulled out more than a mouthful of clear thinking and put it to my lips. It was good and I was ready.

I thought once more about her lips, how good they felt, as good as anyone's lips do. But was anyone enough?

I filled the wooden spoon again and used the pizza pan to cover the steamy stew. I swayed down the dark narrow hallway, mimicking her sing-song sassiness.

"Now you're going to get it, I can tell how much you want it." I walked towards her slowly, moving my hips like I know I can. I held the spoon with shrimp and rice and sauce and peppers and offered it to her surprised and gaping mouth, lovingly cupping my hand beneath the spoon so as not to mar her pin-stripes. I bent over all Betty Page like. I blew away the steam à la Marilyn Monroe. And as I shoved the spoon her way, I explained, "There is a fine line between too much spice and just enough ... this has just enough."

DINNER WITH JANE

Michelle Rait

"YOU'RE BACK," JANE SAID as she walked into Regina's office. Regina looked up, trying hard to conceal her delight at seeing Jane.

"Yeah, I took the red-eye back and came straight here to finish a project. I've been up for two days."

"Will you be too tired to go to dinner?" Every Wednesday night for the last two months, the two women had gone to dinner. They'd enjoyed it, and while they kept their distance, they both knew there were too many signals being passed between them for the dinners to remain innocent for long.

"I don't know. Maybe," Regina said. In reality she was exhausted, and knew she should just go home. If she didn't, she wasn't sure that she'd be able to maintain an appropriate level of contact with Jane. Jane – and the fact that Jane was off limits to Regina – was all Regina thought about on her flight home.

"Well, I'll check back in with you later to see if you've made up your mind." With that, she walked away, leaving Regina in a state of turmoil. Seeing Jane bounce into the room and smile at her made Regina's day. She could only think of being close to Jane, holding her, running her hands over her. With a sigh, Regina tried to force the thoughts from her mind and turned back to the computer.

On her way home, Jane again stopped by Regina's office. "I've decided," Jane said. "Like it or not, you are coming home with me and I am cooking you dinner. You said yourself that you've been up for two days. You should eat before you go to bed." With that, Jane grabbed Regina by the hand and pulled her away from her desk.

"All right, I'm coming," Regina laughed. Against her better judgment, and to her delight, Regina allowed herself to be taken to Jane's house.

"I'm sorry it's so messy. We haven't had a chance to clean the house since Kathy started working nights." Regina looked around her. The house was modern, with sleek furniture and polished wood floors. Bookshelves neatly lined the walls, but the dining room table was littered with the documents Jane's lover had been working on before leaving for work. The coffee table had piles of month-old magazines on it, and CDs were scattered on the floor. "Do you mind if we just take our plates and eat on the couch?"

"Sure," said Regina. When dinner was ready, she curled up in one corner of the couch to eat as Jane sat on the other side. Outside, the sun had begun its descent behind the trees. As dinner progressed, Jane's legs slowly rubbed against Regina's, at first almost accidentally, but gradually more deliberately until Regina responded in kind. By the time they were done eating, the daylight had faded, and the two women sat facing each other in the growing darkness.

Then, without saying anything, Jane reached forward and pushed a strand of Regina's hair away from her face. Her hand lingered in Regina's hair before gliding down the side of her face toward her chin. Regina was enraptured. She had wanted this to happen for too long to stop it. Regina looked into Jane's eyes and smiled. Jane continued to softly stroke Regina's cheek, hair, and neck. Her touch was so light, Regina could scarcely believe there were fingers touching her, but every inch of her body realized it, as a shiver went down her spine and a warm feeling spread through her. Not wanting Jane to stop, Regina carefully reached her hand out and began reciprocating. Her hand caressed Jane's cheek, and followed the line of her face to her chin. Regina's fingers moved closer to Jane's mouth – the mouth she dreamed about kissing – then down her neck, around to the back, then up to her hair. Both women leaned closer towards one another, drawn together without words. Jane's hand was on the back of Regina's head, pulling her close. Regina looked at Jane's lips, wanting to feel their warmth on hers. They moved closer, close enough for Regina to smell the faint scent of the lotion Jane put on her face that morning, close enough for Regina to tingle with the anticipation of finally kissing Jane.

Regina pulled away. "I need to go home. I want to stay, but I can't do this until you're ready – until we don't have to hurt anyone. Until I can kiss you all night."

Jane again touched the side of Regina's face, then let her hand drop to her arm. She didn't say anything, but nodded in agreement.

Not wanting to leave, Regina held Jane's hand for a moment, then reached out to run her thumb gently across Jane's mouth. Jane kissed it lightly and Regina stood up.

"I'll see you tomorrow," she said quietly, and left without turning around, knowing that if she did, she would not leave.

LETTER DELIVERED AS A DREAM

Marcy Sheiner

DO YOU REMEMBER THAT SUMMER when our biggest problem was ants? We who were so thoroughly versed in the habits of the cockroach were astounded by the rapidity with which ants reproduced. By mid-July it had become impossible to use a honey pot, or to leave garbage out overnight. Our lives revolved around maintaining a crumbless kitchen.

We bought dozens of round red traps, identical to those we'd used in the city to capture roaches. The ant population diminished, but by no means disappeared. I suggested my mother's method of smoking them out of their holes; you remembered your fifth-grade ant-farm-in-a-fish-tank and wouldn't let me do it.

It rained a lot that summer; no one had prepared us for the mugginess of the mountains, from which you suffered terribly. We'd planned to do a lot of hiking and antique-hunting, but ended up playing Scrabble and going for walks in the cool moist evenings. We held hands as we walked into the village, and ate Häagen-Dazs ice cream cones on the way home.

Meanwhile, the ants kept coming, a determined army of ruthless marauders. When I brushed one from your leg you confessed that you liked the way they tickled your skin. And so I discovered a new way to delight you: like an ant I crept lightly up your calf, past the hollow behind your knee, lightly, lightly up your thigh, until you pulled me into you.

Ah, that summer. How old were we then? How young? What were we thinking when we rented that little cottage in the mountains, knowing little of the country, anthills, each other?

By late August we'd given up on ant control; they traipsed freely across the mound of spilled sugar, or clustered greedily around a cake crumb on the floor. Our armed truce was such that when one squished beneath the heel of my sneaker, you actually cried.

The morning after Labor Day we washed the linens, packed our unused tennis gear and retrieved odds and ends from beneath the bed. What about the ants? I asked; the landlady will be horrified if we leave them behind.

Against your protests I bought a can of Raid, and while you waited in the car, carried out a search and destroy mission. When I emerged, you grimly started the car and we headed back to the city – I to Brooklyn, you to the Upper West Side – both our apartments overrun with cockroaches after a summer of neglect. That night on the telephone you admitted you'd had no qualms about squirting and smashing the nasty little creatures, infinitely more repulsive than our industrious ants.

Over the years I seem to have developed an aversion towards killing ants. But this morning I discovered one already dead near the sink, a victim of cockroach poison. Hastily I flushed it down the drain and wondered, where are you?

A LOVER'S MOON

L. M. McArthur

SARAH GRIPS THE STEERING WHEEL TIGHTLY with both hands. The car bumps over the windy roads and steep inclines of the Rocky Mountains.

"Come on baby, talk to me. You can't be mad at me the whole vacation?" Sarah asks, not daring to take her eyes off the road.

"Wanna bet?" Diana says icily.

Sarah can feel Diana's glare without looking. "You know I hate it when you don't talk to me." Diana does not respond.

"This is our holiday. Are you going to spend the next three days not talking to me?"

"Possibly." Diana flips down the sun visor, checks her hair in the mirror.

"What was I supposed to do? You know my brother is going through a hard time right now." Diana pushes the visor back up. "Support him, yes. But to invite your brother and his three kids on our vacation is a bit much. Especially without asking me."

"Look, it'll be fine," Sarah assures her. "They'll go off and do their own thing and we can do ours. Besides, I bought you a new camping chair, so you can put your feet up and relax. Remember?" Sarah leans over, flashing Diana her biggest smile, praying her peace offering will make up for the intrusion of her brother and his kids.

"Yeah, I remember."

Sarah notices Diana's shoulders drop, just a little.

At the campsite, Sarah raises the hammer to drive in the last tent peg. She tightens the rope and scans the campsite. There is a thick line of trees around the site for privacy, a lake within steps, a white sandy beach, and a forest with hiking trails. Sarah combs her fingers through her hair. There are places nearby to be romantic with Diana. A bit of a challenge at best, but having her brother and his three kids along? What was she thinking?

Benjamin and the boys return to the campsite, arms piled high with wood for the late night marshmallow roast. Diana is curled up in her chair with the latest lesbian novel. Her denim shorts ride high to show off her muscular thighs, and her strapless emerald shirt with a plunging neckline lets the warm sunlight shine down on the bare skin of her shoulders. Her blue eyes sparkle as she devours her book. Maybe an afternoon walk in the forest would be a plan. Sarah saunters over to her lover's chair.

"How about a walk?" she asks, gently caressing Diana's arm.

"Sure," says Diana, closing the book.

"That's a great idea. Let's all go for a walk. The boys have been pestering me to go exploring," says Benjamin.

Sarah snaps her head around to see him gather the boys, their faces bright with excitement. There goes their romantic walk. All Sarah can do is shake her head during the hike, grumbling. The only sympathy she gets from Diana is a smile and a snicker. She puts her arm around Sarah's shoulder and whispers triumphantly, "I told you so." Before she pulls away she licks the outer edge of Sarah's ear and nibbles her earlobe, sending shivers down Sarah's back.

Later, as darkness blankets the campground, the boys decide to venture down to the theater stage for the evening entertainment, scurrying down the path with their father trailing behind. Diana has her nose back in the book, curled up in her chair by the fire. Sarah sulks at the table, drumming her fingers on the red checker tablecloth, not knowing what to do next. Diana glances over, closes her book.

"How about a stroll down to the lake? All the campers should be watching the entertainment," she suggests, drifting over to the table. Sarah's heart beats faster at the prospect of actually sharing an intimate moment together. They stroll down the dirt path to the lake holding hands, caressing fingers. At the lagoon, they watch the moonlight glimmer on the water.

"It's so beautiful here," Diana says.

"Yes, it is." Sarah wraps her arms around her lover. She leans in, kisses the outer edge of Diana's mouth. Sarah's tongue traces her lips and coaches her tongue to escape. Mouths open wider, tongues slide together deeper and deeper. The kiss continues until both are breathless. Sarah reaches under Diana's shirt to feel the silkiness of her skin. Caressing each nipple, Diana moans her desire from deep within.

Thundering footsteps pound down the path. A flashlight beam blasts into their eyes.

"Auntie Sarah, are you down there?" echoes a voice.

"Oh, god no. Not now." Sarah releases Diana abruptly. Three excited boys barrel down the path to the sandy beach.

"Hey, it's time for the marshmallow roast. Come on!" Sean grabs Diana's arm and pulls her back up the path. All Sarah can do is amble up after them.

As the evening winds down, the campfire dies out. Sean, the youngest, is snuggled tight in Diana's arms, asleep from the long day. She moves to release him to his father. Sean, feeling a disruption, holds on tighter.

Benjamin smiles. "Looks like he's yours for the night."

Carrying him inside the tent, Diana snuggles down on the sleeping bags. Sarah glares at her brother before entering. He shrugs, smiles, then enters his own tent. Sarah looks up at the full moon. It's a lover's moon, big and romantic. She lets out a heavy sigh, ducks her head under the flap and into the tent.

THE DINNER

Midgett

THE PHONE RINGS. I'm in the kitchen skinning and boning chicken for dinner. I stop what I'm doing and wash my hands. Put the phone to my ear. A familiar voice says, "How are you doing?"

"Missing you, my honey," I tell her. My heart beats a thousand miles a minute.

"What are you doing?"

I grope for words. "Cooking something nice for you." I hope she won't ask what, because I like to surprise her.

"Okay, see you soon," she whispers.

She hangs up the phone. Even after twenty years, my heart still races every time she calls.

Dinner is ready. I decide we'll eat in the living room, on the small table, Chinese style. I put candles and flowers in the center of the table, set the Oriental dishware. I bring the food from the kitchen and place it on the side table which I use as the serving space because I never know what to expect when she walks in the door. We might eat right away or she will want to make love for an hour before dinner. Depends how her day went.

Even after all these years together, she is just as passionate, horny, and unpredictable as she was when we first got together. I remember the evening she invited friends over for dinner. She charmed them, like she does, with her smile as soon as she walked in the door. After fifteen minutes she excused herself and asked me to do the same. She took my hand like the gracious butch that she is and led me into the bedroom, closed the door, cupped my face with her hand and said in the sweetest tone, "Suck me."

I could not believe what I heard. "Honey," I said, "we have company out there."

149

She didn't respond, simply unzipped her pants. I shivered slightly, put my arms around her neck and pecked her on the lips. Then I pushed her gently onto the bed, and in a quiet voice I asked her to sit still. I got down on my knees and pulled her pants down. With a soft touch I kneaded her hardness, and with each stroke her clit got harder.

I licked her with light strokes, then faster all over her hard clit. I took in her juices, sucking and licking her like a cold Popsicle. "Quiet," I warned as she came. "We have dinner guests."

The door bell rings and I know it is her. There she stands with a mischievous smile on her face, caramel complexion, mixed grey hair. Her large frame is evenly distributed. Her buttocks are round and inviting. Her chest is firm with small breasts. She stands at the door with a twinkle in her eye that is indescribably delicious.

I kiss her briefly, and wonder what is in store for me this wonderful evening after dinner.

BUBBLES

Zamina Ali

WE SAT FACING EACH OTHER. Her beauty in the candlelight was blinding. I was afraid to move, wanting to capture every second of this moment. My eyes rose from the drop of water on my arm and met hers, heart racing faster.

"What's on your mind?" I asked.

She smiled playfully and whispered, "You know what's on my mind." She closed her eyes and smiled.

I felt her leg lightly brush against mine. "Are you comfortable?" I asked shyly.

Her eyes opened and she breathed in slowly. "More than comfortable. This feels like heaven."

I sighed. Our heaven. It surely felt like something beyond our everyday routine. When did we ever make the time like this, to lie with one another in a sea of happiness? I felt much comfort, but could not leave. I was pressed for time, but the pulse between my legs was increasing as her heat projected toward me. I felt her eyes all over my body. I wanted to lift her up and put my hands on her ass, have her at my tongue's reach. She came toward me, water dripping from her chin, soap all over her smooth skin. Her nipples were disguised in white bubbles, leaving more to be desired than I could imagine. My body quivered at the touch of her hand on my knee. The water was still warm and her heat combined with mine was making it our own whirlpool. Leaning over slowly, she ran her gentle hands up my right leg and along my waist. I felt her moving toward me, her wet body on mine.

"I want to feel you. I want to feel you against me," she whispered.

I rose up and she pressed herself against me. Her tongue was on my neck as she licked her way up to the back of my ear. I pulled her close and wrapped my legs around her bare ass. She moaned with pleasure as I ran my fingers along her spine and pressed hard. We locked eyes as we licked each other's tongues. I had never before felt so close to someone. I wanted to please her, to taste her. I stood up and slowly pulled her up with me, pushing her against the tiles. Our bodies slid together as we kissed passionately, my tongue on her neck, circling her upper chest as my hands caressed and massaged her nipples. Her breasts so full, so desirable, I licked them slowly as she moaned and touched her inner thigh. Longing to taste her, I knelt down before her. It was an awkward position, but the pain from kneeling in the tub was exceeded by my desire to please her. She cupped my head in her hands as I ran my tongue along her inner calves. I slowly worked my way up to her right inner thigh, massaged her ass. Her moans grew louder.

I continued moving my probing tongue between her legs. She pulled my head closer and closer. My tongue had a life of its own, licking faster and faster. I wrapped my lips around her clit and she screamed. I inserted two fingers into her, wanting to be closer to her. I looked up and met her eyes, then moved back and licked her again, bobbing, tongue moving in a circular motion, back and forth, faster and faster. I could feel it coming. She violently thrust her hips when the explosion came right into my mouth, her body quaking. My hands slid from her and I sat back, thinking I was in bed. I slipped into the tub and she gasped, "Are you okay?"

I raised my head from beneath the water and she giggled.

"What?" There was a large glob of bubbles on my nose. How romantic. She smiled and leaned over to kiss me. I looked at her, now with bubbles on her face too. Bubbles will never be the same.

WOULD YOU?

Rosalyn S. Lee

YOU CROON THROUGH YOUR WHISPERS about the things you feel, itching to explore me, an endless dream, to touch my warm center and make me scream, but do you dare reach for your share? Would you allow all the emotion that has been gathering with such force let you do what you've always dreamed of, as your own heart quivers with delight? Would you give in to your longing to taste this fruit, forsaking all others, to find your firm yet tender hands wandering beneath my dress, stroking my sun-tanned thighs, moving up to meet the crest of my full and solid buttocks as your own cheeks tighten with sensation?

Would your impatient fingertips tug at the edge of my panties, eager to caress my mound, weeding through the thickness of my forest, only to find the center of my universe moist and becoming harder with each stroke as your own wetness flows? Would those powerful fingers slide their way around my succulent pearl then enter me, one digit at a time, until I am filled with your ravenous desire as your own needs begin to swell? Would you spread my warm, eager thighs and toss my legs over your capable shoulders so my wet, pink and brown pussy is exposed to your baited tongue? Would you pull my hips close to your nostrils and inhale that which is fragrant with my womaness?

Would your wanton passions make me naked before you, exposing my full, brown breasts to the raw sunlight and would you begin licking my nipples with purpose and pleasure until they stood so tall they would salute and beg for more? Would you then pull my joy to your mouth and lay your tongue on it like a hot fudge sundae, moving gracefully to catch all of the drippings from the corners of your hungry mouth as your own fountain overflows? Would you dine at my table, this gourmet meal, such a queenly dish, inside out, licking me dry, from front to back then catch me as you bring me to my judgment, your own convulsions beginning to take hold?

Would we ride the wave together, your eager tongue still surrounding my swollen bud, moving me from barely audible to waking the country side as I cum in you mouth, your hands, your heart? Would you hold me close as I collapse from our interlude, in the warmth of your sweat-chilled arms, spent and naked, surrounded by the glow of our fulfilled longing?

Or will this remain a heart-felt secret, living in your memory only while waiting for the oven bell to ring, calling you to evening meal then off to the cold of your empty bed?

DON'T TELL

K. Lee

DEAR LIZZIE:

I turned fifteen yesterday, and I set all my dolls on fire. I piled them all up in the alley behind our condo where the shed is and I poured gasoline on them, because that is the best way to start a fire, and burned them. How are you? How come you haven't called in a while? Are you okay?

You don't have to worry because I didn't tell anyone, especially not my parents, but I think about it a lot. Are you mad at me? Even though you go to a new school and I am still in the old one you are still my best friend. I think about you a lot when I am in the backyard and when I am alone and when it still smells like summer. It was so hot, remember?

The only thing that's different is that my mom told me that it was fine if I didn't want to wear underwear anymore, but I just got my period again and she said I have to wear them when I have my period, but that's okay I guess. Don't worry, because she didn't see me naked or anything, and the little red mark that you made on my bum is almost faded away.

Did you know that my brother is going away to school? I asked my mom if I could have his bedroom, I said that it's because it's bigger, but really it's because it has a big window that faces your window. We could talk all night if we wanted to, or send each other messages. I can change into my pajamas and you can watch me, I'll even show you my vagina and spread my legs so you can see all of the inside parts. But if I do that I'll just wish that you could touch me. Hey! Maybe we could build a ladder or something, and then we could climb across in the dark and sleep in each other's beds! I promise I'd let you touch me everywhere, even my face.

Just so you know I don't mind that you didn't come to my birthday. It was boring, anyway. My mom invited my old grampa and some of her friends. We had a big cake that said "Happy Birthday" and one of her friends named "Stick" put his face in it. It was so funny; he had icing all over his face. He's dumb but he's funny; he sleeps over sometimes.

I miss you a lot, and I wish that you could just live with me. I hope your dad isn't being mean. Do you know if your mom's coming back?

I go sometimes and make sure that the place where we carved our names in the fence is still there. It is, except someone wrote the word "dicks" beside it, but they spelled it wrong, they spelled it "dyks" or something. Do you remember when you said that you loved me better than any man could love a woman? I believe you because I feel the exact same way. When I think about what we did in the alley by the shed, I just smile, and I can feel myself getting all wet and warm in my vagina. I can put three fingers inside of it now, but it's not the same because I want you to hold me and kiss me. There, I'm getting wet just by thinking about it.

You're my best friend, Lizzie, and I think I love you.

Write back soon.

Jill

FLIGHT

Barbara Brown

I'VE COME TO ACCEPT AS TRUTH that there will never – I mean never – be a time like it. I've tried all sorts of tricks and toys. Most folks who know me will tell you I've tried all sorts of women. But there's no comparison.

How old were we? I think I was ten, maybe eleven. You were older, half a year older. Back then, the difference was important. Of course, you knew more. You taught me how to "gonchi" my brothers by pulling their underwear up their bum. You taught me how to laugh Coke through my nose to gross out my mother. And you taught me that there can be truly indescribable pleasure in this world.

You were the girl with the space between her two front teeth. All the kids teased you about it – "Bucky," "Chewer," "Beaver," and "Space Cadet" were my favorites. But I liked the way you could whistle through that space in your teeth. I liked how you squished food through the hole – foods like split pea soup and strawberry-flecked yogurt.

When I try to remember, I don't know quite how it happened – how I managed to get you, and me, alone, naked, and staring at each other. Or maybe it was you who managed to do it. I don't know how we started (and continued) to rub each other's nipples until they were sore, pink, and standing up. I have to say, I was pretty surprised that nipples could even do that. Back then I mostly thought that nipples were left over from the dinosaur era and had no use whatsoever, especially when I heard what the boys said to the twelve- and thirteen–year-old girls. Those girls would just shrivel up, literally, slump themselves over, blush like a radish, and go hide with the other slumping girls. Breasts and nipples seemed like a curse.

Until you let me touch your bright red nipple with my

tongue, and I got dizzy and had to lay down. Until you touched mine with your gym-calloused hands and said, "Cool."

But the best part of all, the moment that I will never forget, the moment that I have searched high and low to have again, was when you smiled at me and said, "I've got an idea." At that point, I couldn't have had an idea if my life depended on it. You said, "I've got an idea," slipped down between my legs, took a mouthful of yogurt, and began squeezing it through your front teeth. You smeared my clit with it. You ate that yogurt off. You squeezed some more on – it came through your teeth so slowly. You licked it off. Then you opened your mouth, bent in even closer and slid my clit between those two front teeth.

Oh my god.

Your teeth, sliding in rhythm with your tongue. Your tongue tickling the tip of my clit. My clit swelling between your teeth. Flying. I was flying, lost on some other planet or cosmic zone. I didn't want to stop, ever, but as I was floating somewhere above reality, you were hitting solid ground. Hard, dry, unrelenting dirt. And then you took me with you.

Without warning you sat up, saying, "What a dumb idea." You got up and went home. Did you really say "I'm bored," before you left? Unbelieving, I lay there as my head reeled from the kamikaze landing you commandeered. Eventually, my mother made me eat dinner, take a bath and go to bed on time. And then. . . .

I think maybe you moved away, or just stopped squeezing food through your teeth and didn't want to play with me any more. I've spent my life seeking that flight, trying to find my way back. And you – well, personally I think it's a vicious rumor but – they say you, with the perfect whistle, with the perfect smile, with the perfect teeth, became a dentist.

SCHOOLYARD ACROSS THE RIVER

Florence Grandview

I HAD NO IDEA HOW TO DEFEND MYSELF. Too inexperienced, I guess. I was fourteen and the school semester was winter 1969. The tough girl gangs were plentiful.

Lynn's gang was always stealing my math homework, copying from it and not giving it back. One day after school they weren't interested in my homework; they just wanted to beat me up. That is to say, they shoved my face in the snow and dragged me around in it. Too bad they picked this day because it was the only time that particular winter when the snow stayed long enough to be mucky slush.

Other kids stood and watched, which was typical. My math books were buried in the snow someplace. I eventually found them, once Lynn and her gang ran off. My classmates who hung around for the fight lost interest when I was only hunting books, so they resumed their trudge homeward.

Lynn's gang wanted to beat me up, I presumed, because there was some gossip going around the school that I was queer. I don't know who started it, maybe Sandy because I heard her whisper in the girls' can two weeks before, "I know some things about her that you simply would not believe." She was glancing in my direction. I got all cold and shivery, even though I couldn't think of a thing about myself that no one would believe.

The thing that finally came to mind was, my heart used to speed up considerably whenever I was near this blonde hippie girl Karla. I tried to hide my feelings. Karla was always skipping school and thumbing a ride into town, so it wasn't as though I could hang around her much. I walked her home only when I had the rare chance.

There was another gang, Beverley's gang, who were beginning to give me a bad time soon after Lynn's gang threw me in the snow. The reason for Beverley's contempt was more vague. Beverley said that Lynn said that I gave Lynn all of Beverley's notebooks. I had no idea what Beverley was talking about. Lynn was definitely in possession of Beverley's notebooks, I could see that, but I sure didn't take them and give them to Lynn. Lynn must have stolen those books herself.

In any case Beverley said, "Me and my gang are gonna lay a beatin' on you after school one of these days," and she wouldn't tell me which day. This was when the first buds of spring were beginning to pop out, and I was feeling pretty good in spite of myself.

Still I couldn't help bristling with fear every time the 3:30 bell rang and I had to walk home from school. I usually had friends to walk with but they were like me: A puny match for the tough girls.

You could be walking along chatting with your friends when someone would rush up from behind and shove you. Then someone else would jump in. You'd get your hair yanked, your plastic hair band would fall off, and you'd know better than to bend over and pick it up. Not right then, anyway.

I always felt better when my personal things didn't get kicked away, especially my valuable, near-completed homework assignments. Having a friend or two who didn't take off helped a little, too.

There was another gang, Joy Ann's gang, who were reasonably nice to me because they were all in love with my older brother Lester. Lester had already quit school by then, and he taught guitar at Reno Music Store. Only the girls who hung around the shopping centre where Reno Music was located knew much about Lester. He was indifferent to me at the time, but I still had some status as his little sister.

From a distance Joy Ann must have observed Beverley's gang threatening me, or scowling at me, or doing something along those lines, because Joy Ann said, "I see Beverley's giving you a lousy time. Me and the gals can have a word with her."

"Can you? When?"

"The next time we see her alone. We won't waste any time if she's bugging you. Can't have her making a habit of it."

"Gee, thanks," I said. I didn't have a clue what Joy Ann's gang might do to Beverley, and I really didn't care. If Joy Ann could solve my problems for me, great. I sure couldn't.

As it turned out, all Joy Ann and her gang did was crowd around Beverley on the playing field, in a manner so she couldn't make a getaway, and say, "If you give her a hard time anymore, you're asking for it, girl. Got that? You're asking for it."

The next morning on the way to school, Beverley was not surrounded by her gang, for a change. She came up to me and said, "Joy Ann and her friends all gave me shit yesterday about bugging you. Did you tell them to do that?"

"Yup."

"Well, why don't you fight your own battles?"

I didn't reply because I didn't have an answer to that. Well, I guess one answer would have been I didn't fight because I was small for my age, had a picky, poor appetite, couldn't manage my own teenage mood swings and was totally floored by the thought of being talked about behind my back.

Beverley repeated, "Why can't you fight your own battles?"

I didn't say anything.

"Fight your own battles," she said over her shoulder, walking away from me. Beverley didn't threaten me anymore after that. Nobody did. The most I got was an indecipherable mumble sometimes when one of the tough kids swaggered past.

The rest of that school year, what was left of it, was pretty good except I felt a lot more jittery all the time, in school and out. There was nothing immediate to be jittery about, except my own lack of fortitude; a hollow lack that followed me wherever I traveled.

Sometimes I'd feel so nervous I'd talk to myself in the relative privacy of my bedroom. I'd say, "You practice talking tough, or else. And learn to defend yourself verbally, since you can't defend yourself any other way." Then I'd go on to have imaginary, tough–but–defendable altercations. This went on for years, long after all the gangs at school crumbled into nothingness.

CONQUERED AND COMPROMISING

Dana Shavit

THEY SAY YOU NEVER FORGET YOUR FIRST. When my first lover returned to her girlfriend after our brief affair, I ran away and resurfaced in my upturned world. Gossip and condolences. Images of dykes with daggers out to get me as my grandfather's body was lowered into the ground.

Death places other losses in perspective.

Papa, you have been gone for eighteen days. A sudden death. A heart attack.

One would think that losing a much loved grandfather would make a failed love triangle seem irrelevant. One would think. Their losses are incomparable.

It's hard to get you out of my head. The fantasies I've created are palpable, even probable under different circumstances. I can see us walking down the street, me standing beside you on the escalators, in line by the fresh bread counter – a silent dialogue continually expressed in a slight touch or in your blue eyes.

I missed you before I knew you. I fell bent to your bluff. One night.

She told me she was mine. And then she called to explain, "Something happened between me and my ex last night," and I heard myself say, "Shit happens." She apologized. I wished her, with all the sincerity that I could muster, "All the best, and take care," and hung up.

If I were to look up and into you, following the grace of your curve and the rhythm of your life, would I shatter in your sight? Would you laugh at my state – unconquered and uncompromising? You make obvious to me a path that was always there but which I am unable to reach. Take me to where you've been, show me your sights, burden me with your scars and I will lick your wounds, turn salt into sugar, blood into wine. I want to know your textures against mine, feel the weight of you, hide my face in your breasts, and scratch my name on your back.

Is significance measured by time? Your valleys and curves held so much promise from virgin height. The first and further loss of purity and denial of my lust, my love.

"Papa, I miss you."

I can't describe what she looks like any more. I can feel her. But I will never look at her again, never see her raise a hand to her ears casually as she speaks and plays with her earrings. I pointed her out to my friends that night. They couldn't understand my infatuation, but I told them, "She's the one. She will be my first lover." They encouraged my pursuit and I found a daring in me that only surfaces on the odd and desperate occasion. I approached her. We left together in a taxi.

Lately life has become like a labyrinth. Head hitting wall, body aching for sin, mind clutching the few past fragments that remain worthy. Past moments creep up on me. I scare myself. The weakness is within. And it's real. There is a point. Even circles have points. Down the slippery spiral dip, expecting Papa's arms held out to catch me before my pretty red shoes touch the ground. The only arms are my own. "Everything is going to be all right," Papa said.

"Who do you miss more?" That's not it at all. It's just that too much happened at the same time and I can't think about one without getting the other somehow horribly mixed up.

I get dressed up, war paint and all, and go to a club. Strut my stuff half-heartedly. I am sick of looking, lusting. Sick of the scene. Sick of being seen, sick of acting like a player in a game I've never liked. I've learned the secret handshake and now I'm back at square one, not straight but rooted and imaginary. And I'm fishing for memories best left under tires. I leave the club – stunted growth and ash in eye.

My grandfather had a younger brother killed in a concentration camp on the same day and month that I would celebrate my birth, years later. My grandfather had nicknames for his five grandchildren, and a pug named Mickey. They would sit and snore together by the TV. I was told that even from his hospital bed he worried about that damn dog. "Make sure Mickey gets his bone, don't forget Mickey."

She called me today. A message on my answering machine, "Hello stranger, give me a call." She called me twice while I was away. What compels me to go back to the slap in the face in search of a smile? This time, I called her back. She is still on-and-off with her girlfriend. How nice. They're trying to stay together. I see. She asks what I've been up to and I tell her my mind has been otherwise occupied. She tells me she's sorry for hurting me. I know. I keep it together and tell her my grandfather died. On our one night together she asked me what my greatest fear was; I told her the death of my grandfather. Her greatest fear was hurting people. Our conversation had nowhere to go; I rounded it up.

I go to my room, climb into bed, hide under the covers. I'm not getting out for anyone. But somehow loneliness manages to creep into my bed, rub against my legs, tease my lips, flirt with my lashes, and laugh at my new-found eagerness. Conquered and compromising.

SPY

ONE DAY BETTINA CAME BY MY WORK FOR A VISIT. She was having girl trouble, and Sarah, the woman in question, worked at the same place as me.

"We made this deal," Bettina told me. "About hickeys."

"Uh-huh," I said.

"We said, 'No date if you've got hickeys from someone else. Just cancel. Don't say anything. Just cancel.' Like, if we had a date and either one of us had hickeys all over her neck, then they'd just cancel the date."

"Did you really think it would happen? Like was this serious deal-making?"

"Kind of, not really, it was a bit of a joke, like, I said now I'd be suspicious every time she cancelled, and we laughed a lot. And I know she has other girlfriends, but you know, you don't really believe they're nearly as important as you."

"Yeah," I agreed.

"So anyway, then she cancels a date we had and I'm trying not to think why, and that's okay, and we reschedule, but then she cancels that date too, and I'm starting to wonder, like about the hickeys."

"Of course."

"And then the next time I see her on the street she has a fucking turtleneck on." Bettina looked at me.

"Well, I think she wears turtlenecks a lot," I said. I was trying to remember anything Sarah had worn in the time I had been here. I thought there were turtlenecks. Sometimes.

Bettina went on. "So now we have this date this weekend, and I wonder if I should just confront her."

"No," I said. "Never confront." Bettina had a look in her eye.

"Well, will you spy for me?"

I knew that was coming. "What? Ask her to take off her turtleneck so I can try it on? Maybe start an office-wide neck examination? I don't even know her. Not really."

"Just see if there is someone who comes to see her. Just tell me if she wears turtlenecks all the time."

"And what if the hickeys are on her breast? Turtlenecks or not won't tell you anything."

"Just tell me, okay?"

"Okay, okay."

"Perfect. And our next date is at that work thing you have this weekend, so you and I can be a team while I'm on my date."

"A team?"

I ended up going with Bettina to the work thing. She called me.

"Sarah's got some thing before," she said. "She's going to be late."

"What kind of thing?" I asked.

"A thing," said Bettina. She didn't seem to mind. She seemed to like it.

"Do you tell each other anything?" I asked.

"It's not like that," Bettina said.

Bettina was taking this like a soldier, I had to admit. We hung around the door of the party waiting for Sarah.

"You'll spy, right?" asked Bettina.

"Yes," I said.

Sarah didn't show up in a turtleneck, but practically. She had the scarf thing going. It was loose-ish, and I saw Bettina trying to look down it.

"Don't corner her and try to take it off," I muttered to her when we went to the kitchen. "I know you, Bettina. Just don't."

"Why not?"

She was looking at Sarah.

"Just don't."

Sarah was looking at her and fingering the scarf.

"Maybe she's overdressed. Maybe she needs to take it off."

I felt like I should keep an eye on Bettina. I mean, I had to work with these people. But no one can do everything, and before I knew it I was enmeshed in meeting someone, then picking music, and then Pride Day politics. When I looked for Bettina again, I wondered if she had already left. I checked the dining room, the smoking area. I was about to walk into the bedroom full of coats when I saw them inside, Bettina and Sarah. Bettina had her hands on the scarf, and they were talking. Sort of. A certain kind of talking. The kind with locked eyes and travelling hands.

"Take it off, baby, please?"

"Why?" Sarah smiled. "I'm cold. I don't want to take it off."

Bettina toyed with the scarf.

"Oh please, I just want to look, just for a second."

"Look at what?"

"You know. Please."

I considered interrupting, pretending I hadn't heard anything. I considered walking away, too. This was private. Instead, I stayed by the door, in the hall, leaning as casually as possible where I could both see in and spot someone coming. I told Bettina I would spy for her. I was spying.

"Don't you want to know where I went tonight, Bettina?"

"Maybe."

"Maybe?"

"Yes, yes. I want to know. Please tell me. Please."

"I went to my other girlfriend's house."

Bettina bit her lip. Her eyes were on Sarah. "Yeah?" she said finally.

"Yeah, and we talked about you, Bettina."

"You did?"

"Yeah, I told her all about how you like getting fucked and how you want me all the time and how you're always wet." Sarah ran her hands over Bettina's nipples, then pinched one. Bettina sucked in air. She looked away for a second and I swear she saw me. She looked right at me, then she looked back at Sarah.

"I think I'm wet now," she said breathlessly.

"I know you are. You always are." She pinched again.

Bettina gripped the scarf. "Just for you," she whimpered.

"I get wet for you, too. I was wet for my girlfriend today, but it was because we were talking about you."

Bettina gasped, but managed to talk. "Did she get wet?" She rubbed herself on Sarah's hip.

"Oh yes. Hearing about you made her really wet. She kissed me and sucked me all over when I was telling her." Sarah's hands were all over Bettina's ass. Bettina moaned and twisted, holding the scarf as best she could.

"Did she leave a hickey?" she asked at last. It sounded like she could hardly get the words out.

Sarah watched her struggle. Good, she seemed to be saying. This is where I want you. "That's for me to know, honey, and you to –"

I didn't hear the end of the sentence. Suddenly music blared into the hallway and what seemed like twenty but was probably three or four partygoers pushed past me to get their coats. I slipped away in the fray. I sat on the couch.

I watched Bettina and Sarah leave.

Bettina waved at me. Sarah winked, I swear.

CRYSTAL NIGHT

Wendy Atkin

THE ONLY EVIDENCE OF MIREILLE'S PAIN was the blood that appeared on her hands as she picked up shards of glass from the carpet. *I bled*, Mireille thought to herself. *I must have been present in the flesh*. Yet Sarah's hands had left no marks upon her skin.

Mireille walked out into the cold night, which was silent now that the traffic had stilled. The crisp dry air struck her face and she burrowed into her coat. Ice crystals twinkled darkly under pools of streetlights, like tears on the face of the winter ground. Only the sound of them splintering under her heels marked the passage of the dozen city blocks between her home and Judith's. Panting as she turned into her friend's walkway, a puff of grey steam appeared as her exhalation, a sure sign that Mireille was still breathing in spite of the deathly grip on her heart.

Only after Judith admitted her into the warmth of the house did Mireille begin to shiver uncontrollably. Her teeth chattered together like hammering nails and she begged to leave off talking until morning.

"Do you want to sleep in the guest room?" Judith asked with her hand placed on one athletic, bejeaned hip. "After all, you are still Sarah's, aren't you?"

A sudden hot tear welled on Mireille's flushed cheek, threatening to dive and crash on her soft red mouth. Her swelling chest signaled her deep distress to her friend, who awakened to the fact that this was not going to be a flirtatious interlude.

Mireille could not yet bear to crawl into a cold bed alone. Not tonight. She asked, lips trembling as if with desire, if it would be alright with Judith if they slept together. At that moment Mireille shattered every carefully constructed boundary between these two intimate friends, both of whom had lovers who viewed their bodies with fierce and passionate possessiveness.

"Of course," said Judith without hesitation, and led Mireille to her bedroom. She slipped off her jeans in the dark and turned back the thick navy duvet, allowing Mireille to crawl in first.

Mireille turned to face the window and tried to relax into sleep, knowing how hard and yet how necessary it was to sleep beside this new body. Judith reached over and enveloped her with her long arm.

"Is this okay?" she ventured.

"Of course, you always know what I need," replied Mireille, startling herself as words she normally used only with her lover sprang from her mouth.

Mireille's body tightened a little beneath the unfamiliar touch. Very soon, however, a steady warmth began to seep into her from Judith. She fell into a soothing sleep. Judith held her close and slowly moved her hand to form a protective circle around Mireille's middle. When her hand touched Mireille's hip, she stirred a little.

Mireille came close to waking at the peculiar sensation of a thousand tiny warm bubbles circulating in her veins. What had Judith done? It was as though she were signaling from her own deep center a transmission of love and caring such as Mireille had not felt for a long time.

Mireille nestled in Judith's arms and slept more soundly than she had in ages. She inhaled the smoky sweetness of Judith's exhaled breath. She felt something long buried begin to stir deep in her body. It was cold in there, but the relentless warmth of Judith pulled it into the warm protective circle of the embrace.

Mireille was surprised to feel desire awaken in her. Deep frozen ponds inside had thawed and released a steady melt of longing. All night her desire mounted. Sleeping with someone is a more intimate act than fucking them. The steady light touch and the scents released by Judith's body in repose filtered through Mireille's consciousness in a way that none of their casual daytime contact had ever done.

When they awoke the next morning, it seemed only natural that they arose from the same bed. Mireille still felt the heat of Judith's body and checked the skin on her hips and arms for signs of the healing hands that had stroked them. They had left no marks.

She went into the washroom and watched the warm water in the sink bubble around her fingers. Tiny cuts glowed rosily through the clear fluid. She lifted the water in cupped palms and splashed the sore fatigue from her cheeks. The water fell in a thousand crystal droplets sparkling in the morning sun.

The mirror's glass reflected back to Mireille the deep pain behind the transparent blue lens of her wide eyes. For a moment, a chilly thought threatened the thaw inside, but just then Judith appeared behind her, encircling her sore arms gently with her long fingers.

Mireille turned her head away from the anguish she had seen in her own eyes, as if to divert Judith's attention away too. But this move only caused their eyes to meet. Judith's shone green with longing and in a split second their lips connected, searing a bond between the two friends in the swift heat of this moment. Mireille felt her clit inflamed with a longing to be stroked to that miraculous point of no return. All her scattered emotions crystallized into one diamond drill of desire that pierced her resistant libido, her heart aching almost as much as her battered flesh.

The pain won out. The moment passed and the friends pulled away, staring into each other's faces with the tremble of illicit lovers who have started something and then tacitly decided to refrain from stroking each other to the point of painful parting. But like the first ray of spring sunshine pooling a thin layer of ice into water, Judith's warm touch reverberated deep inside Mireille's body for as long as it took for that winter to give way to spring.

CITY HEAT

Andrea Richardson

I RETURN TO THE CITY where our passion ignited. Ten years have passed. I am alone. This time you have not followed me. But, in the summer heat of August, memories of my first lesbian love surface as fragments of innocent romance and fiery desire. In these hazy days of my return, you reappear as a mirage rising from the blazing pavement, and I am immediately transported back to that time and space.

Do you remember the summer heat, the sleepless nights? The sheets were tossed from the bed; the fan circulated the hot air and lovers lay side by side in their stickiness.

One morning I laze in bed lingering between the sheets. I was bored by the drone of morning traffic. Then there came a music apart from the urban soundscape. The wind was blowing and suddenly I saw the trees dancing. I was drawn into the past.

From my bedroom on Fairmount, I can see the swaying trees. Beyond them lies Mont Royal, a refuge from the city grit. You are there with me. The wind is singing and we are dancing. Our sweating bodies taste of salt. This was not our first night.

The first night. You moved through the room with hints of seduction. The house bathed in its warm evening light. You seemed aloof, but I could sense your burning impatience in that guise of nonchalance. We were like cats at play. Who would pounce first? The music was your invitation to dance. I think there were flowers. I seem to remember the sweet scent of jasmine in the spring air. You brought a platter of fresh fruit and we laid on the bed eating sweet juicy strawberries. Did we eat mangoes that time too? We initiated touching, a long hour of caressing only our hands. Ten long years later, this would also be our parting ritual. I felt the imprint of your hands on my flesh, branded by your love.

I pass by the El Dorado. Another fragment. Another time. An even earlier memory of when I was in full pursuit. It was in a small café that I touched your vulnerable heart with the simplest of gestures. It was the first of May and I greeted you with a bouquet of lily of the valley. This flower is intoxicating. My small gift was full of intent and did not go unnoticed. It was the hour of my conquest. I even surprised myself.

In this city, I see spontaneous expressions of love on street corners. Couples feeling the heat, enraptured in their desire for each other, captive of their pressing lust. Across the street, a man and woman suddenly stop and melt into each other. I am tricked by my own eyes. I now see women embracing women at my every step and turn. What were tinges of desire are now scorching moments of burning excitement. Where are you? You are but a memory, fragments from the past.

I am riding up the Main on the 55. I notice how the boulevard has changed from its days of smoked meat and haberdashers to the slick pretentiousness of an artsy world for those who want to see and be seen. Then I see that funky boutique, Scandale. You wanted to buy something extravagant. You saw this elegant blouse in white cotton which evoked the medieval period. There was no restraint. You pulled me into the change room. You wanted to do me there and then. We emerged with your purchase and hurriedly went home to bed. That evening we dressed each other to go for dinner. It took forever as I caressed your waist and hips and thighs, tugging you back into bed, dressing and undressing you, feeling the silk slide over your silky skin. We dined for hours. You wanted me to taste everything. I only wanted to taste you. When we got home, I finally did, long into the dark night.

The body remembers. I am aroused by memories of our young love. Many miles lie between us now. Our many conversations have fallen into silence. It is true we are older, perhaps softer and riper for what life has to offer us. This movement through time and space seems so bittersweet. Bitter and sweet.

BITTERSWEET

Miljenka Zadravec

SQUINTING THROUGH THE FLICKERING LIGHT of the dance floor, I see her. She leans against the bar, her left hand shoved into the pocket of her black jeans, cigarette dangling from her lips. Her white t-shirt gleams beneath the black light, revealing the contour of her small breasts.

She has already noticed me.

We haven't spoken in five years. Yet Jude holds an intense space in my heart. Still. Despite ... everything.

She looks adorable, her brown curly hair shadowing those liquid green eyes. I watch her, remembering. How her energy merged with mine. How in the heat of lust, we could hear each other speak without saying a word; remembering her eyes crying, radiating love, for me. How her hands held and stroked me, tenderly. She said she could never live without me.

We had no boundaries, no skin, we were two souls merging.

I moved out while she was at work. I packed my van with books, clothes, pictures, crystals, boxes thrown together. I left what was questionable, shared. I took the microwave, later regretting this practicality. I didn't leave a note or explanation. A salmon struggling for her life. I left in January. Like a thief, I slipped away in broad daylight. Grabbing bits of myself back.

From across the room, Jude stares at me and in that moment I know she still loves me.

It was my friend Sarah who helped me. She heard Jude yelling at me one day. Screaming obscenities. Sarah had come to the door, invited for breakfast. She left without knocking. When she didn't show, Jude phoned Sarah and asked when she was arriving. She said she wasn't. Later Sarah asked me what I was doing. Why was I allowing myself to be treated so abusively? Me, such a strong feminist.

I felt ashamed; exposed.

I stare back at Jude remembering the nights our bodies melted away.

I had to leave without a note. The roller coaster ride of thrills and terror had to come to an end. I could not listen to her screaming accusations for one more day. I would not say sorry again. I did not want her to talk me into another passionate new beginning.

Yet as I look at her, I remember. How soft she was, so warm, exuding innocence in her pink tank tops, purple shorts. She wore a leather skirt, just for me. She was beautiful, seductive. Irresistible.

I left to save my life. I started out with Jude: strong, happy, connected to community, and I left six years later: ugly, sad, worthless, and very alone.

Now here I am, strong again. At the same gay pride dance as Jude. I make my way across the room. Confident, as an old Whitney Houston song plays. I ignore the memory of her cold steel eyes piercing through me as she threatens to kill me. Her hands gripping the steering wheel of the car that tries to run me over.

Looking right into Jude's eyes, I smile, say, "Hi."

I feel her sexual energy rise, meet mine, jerk away. She half-smiles, stiff, as her long- haired, short-skirted lover puts a pos-sessive arm around her. Jude nods, then smiles wider at my lover, who keeps her distance. Jude's girlfriend turns her back on me and moves in front of Jude. A solid fortress. She ignores my presence. I am not impressed by her.

In this moment, I am grateful for my friendships. My running partners who keep me fit. My dogs who keep me outdoors and tanned. Grateful that I am feeling beautiful and loved.

See, I did great without you. My ego smiles inside.

Later my lover and I are sitting on a couch, in a different room. Jude walks by without her girlfriend, stops, hesitant, says, "Hello."

I stand up and introduce her to my lover.

Somehow, my hand reaches Jude's. Her fingers grasp mine. We keep holding hands while she is talking to my lover.

Miljenka Zadravec

Neither one of us makes the first move to let go. The energy between us is strong, sad, familiar.

I loved her.

Then I remember what day it is today.

I smile, eyes full, as I let go of her hand. I glance at my gentle lover. I know I will never be with Jude again. Despite our souls meeting. Despite the passion. Despite ... everything.

She will never be my lover again. Not a lover, and no, not even a friend.

Jude's fingers still extend towards me as my hand drifts away.

She smiles her crooked smile.

I lean forward, kiss her softly.

"Happy birthday, Jude."

MOMENTS IN DESIRE

Fiona Coupar

Stein River Valley, BC
September, 1999
I am sitting on these sun–warmed rocks watching the Stein River rush and plunge past me. It is a clean, wild, light green river, sparkling with white foam. These are the sacred lands of the Interior Salish people, where they came for spiritual renewal. The bright yellow and green leaves of the aspens rustle softly in the wind all along the water's edge.

As I listen to the river and the rocks sing, and feel the heat of the sun on my arms and legs, I allow myself to think of you. I can see your strong and gentle hands, the first thing I noticed about you, where all the long and difficult paths of your life are marked. Your brown eyes are rich like earth, like a deep, lustrous cherry wood. I love how you are wild and tender like this water. I love your fire and insistence, the way you take me like I want to be taken. You have tamed me, and I have let you. Thinking of you like this makes me laugh out loud to the rocks and the trees and the river, it is so good.

It will be so long before I see you again, and San Francisco is so far away. But at this moment, in this sunny and peaceful place, that is somehow all right.

San Francisco, CA
December, 1999
Finally I am here with you, freed from the torturous wanting and waiting of these last two months, and the endless phone calls from Vancouver to San Francisco. I am pretending not to notice you as you come out of the house into the backyard to take my picture. You move around me quietly, crouching and

focussing, trying not to disturb me while I am writing, yet wanting very much to disturb me. I can feel you holding me in your gaze, wanting to reach out and run your hand along my thighs.

The sky above us is unseasonably clear and blue. Next door someone is listening to hard luck music, something with lots of mournful horns. A light wind plays with the chimes above the back door. Clear, delicate notes mark the seconds as they pass, making each one resonate in the late morning heat. I listen to the bright tinkling fragments of sound as they float through the air, melting into each other. Overhead the sky splits with the roar of planes to and from the airport. The music, the chimes, and the thunder of the planes all feel like they are rushing through my arm and spilling into my pen like rain down a window.

My body is languid and relaxed as I sit here drinking the coffee you have brought me. I have been loved and fucked, charmed and pampered, chained and healed by you since I have been here. My wanting you has flooded me like the mouth of a river at high tide, and I feel full and saturated. It is all so sweet, everything about this hot second is so sweet; even more so because I know how our hours and days together are measured, counted, and fleeting.

Tomorrow one of those planes will tear into the sky and carry me away from you, away from this moment. Saying goodbye to you is so hard. One instant I am smelling your hair, looking into your eyes, waving to you, and the next, you are gone. But right now I am here with you, watching the sleepy grey shadow cat lying in the dust scanning for birds, and the dying pink gladiolas fading gracefully into the corner of the garden.

Vancouver, BC
October, 2000
It is a busy Saturday on funky Commercial Drive, Vancouver's east-side main drag full of small stores and restaurants. The autumn day is cloudy and overcast. I have spent the morning wandering without purpose up and down the Drive, buying stupid things I do not want and cannot afford.

I have felt empty since we broke up in August. I don't want anyone to know this part of me, how much I need you, want you, and miss you. How I think about you first thing in the morning, and last thing at night. I especially don't want you to know it. I can feel how you pushed into me with the force and gentleness of a strong, smooth-skinned plant growing through hard earth. You uncovered my loneliness and grief. You released my oldest and saddest tears from the room inside me, where they had sat silent and neglected like forgotten toys. Your kindness opened me, and I will love you forever for that alone. Now I have no idea what the right thing is, or when I will see you again. I am so tired of trying to do the right thing, of listening to this screaming void inside me.

I remember the cry of a wolf I heard this September in the Southern Chilcotin mountains. The howl rose up out of the distant shadowy pine trees on a cold, crisp night, up into the clear sky and the jagged points of the stars. It was a lonely, primal cry piercing the black night. My memories of you move restlessly inside my thoughts always, pacing and roaming, leaving me no peace.

WAITING

Bryhre

THE ACRID TASTE OF HER CIGARETTE FILTER BURNING prompted Jan to cough as she flicked the offensive object in the general direction of the litter barrel. She checked her watch again and realized Angela was now forty-five minutes late. The heavy sounds of rush hour traffic blared from two streets over. At least if she'd insisted on meeting inside the restaurant she could have escaped the noise. Angela's arrivals at their meeting places were definitely getting later and later each time. And her saucy smile and sweet words of apology had lost their effectiveness. Jan angrily pulled another smoke from her pack and lit it. Angela hated her smoking. If the little witch really was thinking, she would have suggested Jan wait inside so she couldn't smoke.

Passersby glanced disinterestedly at the small, denim-clad woman leaning against the grey concrete wall. Jan surveyed herself as though from a distance, and wondered what Angela had seen to attract her in the first place. Maybe just the sight of a genuinely nice person she could toy with and make miserable.

Jan resisted the negative pull of her thoughts and tried to remember back nine months when Angela first walked into the video store where Jan worked and asked to see the catalogue of adult entertainment. Her hair, long and blonde, fell thick and heavy to below her ass, swinging as she moved her hands and body to accentuate her request. Jan watched her surreptitiously as she flipped through the pages, and her eyes widened in apparent shock at the sight of the explicit illustrations. When she asked Jan about the characterization and cinematic quality of one of them, Jan glanced at the page thrust under her nose and said, "Sorry; haven't seen that one yet." The top and bottom, decked out in black leather and spikes – the bottom's wrists manacled tight behind her back as she knelt at the feet of her master, head bowed submissively – did nothing for Jan.

"You can watch it with me if you like." The coy customer raised her brow. Jan felt an ache begin somewhere in her gut. This woman definitely did something for her.

"I get off at midnight," Jan said. "Can you wait that long?"

She responded with a level, straight-on stare and an infuriatingly laconic, "Oh, probably. . . ."

And it had gone on from there. Jan felt herself hooked and reeled in slowly. In small, idiosyncratic ways she fought her fascination. When Angela pleaded with her to move into the loft she rented in English Bay, Jan refused to give up her east end bachelor suite. Angela's switch from sweetness to bitchiness within four months made that decision even more trenchant. Jan's apartment became her refuge from hurled high-heeled shoes and kitchen utensils. Somehow, she'd had the foresight to keep her address private. Angela could certainly find her if she wanted to, but that didn't seem to be part of the game.

Detachment developed somewhere around month six. That was when Jan realized she was actually enjoying herself, if being in a state of continual sexual frustration and on the receiving end of all the female craziness Jan had ever heard of and managed to avoid till now could be enjoyed.

On the day they had met, Jan and Angela never did watch that film. Angela met her at the shop after work, and walked crying into Jan's arms. Something about the abusive ex from hell she had encountered shortly beforehand. Angela cried beautifully and seductively, like a wounded child, and Jan could not fuck a child. Somehow, she had never been able to get past that sense of Angela, despite all the words and wiles. Beyond the surface camouflage, there wasn't enough woman there for Jan to engage with the way she might have if things were different.

There was plenty to keep her occupied, though. Jan recognized herself now as a world-class caretaker. She smiled wryly to herself as she finished another cigarette, and glanced up the street again to see if Angela was in sight. Other couples walked by, holding hands and laughing together; married couples with the kids at home tormenting the babysitter. Not a single long-haired loner among them. Talk about tormenting the babysitter.

Jan did a quick calculation in her head at what she thought might be the current rate for babysitting. She considered canceling the reservation, but decided against it. It was in Angela's name anyway.

Jan whistled to herself as she put her hands in her pockets and strode purposely down the street.

Half an hour later, Angela rushed into the restaurant and listened with a hand to her mouth as the host assured her no one was waiting for her.

At Charlie's, Jan settled into a threadbare chair and placed her pint of Canadian on the glass table top. She looked toward the bar for permission as she pulled her smokes from her breast pocket, and looked expectantly around the bar for a familiar face she could tell her story to.

I SAW YOU

Joli Agnew

"WHAT'S WRONG NOW?"

I look away from the car window. "Nothing's wrong." My voice is quiet, almost dead. So different from the rage screaming inside me. "Why would you think that?"

You shrug and I watch your breasts jiggle from the movement. Your breasts are large and firm, with dark pointed nipples. Tonight you aren't wearing a bra and I can't help but stare at your tits as you maneuver your precious BMW down the highway.

You glance at me. "You were acting kind of pissed off at the party."

Like you would notice. Or care. You were too busy drooling over that slut. I know your pussy creamed at the sight of her. I glance at your leather skirt. Your panties are probably drenched with your juices. If you're even wearing panties. Or did that whore find total access when her hand found its way up your skirt?

I shift around in my seat as I remember how you looked when the beautiful bitch touched your cunt. Your raspy breath hitched in your throat as pleasure rippled across your face. I was fascinated as I watched you with another woman. I also wanted to pull you away and attack you. With hatred or desire, I don't know.

"Are you?"

I jump, realizing I'm in the car with you, but clueless about the discussion. "What?"

"Pissed off?"

Now would be the perfect time to throw a fit. To ask why you keep cheating on me after all these years. I should ignore you and pout, but that never works. Somehow I always manage to look bad when I didn't do anything wrong.

"No," I sighed. "I just have some stuff on my mind." I turn away and look out the window. Stuff like why do I love you when you treat me like this? Why do I stay with you when I could do so much better?

Sex. I shake my head over the simple, painfully honest answer. The sex between us has always been great, even when I hate you. Like I do right now. Right now I want to claw your eyes out. I want to tear strips out of your luscious brown skin and yank out your long straight hair. It would give you an inkling of how I feel.

My losing control over my anger doesn't frighten me. What scares me is how thrilled, how wet I became watching you two go at it when you thought no one saw you. Excitement shudders through me. My pussy blossoms with want as I remember you with that tramp. My heart roared in my ears as you sagged against the shadowy wall while she fingered you. You viciously French kissed her, wildly, desperately. I quivered at your guttural groan when she pulled your shirt down and mouthed your naked breast.

You came so violently, so quickly. She must have been really good. Was she better than me? You got on your knees unbelievably fast, shoving her tight jeans down and sucking her shaved pussy while fingering her ass. The two of you were moaning like animals in heat. You didn't even notice me nearby. I rubbed myself to a climax as I watched you cheat on me.

How I hate you. Only you could turn me on while ripping my heart out. I can't believe I got dripping wet watching you fuck another. What would you do if you knew that I saw and couldn't stop watching? Would it excite you, or would you use that knowledge against me?

It doesn't matter. I'll never give you the satisfaction of knowing that I saw you. Or that it hurt.

REVENGE

Tara Lagouine

IT'S THE NIGHT OF THE BIG HALLOWEEN PARTY. I look dashing
in my black cape with its red velvet lining. A push-up black lace
bra under an immaculate white, almost transparent tuxedo shirt,
fishnet stockings with nothing underneath, and black patent
leather stilettos round out my attire.

The house is full to cracking with beautiful and bizarre
women. A seductive Marilyn Monroe offers me her throat as I
glide by and I back her against the wall, spreading my cape over
her as I take a bite (a nibble, really) and she swoons in my arms.

I feel eyes drilling into my back and glance behind me. You
are there, staring. I lift my upper lip to show you my teeth and
turn back to my willing victim. She reaches up around my neck
with her hands and pulls my face towards her and as our lips
meet, she slides her tongue down my throat. I'm getting hot and
I grind my clit into her leg. I whisper in her ear that I would like
to continue somewhere quieter, and ask her to meet me upstairs.
She agrees and blows me a kiss as she sashays out of the room.

You are suddenly at my side with a look that I've never seen
on your face before. You ask me if I like my new girlfriend better than you. You're just starting to say something about how I
seem to be having no trouble in finding a replacement, but instead of answering, I grab your hand and pull you into the bathroom. I pin you against the sink and kiss you hard, violently.
You don't move but your lips and your tongue respond. I move
my lips to your neck, your breasts, lifting your shirt, pulling
down your pants. I hear your breathing, harsh and labored. Not
a word escapes your lips. I pull your panties down and bury my
face in your sex. I know where your little pearl is, and it's already hard and your cunt dripping. Do you remember how I
used to lick you, suck you until you screamed? My fingers up

your cunt contracting and then ballooning as your back arches up your belly your breasts, you murmuring all the words I can never hear, my face my mouth my teeth straining to enter you, your hands reaching down to clutch at my hair. I shake my head lips teeth tongue on your clit hard slippery hot. And you start to shudder – no screams – I reach up and put one hand over your mouth and I feel your tongue lap my fingers, your teeth bite into my palm. That's what you wanted – you missed it, didn't you? You haven't found anyone to replace me in this department, have you, and I know you want me again – you want to do it to me. I slowly rise from my knees. You smile at me with your just-fucked eyes and you still don't say a word as I wash my face and redo my makeup. I smile back, reach for the door and I'm gone.

Outside the door are a crowd of women, their bladders full, impatient but laughing at what they know just went on behind it. But they don't know really. They don't know that this was just my first act of revenge for the way you ended our relationship.

I climb the stairs. Marilyn is waiting for me.

MUSICAL CHAIRS

Anne Seale

ROSANNA LEIBOVITZ IS THE MOST DESIRABLE WOMAN ON EARTH. I should know. I've wanted her for two years, ever since the night I joined the Lyrical Lesbian Chorus.

I was late to that first practice. A customer had walked into the bookstore five minutes before closing and wouldn't leave until she found the perfect gift. By the time I arrived at the center, a dozen or so women were already perched on metal folding chairs arranged in a U, singing earnestly to the beat of the director's baton.

I found a seat among the first altos and looked around to see if I knew anyone. I didn't, but directly across from me in the soprano section sat the creature of my dreams, giving her well-distributed all to "I Am Woman."

How can I describe Rosanna? She's dark and mysterious, with flashing eyes and wild black hair. She dresses in bright prints, heavy with lace and embroidery. She laughs wickedly when conversing with the other sopranos, but when she sings, her face glows with angelic fervor. Fortunately, she's single.

Unfortunately, I'm not.

I am joined at the hip to Claire Freeman-Bache. I'm the Bache. We hyphenated after our union ceremony in 1992. Claire and I jointly own a house, two cars, and the bookstore. We do everything and go everywhere together. The chorus is the only thing I do without her.

Actually, it was Claire's idea for me to join. "Jeannie, look," she said one day as she leafed through a gay newspaper from a stack that had been dropped off. "They're forming a lesbian chorus down at the center. Why don't you go? You were just saying how much you missed singing."

It's true. I was a strong alto at school and in the First

Methodist choir. Now that I was a well-educated heathen, I had nowhere to sing. "I don't know," I said modestly. "It's been so long. Maybe I'm not good enough."

Claire gave a snort. "Of course you're good enough."

Dixie, our only employee, was dusting a bottom shelf. She jumped up and ran over. "Do it, Jean," she said, "you know you want to!"

Claire tore the article out and stapled it to the wall calendar, saying, "And since the center's so close to the bookstore, maybe you wouldn't mind closing up on Tuesdays so Dixie and I can go to the house and work on the books." We'd lost our last computer in a store burglary a few months before, and had decided to keep the new one at home.

So it's two years later and I'm sitting on the same folding chair at the GLBT Center, spending yet another Tuesday evening watching Rosanna as her breasts rise and fall in deep, controlled breaths and her rosebud mouth curls around "The Impossible Dream." How I want her. But I could never be unfaithful to Claire because I know Claire would never be unfaithful to me.

Rosanna suddenly looks up and meets my eyes in a bold stare. She sticks out a pearly-pink tip of a tongue, and licks the middle of her full upper lip. Then she moves it languidly around her mouth's perimeter as she lowers her music enough for me to see the thumb and gold-ringed forefinger of her left hand pinch her right crimson-clad nipple. My own nipples jump to attention, and fluid gushes into my crotch.

I force my eyes down and try to sing, but all that comes out is a squeak. The woman next to me gives me weird look. I wonder what kind of look she'll give me when she sees the soaked seat of my jeans.

I sit tight, my eyes glued to the music, until the director squints at the wall clock, raps the baton on her music stand, and says, "Take ten." Holding my jacket around my waist, I run out the door and jump in my truck.

When I get home, the house is dark except for the flickering of the computer screen in the den window. Dixie's car is parked behind Claire's on the other half of the driveway.

Mercifully, the stereo is at full blast when I enter through the back door. I tiptoe upstairs to the bedroom, and put on dry un-derpants and jeans. Then I go back down and stop by the den to see how they are doing. I freeze in the doorway when I see the computer screen, on which several nude women are athlet-ically interlocked on a black fuzzy sofa.

That's not the worst of it, though. Claire and Dixie are some-how occupying a single desk chair, and are doing their best to imitate the activity on the screen. I didn't even know Claire could bend that way.

My heart grows light. I float out and start up the truck, revving the motor loudly. As I'm backing down the driveway, two heads appear at the den window. I honk and wave.

Back at the center, I slide into my usual spot. Rosanna eyes me quizzically. I grin and throw her a kiss before joining the chorus in a rousing rendition of "We Shall Go Forth."

BURNED

Jacquelyn Ross

I OPEN THE FRONT DOOR OF MY MOTHER'S HOUSE, walk into the room, and drop my medium no-fat, no whip, decaf Starbucks moccachino when I see my mother kiss my girlfriend, Nicole. It is not a nurturing or polite kiss, but rather a full-fledged "I'm your woman" liplock.

The coffee hits the floor; the hot liquid spreads as quickly as my temper. Deep down I know there is something going on between them. The shopping trips that last past midnight, the way my mom looks at my lover disapprovingly when Nic drapes her arm across my shoulder at the Sunday night family dinner. Here is the woman who brought me into the world, made sure I was happy and cared for, read me bedtime stories, gave me a hug when I was feeling sad, and helped with my homework. Now, she is helping herself to my girlfriend.

Sure, Nic and I hadn't had sex in the last sixty-seven days, but is that the reason she looks for love in the wrong place?

My mother is so saintly. Mary almost became a nun at sixteen, and now look at her - clenched to my boyishly cute lover and paying no attention to any of those Ten Commandments she is always reminding me of.

They stop when they hear my coffee cup hit the polished ceramic tile floor - Mom looks too happy for this heart-wrenching moment. Nic looks like she was the one found at Brentwood with the bloody glove in her hand. I open my mouth, but I can not talk - the shock of the love scene is too intense for my mind to make sense of.

"Oh honey, this isn't what you think," my mother says as she quickly wipes her hot pink lipstick from Nic's upper lip with her thumb, while my ex-girlfriend frantically buttons up the top three buttons of her shirt. Mom taught me to share, but this is ridiculous.

My hands flutter like a bird's broken wing . . . perhaps in sign language to tell then both to fuck off. Nic looks at the floor, obviously embarrassed.

"Honey, we were just talking about you," Mother lamely explains. "Nic is unhappy and I am just comforting her."

"Comforting" is not the word I would use to describe what I witnessed. My mother and my girlfriend are lovers. Couldn't Mom pick up a blonde at church bingo on a Friday night to nibble on? Where is common respect, decency, and a gun when you need one?

This is the last straw for Nic and me. I look as sorrowful as Bambi, only this time Bambi wants to shoot her mother before the hunters get to her. I don't want any explanations now, as I step through the coffee puddle toward the living room.

"Do you mind?" I snap at Nic, who is struggling to do up the last button on the jeans I bought for her birthday three and a half weeks earlier. "My mother? Why?"

"It just happened," Nic tries to explain. "We didn't plan to fall in love."

The "fall in love" part makes me recoil back into the sticky pool of coffee.

"Get out!" I yell at her.

Nic looks away from me. Mom is crying and Nic says softly to her, "I'll call you later."

At that, my head whips around like Linda Blair's in *The Exorcist.*

"You'll call her later?" I repeat, stunned.

Nic grabs her jacket and hurries out the door, as she quietly says something about being sorry to me. I slam the door behind her, and turn around to confront the family traitor I used to idolize.

"You have gone way too far," I say before the tears start. "Out of all the women in the world, why did you pick my girlfriend? And, just when in the name of God did you become a lesbian?"

My mother mumbles something, then looks at me and whispers, "I never wanted to hurt you, honey. I will always be sorry that I have."

"I don't understand. I thought I knew you, but I know nothing about you."

I swing around and stomp out. As I bang the door, I hear my mother sob. For that, my heart hurts. I can actually feel it ache like a rotting tooth. Now I have to deal with Nicole. I want Nic to hurt as much as I do.

I don't remember the drive to our apartment. As I walk into the hall of our place, I can hear sounds from our bedroom. My heart thumps as I make my way to our room, a feeling of help-lessness overwhelming me.

When I enter our bedroom, I watch my partner of five years stuff her belongings in to a black hockey bag. She looks up at me; her eyes are red and vacant. There are razors running across the lining of my stomach. I back out of the room.

I stomp into our kitchen. I feel empty, my two best friends now lost to me. I hear the closet door close. Nic has finished packing. I hear her familiar footsteps walking toward me.

Nic looks at me and asks, "Do you want to talk?"

"Get the fuck out," I say as the lump in my throat spreads.

She hesitates by the back door for a moment, then pushes it open. She doesn't turn back. She keeps a brisk pace as she walks to her car parked in the driveway.

I peak through the kitchen blinds and watch the car lights back out. When I can't see them anymore, I walk back into our bedroom, turn on the light and look at her empty desk. One bright orange thumbtack is all that remains on her bulletin board.

SCOOPED

Shelly Rafferty

for Kathy

I'VE GOT A BUM LEG FROM FALLING OFF A ROOF in another life. Up on the barn at Three Pines Farm, hammering shingles, I dreamed of joining the army, or driving a snowplow, or even being a wildlife officer, but with this bad leg, I've been reduced to reporting for the local paper.

It's a tolerable life.

Our publisher, Lydia Talcott, says I'm reliable and succinct, not given to florid language and hyperbole, and last year, after Bob Haverstack retired, she gave me the sports section.

Now, Hamilton, New Hampshire, is not the most exciting place, but it is the seat of Aurey County, and any sports news worth writing about happens right here. In the winter we've got the regional speed-skating championships, and in the summer, the best small boat sailors gather on the shore of Lake Hamilton for the annual Skarsgaard Swedish Meatball Regatta.

It seems like an unlikely event at which to fall in love, but last week the wind was blowing my way.

The starter's pistol cracked the afternoon air like a melamine plate struck by a falling rock, and twenty-seven Sunbirds pushed off from the shallow water. Sails were quickly hoisted and centerboards dropped, and into the wind they went, headed for Sheriff Fitch's pontoon boat, anchored a half-mile out.

As in years before, Tim Tupper was favored to win, and his fourteen-footer cut to the head of the pack. The wind was brisk; the race would be quick. And it sure was pretty.

We followed the field in Lydia's twenty-two-foot inboard motorboat. The grande dame was at the wheel herself, and I stood next to her, nursing a beer.

We were three-quarters of the way out when Tupper caught up with us. I swung my 35mm up to my eye and snapped a few shots for the paper. A bright yellow sail suddenly burst through the frame of Tupper's jaunty angle and cut off his wind. A red lifejacket, some skimpy mesh shorts, and the most beautifully muscular arms I had ever seen were holding on to a pregnant sail, and I nearly dropped my camera into the drink.

I adjusted my lens for a closer look.

Against my manifest of contestants, I checked number eight: Kit Featherweight of Brattleboro, Vermont.

I backed into Lydia and elbowed her. "Hey," I said, nodding off the port side. "Away all boats."

Lydia clumsily settled her Margarita into a cup holder and glanced over her shoulder. "What are you talking about?"

"A veritable mermaid at ten o'clock."

Lydia shaded her eyes and cranked the wheel around a bit. "She's got Tupper on the run."

"Come in a bit, close on the buoys," I ordered gently. "I want to get a better look."

My boss indulged me. She knew my interest was more than vocational. We drew in nearer, our little cruiser just thirty feet off Featherweight's bow.

"Ahoy the ship," I shouted. "You're upsetting the balance of power, Featherweight!"

The skipper looked up quickly and narrowed her eyes. "Do I know you?" She kept a firm hand on the tiller and let the sheet out just a bit. We were nearing the turnaround at Fitch's boat. It was garishly adorned with logo pennants from the meatball company.

I held up my clipboard. "I'm a member of the Fourth Estate! Local paparazzi, if you will. Do you want to make a statement?"

"You're a little premature," Featherweight called back. She was smiling broadly. "The race isn't over yet!"

"I'm still in this," came a yell from Tupper behind her. "We've still got half a course."

"You're eating her dust," I called good-naturedly to Tim. He followed her by twenty feet or so.

Tim's voice was undaunted. "I know it looks bad now. But when I win, you'll still go out with me, right?"

I rolled my eyes and tried not to linger on how awkward that might be. Tim Tupper had been after me for years.

Featherweight looked over her shoulder. "Hey, is that the prize?" she shouted to me.

"What?"

"Going out with you. Does that go with the trophy?"

Kind of cheeky for an out-of-towner, aren't you? I thought.

Featherweight adjusted her weight in the cockpit of her tiny sloop. She tipped up the brim of her cycling cap and inquired with a look if I was interested. I motioned to Lydia with a finger circling in the air. "Heads up!" I suggested to Featherweight. I gestured over the bow. "You'd better prepare to come about!"

Lydia took the cue and gunned the motor as we swung through the warm summer water in a wide, generous arc. Our turn sent a hungry wake into the sailors. The pitch and yaw of the wake shook the small boats like waving handkerchiefs as they rounded Fitch's boat.

Within a minute, Tim had gained the inside of the wind. On the far corner of the halfway marker, he advanced on Featherweight and deflated her sail. The wind was strong, but stuttering, and as he pulled out in front, her sail filled again.

Water spilled over her deck as she dragged the sheet in, harnessing the breeze. From the squint of her eyes, the freckled shoulders and telltale patch of white on her wrist, I knew she was an experienced sailor. The wash of the frothy chop was soaking her deck shoes. She leaned back, angled at about sixty-five degrees off the water.

"You haven't answered the question!"

"What question?"

"Dinner?" she ventured. "With me."

"I'm here to report the news, not make it."

"So even if I win, you won't go out with me?" Tupper and she were now neck and neck, separated by fifteen feet of open water. "You're not seriously committed to Popeye?"

I ignored the playful disparagement of Tim. He'd survive being stood up.

"If you're interested in headlines, I've got one for you."

"What did you have in mind?"

"How bad do you want to win?"

"It depends on the prize," she called back.

"You'll have to lose the race," I warned. I had her attention. I put my foot up on the gunwale and grabbed hold of Lydia's windshield. My boss and I exchanged a quick glance and Lydia rolled her eyes as I hoisted myself topside. From my vantage point I could now see the strain of Featherweight's thighs and the turn of her waist under the lifejacket. "How about 'Vermont Sailor Rescues Reporter'?"

"You're not really going to jump in!" I detected the slightest amount of panic in her voice. "Surely an old salt like you can swim!"

"Not very well!" I shouted. I took a giant deep breath, and closed my eyes. "And I like my steak very rare!"

The steak was delicious.

And so was she.

ROCKING THE BOAT

Miriam Carroll

THE SMALL SLOOP ROCKED SEDUCTIVELY in the frigid waters of the Baltic Sea. Overhead, in the long day's night, stars sparkled as if holes were poked in a giant black cloak above which some mighty god played a monstrous light.

In the prow, leaning carelessly against the helm, Queen Christina stood, brooding to herself in seven languages. "I need to have a woman. Right now!" The words sounded most seductive in her native language, so she repeated the phrases aloud, balancing the syllables to match the rhythmic tossing of the anchored boat. Her Arctic fox neckpiece slid aside as one regal hand slipped beneath her woolen shirt to stroke her nipples, which hardened to the wind-roughened touch.

On the alert for this sign, a shadowy figure released her hold on the boom, balancing her way to the Queen. Her breathy whispered response caused the Queen to turn, gazing upon her personal servant. Christina coyly moved her shirt to open further, revealing her fullness.

"Your Highness, you must come below. The winds are unkind, and will surely cause you chills." The younger woman's eyes held fast to the lovely open breasts. She felt her own signs of a similar need arise in her belly. She stiffened her legs, hoping to quell the desire.

"I am too hot to worry about chills, my dear Eva. But I will follow your advice." The great lady reached for the strong hand proffered.

The Queen's cabin was luxuriously appointed. No narrow sailor's hammock for her, but a thick down mattress piled high with furs of mahogany-rich sable, contrasting with the crystal white fox collar tossed carelessly on top.

Eva removed Christina's heavy outer garment, then turned to

add some charcoal and an incense stick to the small brazier set in a metal niche, bringing a heady mixture to the air. She removed her own greatcoat, letting it drop.

"Perhaps Your Highness would enjoy a massage, or I could prepare hot poultices?" she queried.

The Queen dismissed these offers with a wave of her hand, permitting Eva to remove her black shirt, then loosen the military belt held with a golden clasp depicting her father, King Gustav's, coat of arms. Eva gently tugged the oilskin pants half way down, exposing the royal hairline. Rather than turning modestly aside, she savored the heat and scent arising from these parts. Gently, Eva leaned forward to brush the creamy skin of the rock-hard belly, imperceptibly curling a finger through golden pubic hair. Now she was unable to quell her body's release of love potion.

The Queen, not insensitive to the moment, began her glistening flow. She lay back on the furs as Eva tugged off the heavy boots and shaggy stockings, kissing each toe as it appeared. Eva was not unused to her Queen's strange proclivity for women lovers, and this was not the first time she satisfied the Queen's amorous desires. But it might have been the last. Eva was well aware that the Queen liked variety.

"Do not the stars show that we are part of a greater plan? Is not love of one's natural ways the only path to God?" sighed Christina, ever the philosopher, even as Eva slowly massaged one calf, then the other. Christina bent one knee up, displaying her sex, teasing, inviting.

Eva knew to bide her time. She deftly removed her own boots, then heavy skirts, leaving only a thin cotton underblouse. She raised herself upon the bed, kneading each thigh now, pretending not to know the closeness of her practiced hands around the juncture of the Queen's legs would soon give rise to guttural sighs of desire. Hers, as well as her beloved Queen's. Eva allowed the pitch of the boat to rock her hands further around Christina's thighs, to the sides of her buttocks. Those powerful legs could outride any soldier's war horse, for Christina had trained as a prince. They would soon clasp Eva in a lock so tight that she must cry for release. The signal came immediately in answer to her prayer for that powerful embrace, as the boat rocked violently against a large undulation of the sea. Eva, much shorter than Christina, laughed, pretending that the wave caused her to roll on top of her lover, as one hand slipped beneath the solid rump to stroke the silky hairs deep within the fleshy fold, while the other held fast to a breast. Eva's head, by coincidence, lay against lolling breasts. She latched on to an enormous nipple thick as her thumb. Around her waist those strong thighs held her fast as Christina clasped the young woman, feeling her stiff tongue vibrate her engorged nipple.

"Now!" Christina gasped, more an entreaty than imperial command. "Enter me now!"

Eva plunged into the wet cavern, probing one finger, then two, and, as her Queen relaxed, worked her entire hand into the tunnel, from which no royal heir would ever emerge. Eva's own body cried for the same release the royal woman now demanded, and found. With her free hand, Eva located her freedom at her own gleaming gate, calling out, "Oh, my King! My King!" For indeed, Christina was King as well as Queen. Eva knew her lover received, but never gave.

Now the women relaxed in the comfort of warm fur, stealing a few moments of sleep.

"Get up, my dear. The State's business is never done, and we must make haste back to Stockholm." The Queen sighed. "Rene Descartes is due here tomorrow. We shall talk of love and hate, hearty subjects both, don't you think, my dear? Now let me loose. Shall I wear that new French brocade gown in the color of burgundy? So much more comfort in military garb, but one must represent the country in style, I fear. Don't look so mournful, Eva. Perhaps we shall find another time to debate our question of love between women."

THE SERVICE CALL

J. L. Belrose

"YOUR FRIDGE IS HAVING AN ORGASM," I tell Martha when I hear the noise it's making.

It's Martha, of course, I want to see have the orgasm, but I'm not making much progress in that direction. I haven't even seen her naked although I've imagined it a gazillion times or more. I even woke up one night and smelled her, the darkness fragrant with her particular commingling of scents; flowers of shampoo, sugar of body lotion, spice of cunt. But I might as well be a piece of furniture, like the old wooden kitchen table she got from the Reuse Center, for all the attention she pays me. She doesn't like my shoes, either.

"What's wrong with them?" I ask.

"For one thing, they don't match."

I look down and, damn, she's right. I've somehow, from the jumble on the floor of my coat closet, managed to find one each of two different pairs of runners and have worn them all day without noticing. My socks match, though.

That's when Goodman disconnects from Women of Wrestling long enough to wisecrack, "You mean you know what an orgasm sounds like?"

Martha giggles. "Maybe she's copping to carnal knowledge involving fridges."

Goody's my best friend, but at this moment I want to transport her into the TV set for some real time wrestling with her idol Tina, The Red Tornado. "Sue's called me twice today looking for you," I tell her. "I should've known you'd be hanging out here at Martha's. What'll I say next time Sue calls?"

As I'd figured, mentioning Sue is all it takes to put Goody on the move.

200

"Are you sure you can't stay?" Martha asks her. "I was hoping you'd stay for dinner."

"Lin here will stay. She's hungry," Goody says, turning to me and winking obscenely as if Martha, standing right beside us, won't notice.

I want to body slam Goody so hard it makes Tina, The Red Tornado, look like a henna'd granny. But I get distracted by Martha turning away and heading for the kitchen, as Goody, giving me a smirking two thumbs up, makes her exit.

"So ... ahh. . . ." I stumble, cataloguing the inviting roundness of Martha's body, the bumps of nipple pushing against her t-shirt, and the way the crotch seam of her jeans emphasizes the cleft between her legs. "I know someone who can fix that fridge for you."

"How much would it cost?"

"A beer or two, probably. Do you want me to call them?"

"Would you?"

I pick up the phone, think for a second, then punch in a number. There's no answer so I leave a message, then tell Martha I've left her number so they can call me back.

"Well, we might as well have dinner then while we're waiting. The frozen stuff's thawing out and needs using up right away."

Maybe my smile's too eager because she does a funny little pouty thing with her mouth while her eyes narrow as if she's focusing on a place dead center inside of my skull. I wait like a confused dog for whatever stick or bone she's going to throw.

"There's fish that won't keep," she says, "and chili. I thought I could break the fish up into some mushroom soup so it's like chowder, then have the chili. And there's a tub of chocolate ice cream to finish up."

"Sounds good," I say, which is exactly what I would have said if she'd told me we were having sawdust meatloaf with axle grease gravy. "Is there anything I can do to help?"

She hands me the can of soup and a can opener, then leaves to wash her hands. Fortunately I get the can open before the opener breaks. I fiddle with the pieces for a minute trying to fix it, then shove it into the back of the drawer under some towels.

Then I wonder if maybe the fridge just needs a jostle. I vise my arms around it, tilt it forward and let it rock back. It shudders. The gurgle that follows is ominously final. I decide I'm not being helpful and get out of the kitchen.

Dinner goes well. I don't spill anything even though I'm more aware of where her legs are under the table than I am of where the dishes are on top of it. When we finish, she suggests I call my friend again. There's still no answer. I leave another message.

"Let's give it an hour," I suggest. "If she hasn't called back by then, I'll go by there on my way home."

So I've wrangled myself another hour. I'm wondering what my next move should be when Martha notices something wrong with my shirt. She pulls at my collar, then pats it back down. Her hand stays a moment longer than necessary, then slides downwards and lingers on my chest.

Automatically my arms go around her. I slide a kiss down her neck. As soon as I hear her sigh, I know my dreams are coming true. I grope for the hem of her t-shirt and lift it. She takes over, pulling it off over her head. As she tosses it onto a chair my hands are already fondling her large luscious breasts, cradling their weight and fullness.

I may be a bit of a klutz in some ways, but I know my way around a woman's body. It isn't long before we're in the bedroom, naked, and the bed is creaking and Martha's moaning and I'm between her legs eating the sweetest pussy ever. The only sounds I hear are Martha praying Oh God yes, Oh please, Oh God, and grunting, and groaning, and swearing damn you, Oh no, Oh damn, and if the fridge was to explode we wouldn't hear it or even care.

When I get home the next morning I hit erase on my answering machine, then I phone Goody. "Hey, Goodman," I say, "who do we know that can fix fridges?"

GOODBYE JOANNA

Stephanie Schroeder

I SEE THAT THEY'VE HIRED PART-TIME HELP while I've been on vacation. I come in to see your bright, shining face and voluptuous figure dancing before my eyes, standing, leaning with just enough cleavage revealed to entice. You throw your head back to laugh at something I've said. You've heard so much about me.

"Let's have lunch," I say, and you agree.

I tell you about my lover and son, you talk about your boyfriend, a former football player, not as intellectual as you'd like, but a good fuck. On the rocks, but trying to work it out, taking "time off," getting to know yourselves before you commit.

We spend a lot of time during the next few days talking and laughing. So much so that my boss tells us to "get back to work" many times. We have lunch and I tell you about my lesbian life. You say you've been "confused," mistaken for a dyke many times, and wonder why. When we get back to the office I send you an e-mail saying that I don't think it would be the worst thing in the world if our coworkers thought we were having an affair (a horror you expressed at lunch because we've been spending so much time together since I returned and you've sensed a flavor in the house), because you're beautiful and if a beautiful younger woman can make a stuck-in-a-rut middle-aged lesbian light up, at least the rumors would have some basis. I couch this in words of caution, don't take it the wrong way, I'm not coming on. But I am. I want you to respond in kind, say you're interested, why don't we just put those rumors to the test. But you don't. Instead you stop speaking to me. For weeks you avoid me except when necessary. When we're alone in the office, I cajole, entice you into conversation, and make you laugh again and see me as a person who can do for you what no one else can do. You come closer, begin, slowly, to thaw. But then tighten up again when people are around. You close the door once again – I've broken through too far.

On your last day, I walk past you and say, "Have a good life." You call me back, "Aren't you even going to say goodbye?"

I take you into my office and close the door. You grab me and lay a big juicy one on my lips, pressing your body close to mine. "I've dreamt of this for months," you admit. "I want you."

And, as no one much is left in the office, I clean off my desk and lay you down, taking your breasts in my mouth through your satin top, teasing, playing: your nipples harden and you moan. You've been waiting a long time.

I reach down your tight pants: your hairy mound is soft and moist, you groan under my pressure. I thrust my thigh between your legs and grind into you with a toughness you haven't seen in me.

You beg, "Give it to me."

I unzip your trousers, pull down your delicate straight-lady, lacy panties and put my full fist into your hot, juicy cunt, twirling it around – no match for that big cock you profess your boyfriend possesses – enough to make you squirm and dance under my touch. I hit all the right places and you beg for more: "Harder, deeper, more." I lick all around your pubis, tasting the salty appetizer – just getting started as far as I'm concerned, teasing you and tasting you and you don't seem to object. I pull my hand from your cunt and enter you with an old water bottle that's sitting on my desk, spinning it around and around. You scream, covering your mouth just in case anyone is left on the floor. I push right in, Hello. How do you do? What can't I do for you today? You are convulsing, sweat dripping from your brow and between your heavy, heaving breasts. You strain under my touch, my pressure in your cunt. I nail you to the desk and shove my tongue into your mouth so that you don't get a chance to breathe. You're huffing and groaning, half with excitement and for lack of oxygen. Finally, you go limp. You are spent and I am satisfied that you are satisfied. A straight lady in possession of a big athlete's cock would rather have a woman's fist shoved up her cunt than waste time with a boring ex-football player who sends flowers everyday begging her to come home. Oh yes, I am satisfied. Someone knocks on the door and yells, "Cleaning lady." We jump and you dress quickly: there's no lock on my door.

I walk you to the train and we kiss goodbye, just a peck on the cheek because I can see the fear in your eyes: a deer caught in the headlights. You go down into the subway and melt into the crowd. And I never see you again.

SCARY DATE

I MET THIS GIRL AT A PARTY. She was short and retro-cute in a polyester A-line dress, Mary Janes, and white knee socks. She had a way of talking that was too casual.

She knew who I was, and wanted in on the action.

"Trish Kelly, if I made out with you, would you write about me in your zine?" It was more a request than a concern. I told her I usually only write about things that scare me, but I gave her my card anyway.

She called the following weekend and invited me to a screening of *Scream 2* at the discount cinema.

Well, she was trying, and even though I have a rep for being an ultra-busy ultra femme, I didn't have any other plans, so I went.

I put the bag of popcorn between my legs, and sucked the straw in my soft drink seductively. I leaned over to ask questions about the very complicated plot. The retro-cute girl ignored everything. When she managed to finish off the popcorn without so much as a handbrushing, I got pissed off. I should have known this would be a lame date when she said she didn't like to sit at the back.

On top of all this, Retro Girl made me promise to stay until the credits finished. She sat slurping her cola. "Pretty scary, huh?" she droned without even looking at me. We were the last people out of the theater. Even the concession girl had gone home.

I had to use the bathroom, and asked her to hold my jacket while I "powdered my nose." In the bathroom, I reapplied my Outrageous Red lipstick, pouting my lips into the mirror. "What a fucking waste!" I muttered as I readjusted my breasts in the cups of my bustier.

I returned to the hall where I'd left my lame date. She was

gone. Annoyed, I made an attempt to crane my neck enough to see down the hall without actually moving.

From the opposite direction, I heard a quiet, but distinct "Boo."

I turned, my mouth open in something between shock and disgust, ready to explain that when I'd said she'd have to scare me, I was talking about a very sophisticated, intellectual scare.

But there was no time.

She clamped her hand over my mouth and pushed me backward through the ladies' room door, and up against the sink.

"Now shut up," she ordered, her hand flying off my mouth and hiking up her skirt. She tucked the front of her skirt into the harness of her strap-on. It was shaped like a porpoise, with only a small fin on top. She pressed her body hard against me, the sink cold against my thighs.

Her hands slid up my sides and pulled on my bustier. She pressed her body harder against me, and I had to grab the sink for leverage, my back arching and my pelvis bracing against hers.

She reached into the cups of my bustier. Her hands were hot little vice grips.

"There's a bottle of lube in my backpack over there," she breathed into my ear. "You are to get it out and lubricate my cock," she instructed, "then I'm going to fuck you in the stall." She released me, and wandered into the stall.

I opened her pack and found a one-liter sized container of Probe. There were also vinyl restraints, a whip, and plain old-fashioned rope.

"Don't touch anything else. Just get in here."

She opened the stall door and pulled me in, slamming the door shut with the weight of our bodies.

"But, what if someone comes in?" I asked rather weakly.

"The cleaning lady does the men's first. She won't be here for a while."

Her hands went up my bare thighs and under my dress.

"No panties. Figures." She muttered.

She opened the lube with her teeth and told me to hold out my hand. "Now, lubricate my cock."

I slid my hands up and down her porpoise, pushing it hard against her pubic bone.

She slid the lubed cock up my skirt and traced the lips of my cunt, zeroing in on my clit.

"You're not wet," she lied. She rubbed the length of the latex between my legs.

She sat down on the toilet, pulling me towards her, grabbing me around the waist with one arm, while the other hand rubbed my cunt so hard, my legs stopped working. Just when I was about to come, I heard a faint whistling from the hallway.

"Oh, yeah, she's right on schedule. We'd better hurry." She pulled me down on her cock.

"Hello, anybody in there?" The woman sang from the door.

"Just be quiet," my date instructed. "Yes ma'am, I'm having a little case of the upset stomach. I'll be out in a minute."

She pushed harder, and I moaned louder. She kissed me, swallowing each of my moans, simultaneously producing a constipated grunt for the benefit of the cleaning lady.

As I came, I reached behind my date and flushed the toilet. She gave a huge sigh and pushed me off her. I pulled down my skirt, and we exited the stall.

"Pick up my bag," she instructed.

"What?" I asked, not quite following.

"The bag over there."

"Oh, yeah, I guess we didn't get to use all that stuff," I said.

"Yeah, that's right," she said as she opened the door for the cleaning lady's cart, "but you've never taken the subway with me before."

FUCKING BARBIE

Cara Bruce

COLLEGE HAD COME AND GONE, bringing me nothing but a good waitressing resumé and the erupting promise of varicose veins. I had passed through my fair share of lovers: my volleyball coach, my best friend's sister, and a couple of girls too drunk to find their way out of the bar. After living like that for the past few years, I felt as if I could use a vacation. I went back home.

The first night, I lay in my bed and thought about Barbie. I knew she was right above me, in the attic, nestled in her pink plastic coffin between twenty or thirty mix-and-match outfits. I wasn't one of those girls who grew up and blamed Barbie for all of their problems. In fact, I was rather turned on by that silky blonde hair and wide-eyed innocence. I will admit I knew Barbie was a bitch, the type of girl who would probably break my heart, use me for her one lesbian fling, trying out the other side of the fence with an unsuspecting dyke like me, and then leaving me for some pretty boy, a latent gay eunuch named Ken who would never be able to give it to her the way I could. He would never want to spank that perfectly round ass of hers or pull on that long blonde hair. So maybe he would buy her that dream house and the pink Corvette she always wanted, but I was sure he wouldn't know how to fist her until she screamed to be fucked like the little plastic tramp she was.

Of course, there was the issue of Barbie being frigid; the stiff plastic, the unbendable knees, legs that only opened one-quarter of an inch. She was just like any other girl I knew when I was ten: underneath that baby-faced demeanor of goodness, a raging slut was just waiting to get out.

The familiar ache was back in my cunt and I started playing with myself. I closed my eyes and began my fantasy. It only took me a few minutes to piss myself off. I was a big girl now. If I wanted to invite Barbie into my bedroom to do dirty things to me then so be it. And if my parents found out I was a lesbian then that was okay, too. I went up and retrieved my princess, gently carrying down her plastic pink suitcase and laying it on my bed.

There she was, already strapped down, wearing an innocent tennis outfit, white, with matching racket. I undressed her carefully. She seemed so small; she wasn't the larger-than-life tease I remembered from my youth. I took off my own clothes, watching her to see if that plastic head could blush.

I ran my fingers lightly over her arched foot. Well, it was more of the straight-up angle than any sort of arch, but I remembered those countless tiny pairs of shoes that always popped off. I thought my doll might have a foot fetish. I thought about foreplay. Then I decided Barbie might like to be treated like more of a slut – that she would enjoy a raw, hard fuck. I brought her down to my clit and started using her like the little whore that she was, making circles with those tiny toes until my own nub was so hard I thought it might burst.

The feet slid in on their own accord. Before I knew it, Barbie's unbendable legs had disappeared up my hungry cunt. I pulled her hair, imagining how bad it hurt. I pushed down on her head, forcing her to give me pleasure. Oh Barbie, you bitch, fuck me like you want to. I arched my back and lifted my hips, offering all of myself to her. Her hard plastic was heating up as I rammed her into myself over and over.

I thought I heard a muffled cry but then I realized it was me who was moaning. I continued my frenzied pursuit of an orgasm-without-batteries. I was sliding my ass back and forth on the bedspread, pushing her up and down inside of me. I bit my lip to keep from yelling, but Barbie was good. She was bringing me to my thirty-first official lesbian orgasm. Her silky blonde hair was soaking wet as I lost it. I came all over her long tan legs, her petite waist, her perfect c-cup tits.

I lay back, shaking while Barbie rested patiently inside of me. There was no quick pull out and roll over. Barbie was a lady all the way. But me, I was a bitch. I rolled over and threw her on the floor without so much as wiping her off with an old, dirty athletic sock. I wasn't worried. She looked blissful, blue eyes wide open and her smooth, flawless skin glistening with my cum.

HOW CARA GOT DISHPAN HANDS

Zonna

"COME ON ... YOU KNOW YOU WANT IT."

"Right."

"You know you do. . . ."

"Go away."

"Stop pretending."

"I'm not pretending, I'm reading."

"Just lay back and let me make you feel good. You don't even have to put the book down."

"I'm not in the mood."

"Bet I can change that."

"How much do you wanna bet?"

"How about ... winner does the dishes for a month?"

"That's a lame bet."

"Afraid you'll lose?"

"No."

"Well, then ... make the bet."

"What is the bet, exactly?"

"I bet I can make you come in the next fifteen minutes."

"Ha! Fat chance."

"Well, put your honey where my mouth is, then!"

"I can't believe you said that."

"Come on. What do you have to lose?"

"I'm not gonna lose."

"You'll play, then?"

"What do I have to do?"

"Nothing. Just let me do whatever I want for fifteen minutes, and see if you don't change your mind."

"This is too easy."

"We'll see how easy it is. Ready?"

"I guess."

Sandy set the alarm clock. "Okay, starting – now. . . ."

Sandy removed Cara's pajamas quickly, tossing the loose, white t–shirt and Winnie the Pooh boxers in a pile on the bed– room floor. When her partner was completely naked, Sandy began discarding her own clothes. She ran her hands slowly across her nipples while Cara watched, amused. She spread open her pussy, letting her lover see how she was already glistening. She dipped one finger inside, moving it deliciously while Cara licked her lips.

"Want a taste?" Sandy offered.

"Nope." Cara resisted.

Sandy smiled and lay on the bed next to her girlfriend. She reached alongside the mattress and retrieved the nylons she'd hidden earlier. She grabbed Cara's arms and began tying her wrists to the headboard.

"Hey, what are you doing?"

"Shhh . . . I've still got twelve minutes."

"You're cheating."

"No, I said anything I want. Stop squirming."

Sandy watched Cara tug at the restraints for a few seconds until she was sure they would hold. Then she reached for her partner's legs.

"No way!"

Cara tried to pull back, but Sandy had a firm grip. In no time she had secured her lover's ankles alongside her wrists, leaving her wide open and helpless.

Cara tried desperately to loosen the bonds, but it was hope– less.

"This isn't even funny!"

"No. It's not. It's sexy."

"Let me up, damn it!"

Sandy touched Cara's face, calming her. "Look, you know I would never hurt you. It's just part of the game. Play along for a few minutes, okay?"

Cara sighed. "How long do we have left?"

Sandy looked at the clock. "Seven minutes."

Cara tried her best to shrug, but in her awkward position, it was more like a wiggle.

"Now the fun begins."

Sandy ran her fingernails lightly over Cara's skin – her arms, her belly, her inner thighs. She watched the goose bumps rise in haphazard clusters. She caressed her lover's breasts, softly squeezing and rubbing them, keeping a close eye on Cara's responses. She felt the heat rise and smelled the warm aroma of arousal as her hands worked their magic. Sandy placed her naked body over Cara's and leaned in for a kiss, grinding herself against her lover's cunt. Their tongues tangled together and she heard her girlfriend try to stifle a moan. She let her lips make love to Cara's mouth, alternating between the barest whisper of a kiss and louder, rougher, more urgent ones, until there was no mistaking the lust in Cara's sighs. Smiling to herself, Sandy worked her way down to Cara's now wet pussy and licked slowly at her partner's swollen clit. The restraints held the girl open in the perfect position, allowing Sandy's hands to remain free to pinch and pull at Cara's nipples.

As Sandy mercilessly teased her lover, she felt Cara attempting to rock from side to side as best she could, ready to surrender.

"Not yet.... I still have a few minutes."

Sandy interrupted her meal for a moment, blowing softly on the steaming cunt before her. She heard Cara whimper. She tortured her prisoner further by licking along each side of Cara's clit but not directly on it. Cara was begging now. Sandy watched the juices dripping from her girlfriend's pussy run down the crack of her ass. She traced them with a finger, exploring. With a little pressure, the opening gave, sucking Sandy's finger inside.

"Oh, Gaawwdddd...."

"I thought you weren't in the mood," Sandy reminded, removing her pioneering digit from its new frontier with a soft pop.

"Shut up and fuck me...."

Suddenly, Sandy's tongue was everywhere: long, lazy laps straight across Cara's clit; deep, probing thrusts into Cara's hungry core. She inserted three fingers all the way to the knuckle and began a rhythmic, pumping motion. Cara was so wet her cunt made a slurping sound, as though it were devouring Sandy's fingers.

Sandy felt the tension growing in her lover's belly, the need to come. She heard the tones emitting from Cara's throat change from low moans to guttural grunts as the woman approached the point of no return. She sucked hard on Cara's clit and felt her girlfriend's body begin to twitch uncontrollably. Sweet, warm juices filled her mouth as Cara came in stops and starts. The buzzer sounded, in harmony with Cara's song of pleasure.

Sandy waited until the muscles in Cara's thighs relaxed. Then she untied her lover and gathered her into her arms.

"Was that as good as it sounded?"

Cara snuggled closer, speechless.

"You lost the bet, you know."

"If that's what they call the agony of defeat, it's worth it. Will you still love me when my fingers get all pruney and wrinkled?"

"Sure, I will. In fact. . . ." Sandy got a mischievous glimmer in her eye, as she thought of the slick, slippery dish washing solution, "how about if we go for double or nothing?"

TWIN BEDS, OR: WHO PUT THE DYKE IN THE DICK VAN DYKE SHOW?

Shari J. Berman

Laura: Millie, it's me, Laura. I've cleaned the house, polished the silver, and baked two loaves of bread and a coffeecake.

Millie: Honestly, Laura, it's only 10:45.

Laura: I know. Wanna come by for cake and chitchat?

Millie: You know me; I never pass up a gab session.

Millie: This cake is delish, Laura.

Laura: Thanks, Millie. It's Sally's recipe, actually.

Millie: Oh. How is Sally?

Laura: Well, Rob talks about her, of course, but I don't see much of her since we broke up.

Millie: You broke up? No foolin'....

Laura: Yeah. It was swell going into the city and secretly meeting, when she could shake that pesky Buddy, but I got tired of commuting. And let's face it ... Sally's been in the life for a long time. She's a whiz at joking and creating imaginary boyfriends, but it was all so new to me.

Millie: I'll say ... I couldn't believe it when you told me you were a le-le-le ... that way.

Laura: Ah, come on, Millie, lesbian isn't hard to say. Some people prefer "queer" or "gay."

Millie: Gay, huh? I can say that. You still keeping it from Rob?

Laura: Oh ... Ro-ob.... *(They sigh in chorus.)* Rob's sweet, but ... the man is dense. I guess you'd have to hit him over the head or trip him with an ottoman for him to figure something out. We sleep in twin beds, for goodness sake. Shouldn't that be a clue?

Millie: Jeez ... Jerry and I sleep in twin beds.

Laura: You know, Millie, there's something I've been wanting to tell you. (*Swallows.*)

Millie: Laura, I really should get home. I'm scheduled to burn a pot roast tonight and. . . .

Laura: Come on, Mil, this will only take a sec.

Millie: Okay . . . may I have another slice of cake?

Laura: Sure thing. (*She serves Millie.*) Coming out with Sal was really neat. She has that gravelly truck driver voice of experience going for her. Commuting and sneaking around in the city was fun. But, I just don't think Sally is my type.

Millie: Oh. What kind of gal are you looking for?

Laura: Someone with darker hair.

Millie: Uh-huh.

Laura: Annoying nasal voice.

Millie: You don't say.

Laura: Kind of scattered about big things, but very knowledgeable about little details and neighborhood gossip.

Millie: Gosh, Laura, if that's who you want, why haven't you picked me? It's the high school volleyball team all over again. Nobody ever picks me. Gee whiz.

Laura: Darn it, Millie, it was you I was describing. I'm in love with you.

(*Dramatic music leads to commercial.*)

(*Millie is wringing her hands.*)

Laura: Is this too much, darling?

Millie: Oh, Laura, I'm dying! Nobody has ever called me "darling" before. Is that what Sal called you?

Laura: No, Sal called me "doll."

Millie: You are a doll, Laura. . . .

Laura: Something Sal taught me is that queer people don't throw Tupperware parties to recruit. You hear folks say they're afraid if they hang out with homosexuals, they'll turn queer, but it just isn't true. I'm attracted to you because. . . .

Millie: I'm . . . queer?

Laura: The queerest, darling.

Millie: Laura ... what do queer gals do in bed?

Laura: Satisfy each other.

Millie: Satisfied ... in bed? Wow. That's a new one!

Laura: Darling, let's ... drat, I hate these twin beds ... how about the New Rochelle Plaza?

Millie: The Plaza? We'd surely run into someone there.

Laura: Good point.

Millie: The Westchester Inn is the place for an affair.

Laura: *(Chuckles.)* Why, Millie, you surprise me!

Millie: I considered an affair once.

Laura: You did?

Millie: Simon Drake. ...

Laura: Simon Drake, the butcher?

Millie: He's not so bad without that bloody apron. It was a game. He'd say, "Simon says give me a little smile." So, I smiled. Then it was, "Simon says let's have coffee." We had coffee. Then, I stopped in for ground chuck and he said, "Meet me at the Westchester Inn."

Laura: But he didn't say, "Simon says!"

Millie: *(Giggles.)* I knew you'd understand, Laura. I looked hard at Simon and saw Jerry in bib overalls. It was just chops and loins instead of incisors and molars. ...

Laura: When you look at me, is it Jerry in cashmere?

Millie: Not even close, Laura.

(They exchange longing glances.)

Millie: I can't believe you paid thirty-two whole dollars. It isn't like we're staying overnight. ... Did you see that color TV in the lobby? What's the big deal about watching Bill Cullen in color?

Laura: Don't ask me. The best shows are black and white!

Millie: I think I'll take a shower. Might as well since you paid for the room and all.

Laura: A shower is a swell idea, Mil. ...

(Millie humming show tunes.)
Laura: (seductively) Well, hello, Dolly. . . .
(Millie screams.)
Laura: What's the matter?
Millie: You scared me. I couldn't imagine who was coming into the shower. . . .
Laura: It's only us, Millie, who did you expect? Norman Bates?
Millie: That isn't funny, Laura. That movie was scary. . . .
(Laura begins to scrub Millie's back. Millie moans softly. Laura fondles Millie's breasts, soaps herself up, and rubs against Millie.)
Millie: Oh . . . Laura . . . that's some touch you have. *(Swoons.)* You really know how to sweep a gal off her feet. . . .
Laura: Let's move to the bed, darling. No sense wasting a king size.
Millie: *(Weakly.)* Not to mention thirty-two whole dollars. . . .
Laura: Not to mention.
(They exit wearing towels. Laura caresses Millie's face and they kiss passionately.)

(Musical crescendo leads to commercial.)

(Laura and Millie are in bed, heads touching, each with one corner of the sheet tucked under an armpit.)
Laura: Are you doing okay, darling? You're oddly quiet.
Millie: Never better. If I smoked, I'd be halfway through a Lucky Strike.
(Laura chuckles, playing with Millie's hair.)
Laura: I guess you don't chatter when you're. . .uhm. . . satisfied.
Millie: Oh, Laura . . . I don't want this day to end.
Laura: Me neither.
Millie: I have ninety-nine dollars saved for a rainy day.
Laura: It's been kind of dry, but it could rain. . . .
Millie: I hope so.
(They embrace.)
(Millie starts humming The Dick Van Dyke Show *theme. Laura joins in.)*

NUMBERS LIE

Ruthann Robson

STRICTLY SPEAKING, INFINITY IS NOT A NUMBER. So when she says she'll love you (or me) (or you and me) forever, it is not exactly fair to blame numbers for her deception. If it is a deception. Perhaps it is merely a wish that did not come true.

A wish similar to "a few." As in the sentence: "You will need a few stitches." She was not the one who said this to me because at the time she would have said it, neither of us believed I would need stitches in any number. The skin was not even broken. It was a bruise. On the lip.

She hit me.

It's not what you're thinking, if what you're thinking is that she did hit me, or that I'm saying she hit me although she did not (a lie!) so that you will think less of her.

You ask me, "How many times?" as if you think you can get at the truth through numbers. "Once," I tell you. Honestly.

I was kissing her at the time. Or more precisely, I was between kisses so numerous that even if I had been counting I would have lost count. Although sometimes it is difficult to decide when one kiss begins and another ends. But this was definitely between kisses, after an ending of one and before a beginning that was not to arrive. My kisses had been thick with tongue. Breathing through my nose had made my nostrils feel clogged with a trillion particles of pollution. I was trying to stretch my neck, a few centimeters from side to side like our chiropractor advised, when I felt the blow strike and saw a galaxy of stars slide past my eyes.

It was an accident.

And I should tell you this: it wasn't her fist.

It was ten times harder. A solid shell of bone.

It was her knee.

Which tells you and everybody else who thinks about it for less than thirty seconds where I was kissing her. Even though I've been a lesbian for over twenty-three years, it's still a little embarrassing. So when the surgeon asked me what happened, I answered that one of my dogs had knocked me in the face while we were "rough-housing."

"How many dogs do you have?" the surgeon asked conversationally.

"Three."

The surgeon nodded, not believing. No lesbian would have three dogs. Three cats or seventeen cats, yes. One dog, possibly. But not three dogs.

That disbelieving nod might explain my failure to ask the surgeon what was meant by "a few," as in the sentence, "You will need a few stitches."

Or possibly, quite (how much is that?) possibly, I was desperate for a cure for my untenable predicament. A spot midway on the left side of my upper lip had immediately swollen purple as an overripe plum and had remained so for six weeks. There was a hard pit at the contusion's center that I could rotate in a tiny circle with my finger if I could tolerate the pain. Which I could only manage for about a split second. Which was longer than I could tolerate kissing.

Even when I could herd my tongue out past the fence of my teeth, my lip would snag on some barbed wire of her flesh, a thigh or cheek, and I would scream a thousand screams of agony. Not exactly conducive to a fine night of romance.

"There are cultures that do not kiss," I reminded her, wondering if there were cultures in which lesbians did not have oral sex.

"Well, we don't live in those cultures," she reminded me.

"It will heal," I promised her.

Can you believe I thought she would feel just a fraction of guilt? After all, it was *her* knee. Can you believe I assumed such guilt was the source of her slight shift of temperament? Can you believe it took me at least seventeen days to guess she was now kissing someone else? And even a few hours longer (all the while rotating that little knot in my huge bruise) to figure out it was you?

In order to preserve the slightest chance at maintaining my relationship, I went to our doctor (we have the same physician, how could we break up?) who most helpfully confirmed that my upper lip, left side, did "look nasty" and was "sensitive to the touch."

"You will need a few stitches."

Perhaps I thought I knew what was meant by a few. Just as I thought I knew what was meant by "forever," as in the sentence: "I will love you forever." Forever means always. As high as I could count without ever stopping. Until I took my last breath and even after. Infinity. That's forever. Isn't that what you think it means?

What do you think "a few" means? Two? Three? Four on a bad day?

Twenty-seven. You're wrong about "forever" and you're wrong about "a few." Twenty-seven stitches to sew up the incision on the outer and inner portions of my lip. You wouldn't think a lip could hold that much catgut, would you? Not even the dissolving kind, which meant that I had to go back and have them pulled out. "We wouldn't want any scars," the doctor said and smiled. There are scars nonetheless.

She left me anyway.

And now you are here, after so many months, sitting at my table that seats three, telling me that she has "terminated the relationship."

Is that a bruise I see on your bottom lip?

What if you and I decided to love each other forever?

What if we decided that zero would be the number of times we would kiss?

You can lie to me if it's easier.

"Shut up," one of us says to the other.

The kitchen floor. My knee; her knee.

Pants down and hands everywhere.

Mouths open only for air.

NOMI'S SOCIAL DISEASE

Karen X. Tulchinsky

I'M WORKING THE SATURDAY AFTERNOON SHIFT at Patty's Place, minding my own business, wiping down the bar for the hundredth time when Betty bounds in, handsome and dashing in her Super Shuttle driver's uniform. She flirts with two women by the pool table, drops some change in the jukebox, takes her time selecting her songs, waves hello to Miss Polly Ester, a seven-foot-tall (in heels) female impersonator who hangs out at Patty's, then plops her substantial butt onto the bar stool directly in front of me.

"What time you off?" Betty asks.

I glance at the bar clock. "Half an hour."

"Good. Give me a Guinness, Nomi. No head."

I glare at her. I don't need advice from Betty. I've been pulling draught all day. I plunk her glass of beer with a quarter-inch head, as it should have, on top of a bar napkin in front of her. She raises it to her lips, drinks enthusiastically, opens her mouth with a satisfying "ahhh," places the mug on the bar. She has a beer moustache. White foam on her chocolate brown skin. It looks good on her. But then, everything looks good on Betty.

"Start cleaning up now. We're leaving as soon as you're off shift," she announces.

"Where we going?"

She grins. "You'll see."

A few minutes later, Betty says, "Okay, you can open your eyes now." She's led me across a street and inside a building. I foolishly agreed to close my eyes until we are inside. It is dark. We are at the bottom of a steep flight of stairs. At the top I can see two women sitting at a table. There is a red light bulb above them, casting a blood-red glow down the stairway. I eye Betty suspiciously.

"Come on." She nudges me up the steps.

"Hi there," the woman seated at the table says cheerfully. "Cover charge is twelve dollars each."

"Twelve dollars!?"

"Relax, Nomi. I'm paying."

I grab her by the sleeve roughly. "Where are we?"

"Here you go." Betty hands thirty dollars to the woman, who makes change. Betty tips her generously.

"Why, thank you."

"Don't mention it."

I'm going to gag.

"Come on." Betty pulls me by the sleeve inside the house. It looks like it used to be an apartment that's been converted into . . . into what? In the first bedroom, there is a couch and a VCR. Three women sit on the couch watching TV. On the monitor is a heterosexual porn flick. A male fantasy of lesbians. There are three "pseudo lesbians" – extremely skinny, straight women, with long hair tied in ponytails, and vacant, stoned expressions, "fucking" each other with sharp, red fingernails.

"Ouch," I say.

"Let's sit down," says Betty.

"No way. I can't bear to watch." It dawns on me where we are. It's a sex club. "Where are we?" I snarl.

"Clit Club. Just opened. Cool, huh?"

"Not really." I look down, realize the linoleum floor is sticky with spilled Coke or beer, or something else.

"Okay, let's check out the rest."

"I'm going." I head for the stairs.

"Hey, I just paid twelve bucks to get you in here."

"That's your problem."

She grabs my sleeve. "Come on, Nomi. You don't have to do anything. Let's just look around."

"You could catch a social disease just from walking on this floor, Betty."

"You are a social disease, Nomi. Come on. You must be curious."

I have to admit, I am curious. I follow Betty. We find a kitchen. The floor in here is even stickier. There is an old fashioned claw-footed bathtub in the middle of the room, filled with ice cubes and cans of Diet Coke, Diet 7-Up, Diet Dr Pepper, Diet Sprite, diet club soda, and Budweiser, Schlitz, and Millers. What a gourmet selection. Cheap, watery American beer, or aspartame-flavored soda. Betty grabs two bottles of Bud, hands me one. I follow her down the long, narrow hall. The walls are painted black. There are photographs of naked men with huge erections, men kissing, touching each other, touching themselves. This place must usually be a gay men's club.

The final room is the largest. It is dark. I can see the vague outline of bodies inside the room. The air is still and stale, the lingering scent of old sweat and cigarette smoke embedded in the walls. I can hear moaning, groaning, and laughter. Slaps. The sqwooshy mouth sounds of kissing. There is a single dim red lightbulb providing the only illumination. The walls, floor, and ceiling are black. My shoes continue to stick to the floor. I don't even want to think about what I might be stepping in.

We walk around the room. There is a long half-wall in the middle. A partition of sorts. On close inspection, I see small round holes drilled into the wall at crotch level. I have heard about glory holes from gay male friends, just never seen them before. I try to imagine standing by the wall, sticking your penis through the hole, not knowing who is on the other side or what they might do. What are we supposed to do with these? Stick our fingers through? Stand naked before them, push our vulvas against the opening? Wait for someone to penetrate us from the other side of the wall? Wear strap-on dildos and pretend to be fags? It borders on the absurd. I don't know whether to laugh or gag.

On the floor in one corner of the room lies a filthy mattress. I can make out the shape of two women lying on top, thrashing around and moaning. Standing against one wall is a well en-dowed femme in a short leather skirt, garters and stockings, a dog collar around her neck, numerous studded wrist and arm bands. A solid silver chain is strung across her naked chest, linked through a nipple ring in each breast. Her head is shaved on both sides. She has a long blonde ponytail sticking straight up on top of her head. In her hand is a large, black leather whip. She cracks it against the sticky floor. It snaps with a satisfying crack. She turns in our direction, sticks out one clawed fingertip, and beckons us forward. The sickeningly sweet smell of too much cheap perfume wafts over.

"Come on," says Betty, practically drooling.

"Uh n-no thanks," I stutter.

"Come on, Nom. Don't be a wimp."

"I won't bite," the femme hisses through bared teeth, "unless you want me to."

"I'll see ya later," I tell Betty.

"Both of you," the femme says. "I like two butches at a time."

Betty grabs my shirtsleeve for dear life, not about to let this opportunity slide.

I pull desperately hard, hear my shirt rip at the shoulder seam. Betty hangs on tighter. I pull with all my might, until my sleeve rips clean through. I am freed from her grasp. I fall forward from the force, toppling onto the sticky floor with a thud. I don't wait to inspect the grimy linoleum too closely. I scramble to my feet. Run for the door.

"Nomi!" Betty calls, my torn sleeve still in her grasp.

Pushing off from the wall on both sides, I race down the stairs and outside in record time.

THE ALTERNATIVE

Lucy Jane Bledsoe

MARCIA LOOKED LIKE A GHOST COMING DOWN THE AISLE. She was no virgin. I should know, but she wore white satin with miles of lace just the same. Her skin was like skim milk, thin and bluish. Her father, by contrast, was radiant. Mr Michaelson wore a black tux and walked ramrod straight, like Marica was some great accomplishment of his. Actually, I have always believed she was. She got her big heart from him.

I wondered what Daddy would wear to my wedding, if I ever had one. All his buddies at the sanitation department would throw him a great party. I couldn't imagine my getting married, but I hated the idea of depriving him of that. Maybe my being in law school made him even prouder than by being married. Maybe.

By now I could see only the back of Marcia and I wished she was wearing jeans. All that flounce completely hid her ass. Her beautiful ass. I'd never said that to myself before. Oh, I'd said, even to her, that she was the most beautiful girl in the world. She is. And she has the biggest heart. Which she got in part from her father, rich and stiff as he was. But I'd never said to myself that I loved her ass.

As Marcia turned to face Jonathan at the altar, I said to my-self, "What are you, Bonnie, some kind of dyke?"

Marcia and I met in English class our senior year in high school. She loved my poetry. It meant nothing to her that her fa-ther was a big shot attorney and my dad was a garbage collec-tor. She wanted me to be a poet. In the end, it was her father who wrote the letter that got me into law school. The Michaelsons are good people.

It was accidental that Marcia and I went to Cal together. By the time we became friends, we'd both already applied. We kissed for the first time on the day our acceptance letters came. Marcia was never afraid of touching. Nearly every Friday night we sat in her bedroom and I'd read her the poems I'd written that week and she'd stroke my hair. My muse was the anticipation of her hands. My poems elevated our relationship to something spiritual. On Friday nights after the poetry reading, when we lay on her floor in exaltation, Marica would say, "This is religion," and I believed her.

Later at Cal, Marcia even convinced her sorority to take me. But I drew the line there. I wasn't sorority material and I wasn't going to fake it. "We could share a room," Marcia begged. The idea of having Marcia every night of the week made my legs feel like giant amoebas. I just didn't have the nerve. Besides, I knew that those other bright, pony-tailed girls would smell us out. Marcia is so good-hearted. She doesn't see blood where I do.

I wore a pale blue polyester dress to the wedding. I got it at Penney's and it didn't fit very well, but I knew this would be the only time I'd wear it. I wasn't going to drop more than fifteen bucks for a one-time deal, period.

Listening to Marcia and Jonathan exchange vows was sort of like doing acid. You just can't believe this other reality has been there all along and you'd missed it. Marcia had said to me, as recently as last week, "Don't you know you're the love of my life, Bonnie?" I had harrumphed. She'd grabbed both my ears, pulled me to her for a big kiss on the lips. We were downtown right at Union Square, too. My embarrassment only egged her on, and she kissed me again. That's when the tears came.

"Bonnie," she'd said, trying to cup my cheeks in her hands, but I had pulled away, told her I was leaving and not to follow, and caught the subway home by myself.

Now the groom was kissing his bride. That's how the minister put it: "The groom may now kiss his bride." Her voice echoed in my head: "No guy has ever kissed me like this." She told me that the first time, in her bedroom on the Friday night we got our acceptance letters. We kissed all night, and I came three times, just kissing.

I didn't look at Marcia when she glided back down the aisle with Jonathan, though I felt their wake. I glanced over and met

Mr Michaelson's eyes. He winked at me. I thought he felt it too.

Driving to the country club for the reception, I worried about my wedding present. It didn't exist. In the trunk I had a box, wrapping paper, ribbon, tape, scissors, and a card. What did I think? There'd be a gift shop at the church? I pulled into a Long's Drugs, then left the parking lot without going in. Next I stopped at a Safeway, went in and walked the aisles, bought three oranges, and left. I sat in a parking space in front of a 7–11 for five minutes, eating one of the oranges, before driving away. Like there were going to be wedding gifts in those stores. Finally, I found a Walgreen's. An iron? A stuffed animal? A year's worth of office supplies? Scented soap? I left Walgreen's still wedding present-less.

I mingled at the reception, avoiding Jonathan's family. "Jonathan is from an old San Francisco family," Marcia had told me, like he was an antique worth millions. He probably *was* worth millions. Jonathan himself, I have no feelings about. None. Although the only fight I've ever had with Marcia had to do with him. I told her, just once, and this was before the time I cried on Union Square, "I don't want you to marry this guy." She said, with an innocence I believe was sincere, "But Bonnie, why?"

"You love me," I answered, my heart slamming against my rib cage. I wonder now how it might have been different if I'd said, "Because I love you."

She stared at me for a long time, then said, "Yes, I love you. Of course I love you. But I still have to get married. What's the alternative?"

For her, it was a real question.

The sugar bowl was crystal. Very pretty. I picked it up in full view of a couple dozen wedding guests and carried it high in front of my chest, as if it were slightly disgusting, away from the table. Anyone watching would presume I'd discovered ants crawling in the sugar, or maybe a glob of coffee-stained crystals. In fact, Mrs Michaelson caught my eye and smiled gratefully. It was appropriate that I should quietly see to such matters.

I carried the sugar bowl into the ladies' room and dumped the sugar in the toilet. Then I washed the bowl in the sink and dried it with paper towels. Mrs Michaelson would probably recognize it. She would tell her husband. One word from him to the dean and I'd be out of school.

The act was so childish, misguided, probably even ignorant, but I felt a need burning in my thighs, a need to disrupt, even the teeniest bit, this ancient ritual of privilege. The crystal sugar bowl traveled up my sleeve as I left the ladies' room. I went straight out to my car. There I wrapped it in the box, tied the bow real pretty, and took out the card.

To Marcia and Jonathan, I wrote. From The Alternative.

CONTRIBUTORS

Joli Agnew writes lesbian, bisexual, and BDSM/Fetish erotica.

Zamina Ali has been writing short stories for over five years, and this is her first published piece. Her focus on short stories has included work related to everyday life as a lesbian woman in Vancouver. She also enjoys writing short crime fiction.

Donna Allegra has published fiction, essay, and poetry in lesbian/feminist journals and anthologies since 1976, including *Hot and Bothered 1* and *2*. Her book of short fiction *Witness to the League of Blond Hip Hop Dances: a novella and stories* was published by Alyson in 2000.

Wendy Atkin coordinates projects on a full-time basis and enjoys writing for its sheer pleasure. She lives in Ottawa, ON.

LaShonda K. Barnett was born in Kansas City and educated at the University of Missouri Sarah Lawrence College and the College of William and Mary. Currently she divides her time between dissertation-writing, creative-writing, and exploring the world's greatest city. She writes and lives in New York with her companion, Wyclef the wonder-toy poodle.

Leah Baroque is editor of *Eroticus* magazine (*eroticus.com.au*), a sex-positive erotic magazine for women. Her articles and erotic fiction have been published widely, including: *Australian Women's Forum*, *Bizarre*, *Libida*, *Paddles*, *Penthouse Variations*, and *Scarlet Letters*. She lives in Australia with two black cats.

J.L. Belrose lives near Blue Mountain in Ontario. She has stories in *Queer View Mirror I*, *Pillow Talk II*, *Skin Deep*, *Best Women's Erotica*, *Uniform Sex*, *Set in Stone*, and *Herotica 7* anthologies, and will also be appearing in the upcoming *Pillow Talk III*, *Contact Sports*, and *Frontiers* anthologies.

Shari J. Berman is a writer, educator and translator. Her novels *Kona Dreams* and *Skipping Stones* are available in German from Elles (*elles.de*), and in English from Justice House Publishing. She and her partner are the editors of the TV parody anthology *Wishful Thinking*, also from JHP (*justicehouse.com*).

Lucy Jane Bledsoe is the author of the novel *Working Parts*, winner of the 1998 American Library Association Gay/Lesbian/Bisexual Award for Literature, and of *Sweat: Stories and a Novella*. She is also the author of four novels for young people. Bledsoe teaches teaching in the Masters of Creative Writing Graduate Program at the University of San Francisco.

Barbara Brown says that fantasy and writing have kept her alive, created new possibilities, and resulted in a lot of fun. "Flight" was produced with the support of the City of Toronto through the Toronto Arts Council as part of a collection of short stories exploring desire, sexual expression, and relationship.

Cara Bruce is the editor of *VenusorVixen.com* and *Viscera: An Anthology of Bizarre Erotica*. Her short stories have appeared in numerous anthologies including *Best American Erotica 2001*, *Best Women's Erotica 2000* and *2001*, and *Best Lesbian Erotica 2000*. She is currently editing *Best Bisexual Women's Erotica* and *Obsessed: Fetish Erotica*.

T.J Bryan AKA Tenacious is a Black conscious, West Indian, working-class, university educated, queer, femme, writer/visual artist and expectant mama. Her works have been published a variety of magazines including *On Our Backs* as well as in nine anthologies including the Lambda Award–winning Black lesbian coming out anthology *Does Your Mama Know?*, *Maka: Diasporic Juks – Writings by Queers of African Descent*, *Queer View Mirror I* and *II*, *Turbo Chicks* and *Hot & Bothered I* and *II*.

Bryhre is a queer female-bodied person currently finishing graduate studies in Vancouver.

Rachel Kramer Bussel is reviews editor at *VenusorVixen.com* and an editorial assistant at *On Our Backs*. Her writing has appeared in the anthologies *Starf*cker*, *Best Lesbian Erotica 2001*, and *Faster Pussycats*. She is co-author (with Lawrence Schimel) of the forthcoming *Erotic Writer's Market Guide* and reviser of *The Lesbian Sex Book*.

Miriam Carroll, at seventy-one, remains an active member of the Community. She loves Atlanta's outdoor club, volunteering jobs, making beaded items, reading, and is currently in college studying Spanish with an eye to future volunteerism.

Connie Chapman is a Vancouver Island writer, part-time farmer, bureaucrat by day and femme by night. Her short fiction has appeared in *Hot & Bothered 2*. She is currently working on a collection of short stories.

Fiona Coupar lives in Vancouver near the Drive, and has spent the last eight years working in an alternate school, which she has loved, and emerging from her writing and theatrical closet. She has also been an artistic director, a clerk, an artists' model, and, briefly and illustriously, a capuccino maker.

T.L. Cowan is a poet, spoken word artist, writer of stories, and other things. She currently lives, writes, and studies in Vancouver. Her work can be found in publications and on stages in Canada and the United States.

Nina D. writes, dances, and plays in lush Vancouver, BC. "Falling" is her first published work of fiction. She gives thanks to the Goddess.

Carol Demech has been adjusting to living in Vancouver, Canada for two years. "You can take the girl outta New York, but you can't take New York outta the girl, eh!" She writes about people who have touched her soul. "Happy" is the first story she wrote, and is her first published.

Elana Dykewomon has been a cultural worker and activist since the 1970s. Her books include *Riverfinger Women, Nothing Will Be As Sweet As The Taste: Selected Poems*, and the Jewish lesbian historical novel *Beyond the Pale*, which received the Lambda Literary and Gay & Lesbian Publishers Awards for best lesbian fiction in 1998. She was an editor of the international lesbian feminist journal *Sinister Wisdom* for nine years, and now lives in Oakland with her lover among friends, writing, teaching, and trying to stir up trouble whenever she can.

lisa g's stop motion videos with Barbie dolls doing sexy things got her hot and bothered. Then she convinced real people to do sexy things on video – this also got her hot and bothered. And now *Hot & Bothered* got her hot and bothered. If the inspiration hits, lisa g is good to go.

CONTRIBUTORS

Erin Graham is a writer, actor, and stand-up comic. Her work has been published in *Hot & Bothered 2* and *Exhibitions: Tales of Sex in the City*. She lives in Vancouver with her cat, Stuart-Louise.

Florence Grandview's story title, "Schoolyard Across the River," was inspired by the B-movie crime drama, *City Across the River*. She also has a story, "Whispers Getting Fainter" in *Hot & Bothered 2*.

Judy Grant likes reading, cold beer, and smart women. "All of It" is her first published short story, and she hopes it's not her last. She would like to like to see more new writers, "So come on girls, let's go!"

Terrie Akemi Hamazaki is a writer/performer based in Vancouver. Her signature piece "Furusato" appears in *Mom: Candid Memoirs by Lesbians About the First Woman in Their Lives*. Her work has been published in *Hot & Bothered 1* and *2*. She is currently at work on her first novel.

Karleen Pendleton Jiménez is a Chicana writer and teacher. She is a member of Lengua Latina, a writing group for Latinas in Toronto. She has just published her first book, *Are You a Boy or a Girl?*, which was a finalist for a 2001 Lambda Literary Award.

Lizard Jones is a writer, interdiscplinary artist, and performer living in Vancouver. She is the author of the novel *Two Ends of Sleep*, about living with MS, and co-author of *Her Tongue on My Theory*, winner of a Lambda Literary Award. She is a member of the lesbian art collective Kiss & Tell.

trish kelly is currently working on a novel called *I Felt The Sun*. She lives in East Vancouver, drinks americanos at Union Market, and publishes her zine *The Make Out Club*.

Sook C. Kong is a poet, fiction writer, literary critic, lesbian, and doctoral candidate. Recently, she collaborated on a sound and video installation on bodies and storytelling, which was featured on CBC-TV. She co-edited the *West Coast Line 2001* issue on power inequities. Her work appeared in *Hot & Bothered 2*.

Tara Lagouine hails originally from Winnipeg, but drifted to Montreal several years ago, where she divides her time between her fantasy world and the sordid underbelly of the village and the strip clubs of Ste-Catherine Street.

Judith Laura is the author of two books, *She Lives! The Return of Our Great Mother* and *Goddess Spirituality for the 21st Century*. Her poetry and fiction have appeared in journals including *Metropolitan, Woodwind, Pudding Magazine, OALM*, and in the 1998 Pudding House anthology, *Prayers to Protest*. She lives near Washington, DC.

K. Lee was born on April 4, 2001. She writes stories, poetry, music, and plays, and lives in Vancouver with her pet snake.

Rosalyn S. Lee is a 46-year-old black lesbian from New York City who writes short stories and lesbian erotica. She has been previously published in *Hot & Bothered 1* and *2*, and is spiritually supported by her girlfriend and Pug.

Suki Lee divides her time between Ottawa and Montreal where she's writing her second novel, *Enchanted*. She has lived in Peterborough, Vancouver, Swansea (Wales), and Seoul (Korea). Her first novel, *Go Through the Waves*, is represented by the literary agency, Anne McDermid & Associates.

Susan Lee has been published in the anthologies . . . *but where are you really from?* and *Hot & Bothered 1* and *2*. She currently lives in Toronto.

Denise Nico Leto is a San Francisco Bay Area poet. She co-edited the anthology, *Hey Paesan': Writing by Lesbians & Gay Men of Italian Descent* (Three Guineas Press). Her work can be found most recently in *Convolvulus, New Blind Date*, and *Curraggia*. She earned her MFA at Saint Mary's College.

River Light is a thirty-four-year-old actor, writer, videomaker, poly dyke switch living in Vancouver. She pens plays, essays, fiction, and poetic prose because she has to. Her work has appeared, among other places, in *Hot & Bothered 2, Best Lesbian Erotica 2000*, and *Wild Child*.

Rosalind Christine Lloyd's work has appeared in many anthologies including *Pillowtalk II, Hot & Bothered 2, Best American Erotica 2001, Skin Deep, Set in Stone, Faster Pussycat*, as well as on *Kuma* and *Amoret*, both erotic websites for literature. Currently travel editor for *Venus Magazine*, this womon of color, native New Yorker, and Harlem resident lives with two unruly felines, Suga and Nile, while obsessing over her first novel.

L.M. McArthur works and lives in Vancouver with her partner and their cat Cali. Her story "Sudsy Affair" was published in *Hot & Bothered 2*. She is also currently writing her first mystery novel.

CONTRIBUTORS

Cathy McKim lives in Toronto where she works as an actor/writer and part-time proofreader. Her writing has appeared in *Hot & Bothered 2*, *Countering the Myths*, and the essay anthology *Letters to Our Children*. Currently, she's in post-production of the film version of her short story, *The Boy in the Attic*.

Mickey is a wanderlustful traveler from Victoria, BC. She makes her bed wherever she lays and may be found at any rest stop, just off every road, near all small towns in the middle of nowhere – and especially wherever there are old abandoned buildings.

Midgett resides in San Francisco. She lectures on human sexuality at the university level. Her experiences includes workshops on sexuality, parenting, aging, and human relationships. She is the author of *Brown on Brown: Black Lesbian Erotica*.

Angela Mombourquette is a filmmaker, photographer, web designer, and writer who lives in Halifax, Nova Scotia with her partner of seventeen years and (of course) their dog and cat. She rides a motorcycle mostly because she really really likes wearing leather pants.

Rita Montana lives in Brooklyn with her partner, Laura. She published a story in *Hot & Bothered 1* and is delighted to be included in this new anthology. Last spring she published a chapbook of her poetry, *Unravelling the Clew*.

Joan Nestle is the acclaimed author of *A Fragile Union*, and *A Restricted Country* and editor of *The Persistent Desire: A Femme-Butch Reader*. She is co-editor of *Worlds Unspoken*, and the *Women on Women* lesbian fiction series. With John Preston she co-edited *Sister and Brother: Lesbians and Gay Men Write About Their Lives Together*. She has won numerous awards, including the Bill Whitehead Award for Lifetime Achievement in Lesbian and Gay Literature, the American Library Association Gay/Lesbian Book Award and the Lambda Literary Award for Lesbian Non-Fiction. She is the co-founder of the Lesbian Herstory Archives, which now fills a three story building in Park Slope, Brooklyn. She lives in New York.

Lesléa Newman is the author of *Girls Will Be Girls, Signs of Love, Out of the Closet and Nothing to Wear, Heather Has Two Mommies*, and many other books. Her newest short story collection, *Where the Girls Are* will be published in spring 2002. Visit her website at *lesleanewman.com*.

Shelly Rafferty is a working writer, student, activist, and parent. She currently writes about sexual assault, women in government, Labrador, and epistemology. She is working on her doctorate and is still afraid of real estate.

Michelle Rait is a slightly neurotic writer who is prone to wandering around North America. She hopes to use her travels as the basis for future stories. Michelle currently lives in San Francisco with her partner and three cats.

Andrea Richardson is a mother, teacher, and activist in varying degrees. She lives in Vancouver with Hestia, her protectress of the hearth.

Ruthann Robson is the author of the short fiction collections *The Struggle for Happiness, Cecile,* and *Eye of a Hurricane* and two novels, *Another Mother* and *a/k/a.* She is also Professor of Law at the City University of New York, one of the world's few progressive law schools.

Susan Fox Rogers is the editor of nine anthologies including *Solo: On Her Own Adventure,* and *SportsDykes: Stories from On and Off the Field.* She received her MFA from the University of Arizona and now teaches writing at Bard College.

Jacquelyn Ross has previously been published in *Hot & Bothered 2.* She lives in Vancouver with her two cats Fiver and Melissa Etheridge-Ross and continues to write.

Elizabeth Ruth is a Toronto-based writer whose fiction has been widely published. Her debut novel, *Ten Good Seconds of Silence,* will be published in the fall of 2001 by Simon & Pierre. She has also written for the CBC, *Write Magazine,* academic journals, and video. Elizabeth is an editor with *Fireweed,* and the founder and curator of Clit Lit – a queer literary series.

Stephanie Schroeder is a writer living in New York. "Goodbye Joanna" was first published in *Bad Attitude, Volume 12, #2,* in a slightly different form.

Sarah Schulman is the author of seven novels and two nonfiction books. She is a 2001 Guggenheim Fellow. Her play, *Carson McCullers (Historically Inaccurate),* will have its world premiere in New York in January 2002 at Playwrights Horizons, directed by Marion McClinton.

Anne Seale is a creator of lesbian comedy who has performed on many gay stages including the Lesbian National Conference, singing tunes from her tape *Sex For Breakfast*.

Denise Seibert is a thirty-seven-year-old lesbian who lives in the Pacific Northwest with her partner of eight years, her dog, T. S. "Eliot," and her cat, Rigel, who helps her write by walking across the keyboard. She has been writing lesbian erotica and literary short stories for twelve years, and is currently working on her first novel.

Dana Shavit was born in Australia in 1974. She has spent the last two years living in New York City and recently graduated from Sarah Lawrence College with an MFA in Writing. She's looking forward to going home to Sydney, and completing her first novel.

Marcy Sheiner is editor of *Herotica 4, 5, 6* and 7 (Down There Press) and of the *Best Women's Erotica* series (Cleis Press). Her stories have appeared in many anthologies and journals. Her book, *Sex for the Clueless*, will be published by Kensington Press in 2001.

Mar Stevens is an African American lesbian living in Oakland, CA. She works for the San Francisco District Attorney's office as an investigator. She enjoys writing, traveling, music, and athletics. She can be reached at Rastawomyn@aol.com.

Zara Suleman is a basic brown girl who lives, writes, and rebels in Vancouver. Her work has been published in various anthologies and journals.

Cecilia Tan is the author of three books of erotica, *Telepaths Don't Need Safewords, Black Feathers*, and *The Velderet*. Her stories have appeared in *Ms., Penthouse, Best American Erotica, Best Lesbian Erotica*, and many, many other places. "La Money Girl" is excerpted from her forthcoming "novel mosaic" of short-shorts, *The Book of Want*. Read more at *ceciliatan.com*.

Jean Taylor is an Australian writer based in Melbourne. Her latest book, *The C-Word*, which documents the experiences she and her partner went through before her partner died of ovarian cancer, is published by Spinifex Press.

CONTRIBUTORS

Jules Torti has been *Hot & Bothered* three times now. Her work has been published in seven different anthologies, and sits in several un-published heaps around the house waiting for a J. K. Rowling miracle. She lives on the banks of the Grand River in Dunnville, ON and hopes to write more books instead of checks this year.

Jess Wells is the author of twelve volumes of work, including the novels *The Price of Passion* (firebrand.com) and *AfterShocks* (the-women's-press.com). She is the editor of *HomeFronts: Controversies in Nontraditional Parenting* and *Lesbians Raising Sons* (both Alyson, alyson.com). A two-time finalist for the Lambda Literary Award, her five collections of short fiction include *Loon Lake Duet* (publication pending), and *Two Willow Chairs*.

Sarah B Wiseman lives in Kingston, ON. Her work has appeared and/or is forthcoming in the literary magazines *Queen's Feminist Review*, *UV*, *CV2*, *Grain*, *Fireweed*, and the erotic anthology *Faster Pussycats* (Alyson). She is a carpenter's apprentice.

rita wong is the author of *monkeypuzzle* (Press Gang), a recipient of the asian canadian writers' workshop emerging writer award, and a founding member of direct action against refugee exploitation. she acknowledges the support of the social sciences and humanities research council of canada.

Karen Woodman is a visual artist and writer. Her work has appeared in *She's Gonna Be* (McGilligan), *Pottersfield Portfolio*, *The Church and Wellesley Review* ("All About Chiffon"), *Queer View Mirror 2* and *Hot & Bothered 2*. She lives in Canada.

Miljenka Zadravec is a working class Croatian lesbian. She is a Vancouver dyke on a bike, a long distance runner, and a full time mom of two beautiful dogs. "Bittersweet" is a an excerpt from her first novel, in progress.

Zonna is forty and living in New Yawk – can you tell from her accent? You may have seen her stories in anthologies by Alyson Publications (*Skin Deep, Dykes With Baggage*) and Arsenal Pulp Press (*Hot & Bothered 2*). When she isn't writing, she's usually changing her cat's litter box.

ABOUT THE EDITOR

Karen X. Tulchinsky is the award-winning author of *Love Ruins Everything*, named one of the Top Ten Books of 1998 by the *Bay Area Reporter*, and *In Her Nature*, winner of the 1996 VanCity Book Prize. She is the editor of numerous anthologies including the critically acclaimed *Queer View Mirror 1 & 2*, the best selling *Hot & Bothered* series, the Lambda Literary Award Finalist *To Be Continued*, and *Friday the Rabbi Wore Lace*. She has written for many magazines and newspapers, including the *Vancouver Sun*, *DIVA*, *Curve*, *Girlfriends*, *The Lambda Book Report*, *Herizons*, and *Writer's Digest*. She has completed two new screenplays which were shortlisted in the Praxis Screenwriting Competition and the L.A.-based Chesterfield Film Writer's Project. Her most recent novel, a sequel to *Love Ruins Everything*, will be published in the Spring of 2002. Check out her website at *karenxtulchinsky.com*.

photo: Dianne Whelan